Be Your Everything

Vera Soulis

Contents

Chapter One: Moody

I sat on my bed, lying flat on my back as I held my arms in front of my face. My eyes scanned the words my book contained as the story went on.

I thought about how I want a story of my own, maybe my life was already a story. A one of a kind. But sadly, I think i'm a little mistaken at the thought considering I don't go on adventures. Yet, I do at the same time. My books take me on adventures that no one else can see unless they read themselves.

Just as I am about to get to a good part in my book, my door swung open and in came my 7-year-old brother, Matt. His shaggy brown hair was ruffled and spread across his forehead.

I smiled and sat up just in time for him to jump onto my lap. I quickly marked my page in the book and sat it aside as I wrapped my arms around Matt. He giggled and squirmed as usual trying to get out of my grip.

"Mommy says it's time to go to school." He mumbled. My dark wavy hair fell into his face and he swatted it away. I smiled and kissed his cheek before allowing him to leave. I stood up and straightened out my skinny jeans and jacket. I slipped on a pair of shoes that were sitting by my door and went downstairs with my backpack on my back.

As usual, my hands automatically clung onto the straps on my backpack when I walked. It was a habit i'd formed ever since starting high school since I have to take my backpack practically every where with me.

My mom and dad were there to give me goodbye hugs and kisses before I headed out the door. Matt also gave me a hug before I began to walk down the sidewalk toward the death trap I call school.

We live about a mile away from the high school. It came in handy because other wise, i'd be riding the horribly stinky bus that I did when I was in elementary school. It was full of obnoxious teenagers that didn't care whether they got kicked off the bus or not.

The only bad thing about walking was, like now, when it snowed or rained, I always froze to death. Snow wasn't covering the ground, but it was flurrying around and trying to.

It wasn't long before I reached the school. It stood tall, made completely out of bricks except for the occasional white that was put there for decoration I assumed. When I stepped into the hallways of the school, chatter was everywhere. From freshman to seniors they were piled in the halls talking back and forth. Talking about their drama filled lives.

Inside my head, I laughed. Some people are just to stubborn to understand life isn't all about getting back at each other. Or cheating on their boyfriend or girlfriend.

I passed by the front office and take notice of all the wonderful drawings that were hanging on the glass windows.

One, a girl that sits at my lunch table, was a drawing of a sun and the moon together. It was perfectly detailed and shaded just how I would have done it myself. Her name was Amber. She had long, blonde hair, and warm Blue eyes. She was a sweet girl but was so quiet all the time. Her and I used to be good friends during basketball season. We both became outcasts, her reason I'll never know.

That's why her and I get along. Although, I talk much more and get sociable when I want.

I continue down the hallways towards my first period which was my English and Reading class, one that I loved. Mrs. Foster was the teacher and she was a kind one. She knew all her students' names, parents, and for the bad ones, she knew their home number because if the countless calls home.

I walk into her room and sit down in my seat in the front row. I take my book out of my bag and open it up, eager to continue the story it was telling.

The bell rang after I had read through a few chapters. I put my bookmark in my book and shoved it back into my bag.

"I have your tests graded, class. I'll hand them out in a moment." Mrs. Foster fishes around in her desk drawer in search of a thick stack of papers. Our Reading exams were literally 10 pages thick, front and back. The school was trying to torture us. I was sure of it. As Mrs. Foster continues to look for the papers, I look around the classroom and take in all the appearances. The usual group of boys sat in the back, talking loudly and throwing paper balls at a girl that sat a few seats in front of them.

The group of boys consisted of the basketball team; Cody Stevens, he could jump so high that he could dunk a ball. Although I've never seen him do it, he talks about it a lot. His short black hair and dark skin goes well with his chocolate brown eyes. But don't be fooled by his charming looks, he's a player. Just as much as his other to friends are, Wesley and Zachary Montgomery. Otherwise known as Wes and Zach. They were identical twins but it wasn't hard to tell them apart. Wes had anger issues and seemed to always have a scowl on his face, but besides that, he had a small freckle beside his nose. That was one of the only ways the teachers tell them apart besides their voices.

Zach, on the other hand, was mischievous. He could also have his anger problems but any other time he's fooling around. Whether it's with a girl, or his friends.

Beside the twins was Adam Baker. His tan skin and blonde hair set him off from the others. He was the only one with that color hair. He seemed to have a heart of gold for a kid that hangs out with nothing but trouble-makers. Except for his best friend, Cameron Bridges. With his bright green eyes and short brown hair, He was tall, muscular, of course, and stole a lot of girls' hearts. He doesn't date very often considering he's big on sports. But for some reason, when the girls at my lunch table talk about it, I think there's some other reason behind why he doesn't date. Or maybe I'm just being weird.

Cameron was fixated on a paper he was writing on. One more glance back at it and I saw he was trying to write a paper. Must be for another class. Like Rodgers'. We had a paper due in there today. I wonder if I did that... most likely. I can't risk my grade if I'm going to do college classes my senior year.

"AH! Here they are." Mrs. Fosters' voice made an appearance right as I turn my attention back to her. Her gray hair was in a poof on the top of her head. That's how most old women keep their hair nowadays for some reason.

She laid a paper on my desk and gave me a thumbs up as if to say I did a great job, as usual. Not to gloat, honestly. I just make sure I do good on my grades. It's one of my top priorities at times.

"Now, Mr. Bridges, you need to study better. I know you have it in you." Mrs. Foster was bent down next to Cameron's ear but it wasn't doing much good. His face didn't show much embarrassment but his actions did she that he was upset about it. His facial expression was blank as he pressed his hand against his forehead. I felt sorry for him for a short moment. Frustration was clearly in his face and he wasn't making eye contact with anybody.

I noticed that his friends weren't even paying any attention to what was happening. Unlike his friends, Cameron seemed to really have to crack down on his grades. Especially this class.

The time passed by quickly before it was time to leave for the rest of the day. I was now leaving my last class when I saw Cameron sitting on the bench that was placed between two maple trees in the courtyard. He was bent over with a cell phone pressed to his ear. I decided to ask if he was OK since he seemed really stressed out since the last time I saw him in Mrs. Foster's class.

I waved goodbye to a couple of girls that I have classes with and are my friends. I don't really have a best friend, maybe because sometimes I to involved with other things to get to know people.

"Hi. Are you OK?" I asked as I sat down beside him on the bench. The phone was now resting on his thigh and was off.

"No." He answered almost angrily. I crossed one leg over the other and intertwined my fingers together, scooting closer to him.

"You don't have to be so grouchy, you know?" I told him. I kept my voice calm. Like the way I do when I'm trying to get Matt settled down. It seemes to help at times but if he's wound it doesn't. I smiled at him although he wasn't looking.

"I have every right." He said matter-of-factly. OK, so he's the sassy type.

"OK, OK. Well, I just wanted to make sure you were all good. You seemed really stressed out." I pressed my lips together and blew air into them making them look like a squirrel's cheeks. Cameron turned his head and looked up at me as I stood.

He acted like he was about to say something but backed down, looking at his phone. My phone vibrated in my pocket and I plucked it out, pressing answer.

"Hello?" I pressed it to my ear and walked away from Cameron, giving him a small wave.

He didn't notice, so I turned towards the sidewalk. My mom's voice came through to the phone, "Sophia, remember to get Matt from school so you can take him home. He's got a game in a little while." She told me. I nodded my head although she couldn't see me do so.

"OK mom. Talk to you later." I said before hanging up the phone. I changed my direction and walked the opposite way so I could get Matt from school. It was cold outside, no snow was coming down but the sky was dark and indicated that it would be soon. I picked up my pace and rushed the few blocks to the elementary school. Standing by the front door was Matt with his backpack on his back. He usually rides the bus home and I'm there with him, but today we had to hurry since his basketball game was in a short bit. Since he's seven, Matt can only play Jr. League. It includes kids from kindergarten to second grade. Matt's in second grade so it's his last year of it then he transfers to Little Leagues, something that I played when I was younger.

"Matt!" I called out to him. His head snapped over to me and a grin surfaced on his face. He took off out the door and jumped into my arms, clearly happy to see me. I hugged him back and pulled him close to my side, letting him sit on my hip.

"Look sissy I lost a tooth today." Matt pulled his bottom lip down so I could see where he lost his tooth. I smiled at him, "Now you're going to have a big boy tooth soon. Did you keep the one that fell out?" I let him walk on his own and he wrapped his hand tightly around my own. Matt reached into his pocket and dug around a bit until he pulled out what looked like a tiny yellow treasure chest.

"Here," He shook it so I could hear the tooth rattle around inside it. I nodded my head chuckled as he shoved it back in his pocket.

It wasn't long before we got to the house. Snow was beginning to fall from the sky and leaving bits of white on the green grass. I directed Matt to go get his uniform on for his game. He dropped his backpack on the floor and rushed up to his room. I took mine off as well and hung it across a bar stool. Knowing Matt, he would want a grilled cheese so he wouldn't starve to death.

As I searched through the fridge, the front door opened and my mom stepped in. She shook the fresh snow off the top of her head and hung her jacket and scarf up.

"Hey, mom." I said as i continued to make the sandwiches.

"Hey." She answered back. I heard her toss her shoes off and leave them at the door as she ran back the hallway to her room. probably to change into more comfortable clothes for Matt's games.

In a short couple of minutes my dad joined us and we were all on our way to the game.

Chapter Two: Family

We pulled into the elementary school's parking lot and stopped the car, each of us getting out and slamming the doors shut behind us. Matt held his water bottle tight in his fingers as he pranced up onto the sidewalk that led to the school's front entrance. He was always happy when he got to play basketball.

He played one other year, last year, since he was unable to play in kindergarten. It may not seem like Kindergartners can play, but they get excited about it.

☆★FLASHBACK☆★

The air in the gym was stuffy from all the small basketball players breathing hard and sweating. It didn't help when parents were standing up screaming at their kids. They were Kindergartens, is what I wanted to tell those parents, but they wouldn't have listened.

I leaned back on my white fluffy coat that I had wrapped around the back of my chair. It gave me cushion since the chairs were a hard, cold metal. My mom sat on my right while my dad was on my left trying to hold it together. He was getting into the game and the fact that Matt wasn't trying his hardest made him even more anxious.

I looked over at my baby brother and saw him running down the court. He glanced up at the clock that had the score and time left on it. His hair was flopping around on top of his head as he ran. Matt glanced back at me, he had worry written all over his face. The next thing I knew, I was watching my brother fall to the ground with his eyes shut.

There was nothing there to trip him, not even his own feet tripped him. The gym erupted in talk as I burst up from my seat, my mom and dad following close behind. I fell to my knees next to Matt's head. He was so tiny, a 5-year-old. I felt tears at fog up my eyes but I couldn't reach up to wipe them away unless I let go of Matt's shirt.

That's when I was practically drug away from him as the ambulance grabbed him up.

That's when the buzzard went off and his team won.

That's when my world came crashing down.

☆★FLASHBACK OVER☆★

We soon learned that Matt had leukemia.

After that he took treatments at our local hospital and started to get better. It was so worrying, that was the time I fell from my social status. I stopped playing basketball with my team and some of the girls decided that I wasn't worth their time for ditching the team considering I was one of the best players. I never told them why, either. I don't ever plan on it.

Matt's in remission now. He has been since the end of first grade. It was the best time ever for us and now he's healthy. We were definitely lucky, that's for sure.

My dad held the door open for us as the warm air from the gym blasted me in the face. It warmed up my rosy red cheeks fast and I automatically felt warmer. Matt ran off to be with his team as I followed my mom and dad to our seats in the front row. I sat between them, like the last time I was here. I suddenly felt myself drifting into one of my daydreams until my mom pulled me back to reality.

"Are you okay honey?" She asked. I looked over at her and saw she had an arm resting on my shoulder.

"Yeah, I'm fine." I nodded my head. She knew though, she knew I was thinking about the last time we were here. She gave me a nod of acknowledgement and turned herself to watch the game. Matt was sitting in one of the chairs they had for the teams lined against the tan colored walls. He was looking at me like he needed me and shook his head.

"Um, I'll be right back." I said lowly to my parents and kept my eyes trained on my brother while I quickly walked over to him. He was still clutching his water bottle in his tiny fingers when I crouched down next to him.

"What's wrong, Matt?" I asked him. He looked at me with his equally sky blue eyes and sighed dramatically. "What if I get hurt again?" He asked. His childish voice made me want to just hug him tight but I resisted the urge to do so. Instead, I pried his sweating water bottle out of his hands and sat it under his chair and made him look at me. "You won't. You're all better now, remember?" I patted his leg and pursed my lips. He smiled shyly and looked down, "OK." He replied. I grinned and wrapped my arms around him in a hug. He didn't hesitate to do the same to me before I pulled away. I gave him a kiss on the cheek and watched him wipe it off in embarrassment while he blushed. I stood up and ruffled his hair before walking back to my spot between my parents.

I didn't expect to see him here. He was standing in the very back beside an older woman. His dark brown eyes locked onto mine for a moment, his face emotionless. I almost wanted to go back there and see why he was here, he never came to any the other year, so why now? Maybe his sibling is playing as well. I thought he was an only child. I tore my gaze from those memorable Brown eyes that belonged to Cameron Bridges.

Why are you wondering about him so much?

I shook my head to clear my thoughts and hesitantly sat down in my seat. My dad roughly patted my back and left his arm to rest on the back of my chair. I shifted uncomfortably in my seat for the next two periods of the game. Matt was put in and was doing great; he made two baskets already. My parents clapped for him right along with me and he jumped around for a second with excitement.

When they took Matt out, I got bored with the game all of a sudden. Curiosity got the best of me and I lied so I could go see if Cameron was still back there. Even if he was kind of a jerk earlier, he struck me as interesting.

"I'm going to the bathroom." I told my mom. She nodded her head and I stood up with my back crouched down slightly. I was attempting to keep my head out of other people's views but that didn't work to well since all the chairs were on one level. I reached the middle aisle and walked through it, my eyes searching through the crowd.

I caught a glimpse of Cameron's head across the room and casually made my over as I tried not ot look to much like a stalker. I was simply trying to make friends with the boy, that's all. I shimmied through the crowd and found myself even closer to Cameron when one of the tiny cheerleaders crashed into me. I tripped over my own two feet and my shoulder hit with Cameron's torso.

He stumbled back, his hands still stuck in the pockets of his jeans. I felt a blush creep up my neck and tried to look away to hide it, but my manners got the best of em first. I looked up at him, just realizing I was so short and he was so...tall. Clearing my throat, I said, "Sorry." He looked down at me for the first time and still had no emotion on his face. Was he always this grumpy?

"It's fine." He said finally. I mentally shook my head and wondered what my facial expression was like at the moment. He must've noticed that he made me just the slightest bit unhappy and shifted his body weight to his other leg, "Uh, why are you here?" He asked me. I knew he was trying to make up from earlier for being so grumpy, but he isn't sliding by that easily.

"Are you to manly to say I'm sorry?" I challenged while trying to suppress a smirk. He gave me a small smile that didn't reach his eyes and shook his head, "Of course," He looked down at his feet. I crossed my arms over my torso and turned myself so I could see the game. As I watched Matt run across the court, I remembered what Cameron asked me. It wouldn't be polite of me to ignore the question, wouldn't it?

"Oh, and I'm here watching my brother. Number two." I told him without looking up at him. I trained my eyes on Matt as I watched him move graciously across the court. All the things I taught him outside of our garage door with our basketball hoop hanging above the door, he was using them. "He's pretty good." Cameron piped up. I glanced at him and saw he was already looking at me. I nodded my head, "I know." With a cocky attitude that I never ever get, I started to walk away. My face contorted into a scowl meant for myself. Where did the cockiness come from? I shook my head, confused at myself.

I turned back to Cameron to catch him quickly looking away from me. I was going to ask him about it until I saw a short little blonde girl come running towards him. Her light blonde hair was tied back into two ponytails that cascaded down off her shoulders. Her little cheerleaders uniform was a bit baggy on her and as she jumped up into Cameron's arms. He swung her around in a circle and watched her giggle, dropping her fluffy pom-poms to the floor. Her uniform was the same color as my brothers uniform and had the same sponsor name written across it.

I walked up to them just as Cameron was propping the little girl on his hip, like I did with Matt often. "Who's this?" I asked as I picked up her pom-poms and held them in my hands. The little girl shyed away and hid her pale adorable face in the crook of Cameron's neck.

"This is my niece, Ella." Cameron seemed to have a glow on his face when she giggled. A real smile -one that I hadn't seen before now- was on his lips as he craned his neck to see her face, "This my friend, Sophia." He finished. I was take aback at how he called me his friend and knew my name. I smiled brightly at Ella as she rose her head up, that smile of hers not faltering even a little bit.

"Well, hello there, Ella." I playfully stuck my hand up for her to high-five. To my surprise she smacked it. It seemed to surprise Cameron as well. A tall, blonde woman came up behind Cameron and played peek-a-boo with Ella until Cameron turned around to see who it was.

"Hey, Callie." He greeted her. She gave him a side hug and took Ella out of his hands while she was saying "Mommy!" over and over again. I handed the pom-poms to Cameron and watched as he handed them to Ella's mom. Her and Ella looked an awfully lot alike with their Blonde hair and brown eyes. Beside hair color, Cameron and his sister looked alike as well.

"Hi!" Callie stuck her free hand out to greet me. I shook it, noticing how she seemed kind of out of breath. Cameron introduced us and we stood there while watching the game a little. I couldn't help but notice how he seemed so relaxed around his sister and niece but in a classroom he couldn't be relaxed. It was like he was always stressed. But the weird thing is, He only seemed stressed when he had to read. Or focus on anything in the same area.

I sat back down in my seat and watched the game. Matt was still running across the gym and I could see the energy draining from his small body. Ever since his sickness, he's been running out of energy fast. He can get back on his feet after a small rest usually, though. The buzzard went off a little later confirming that the game was over.

I stood up with my parents and was hit by a weight with hands wrapped around my neck. Matt laughed into my ear and pointed up to the score board with a giddy smile on his face shouting, "We won! And I feel good, sissy."

Chapter Three: Goody Two Shoes

C hapter Three:

Goody Two Shoes

Cameron's POV

I stepped into the front door of my two-story house, taking in the scent of tacos filling my nose. The TV was illuminating the living room while I looked in and saw my dad asleep in his chair. He must've gotten off work late. My mother was talking to herself, babbling on about something that I most likely wouldn't understand. I walked into the living room, the events of tonight on my mind. What was up with Sophia being so interested in talking to me all of a sudden? She used to be popular, and quite irresistible according to what Adam says. There a small part of me that would like to know how she suddenly fell from her high status, but then she'd probably just call me stupid. Sophia isn't like the other girls. She doesn't judge people, at least not out loud. I've noticed how she's always talking to someone different at school.

Maybe she talked to me out of the goodness of her heart earlier today and was just trying to see if I really was OK. It seemed unlikely though because most girls at school only talk to me to 'get to know me' as they call it. Then again, she doesn't seem like most girls...

"Hey, son." My dad's sleepy voice broke me from my thoughts. I sat back on the couch and propped my feet up on the coffee table. "Hey Dad." I replied. Today wasn't exactly a good day for me. I'm almost a hundred percent sure that Mrs. Foster called my mom and told her about my poor grades. Of course, my mom knows I have trouble in reading for reasons I've never told. But you can believe that she's going to yell at me. Any other time I get a poor test grade she doesn't do much but tell me I need to do better.

"Are you ready for your game this weekend?" His rough voice asked. I nodded my head, "Sure am."

"Dinner's ready!" My mom called. Dad and I shot up and made our way to the dinner table as usual. With only the three of us here now, it felt kind of empty. Callie graduated college a few years ago as a teacher and now she's raising her 5-year-old daughter with her crappy fiancé, Lance. I don't know what she sees in that man honestly. Once you meet him, you automatically want to punch him in the face. Even my parents aren't big fans of him but they put up with him for Callie's sake.

I noticed my dad had some gray hairs coming through on his close cut beard. It's always cut short with a little bit of a mustache visual. My mom was aging to. Her stress mostly came from my sister and I. Being nine years apart, my sister and me didn't always get along. Now that she's 26 and I'm 17, we can control our rage.

"Dig in!" My dad sang. The tacos were a bit messy but delicious. My mom was a pretty good cook if I may say so myself. "So, your teacher called today." Mom began as she took a bite of her taco. I quickly stuffed a giant bite in my mouth to avoid conversation about this subject. "Cameron, stop it. You're gonna choke yourself." Dad butted in. I let my gaze fall onto my plate and kept it there so no eye contact was needed.

"Why did you fail your test?" Mom asked. She had finished her bite and had her fingers tapping along on the table. I swallowed, taking a gulp of my water to wash it down. "Mom," I drug out in annoyance, "Do we have to talk about this now? I have a game coming up and-"

"That's no excuse for bad grades! Cameron Walter Bridges Dyslexia shouldn't be problem for you, either. I know that's why your doing poorly in your reading class." Her voice calmed as she talked. Bringing up the whole Dyslexia thing makes me spaz out sometimes since it is hard to deal with, especially when your a basketball player like me and have to keep your grades up if you're going to play.

I clenched my jaw to keep it from opening and saying something I'll regret later. My dad had an easy look on his face. It simply said "I'm just going to eat my food and be quiet". While mom on the other hand, was not backing down.

"What can you do to get your grades up?" She chewed her food slowly and gripped a form tight in her hands. We may be eating tacos, but she always uses a fork. That's something I never will understand.

"I don't know, Mom." I answered, "Study more? Try to cure my Dyslexia?" Sarcasm was dripping from my words. Mom shook her head and looked down at her food. The look that always means she's thinking crossed over her face. Her brown eyes looked up at mine before she said what I dreaded most;

"You'll get a tutor. And if that doesn't help, then no more basketball."

•

"Are you serious?" Adam, my best friend since Pre-K, said. He clutched his under armour backpack as he unloaded the unneeded books into his locker.

I shrugged my shoulders, "She doesn't understand anything." Even Adam doesn't know about my Dyslexia and I'd really like to keep it that way. Nobody needs to know my weaknesses except for myself.

"Does she know what'll happen to the team if you can't play?" Adam's eyes were wide now with curiosity. Over the years he's gotten close to my mom and she's like a second mother to him. He knows how she can get when she's mad and how authoritative she thinks she can be. My dad is scared sometimes... OK so scared isn't the word. It's somewhere around that, though.

"She knows." I replied with a deep sigh. Adam closed his locker now with only few books and notebooks zipped in his bag. We started to walk down the hallway towards our classes.

"You're gonna have to get a tutor then, dude." Adam patted my back and started into the classroom. My hands hung in the air as if asking 'What the..?' Shaking my head, I made my way into Mrs. Fosters class. Suddenly, the idea hit me.

I could easily tell my mom I have a tutor and just spend my evenings hanging out with friends when I'm supposed to be 'tutoring'. Mrs. Foster wouldn't know either. This plan is fool proof...

"Mr. Bridges?" Her voice stopped me before I could reach my desk. I winced at my name being called before class even started. This can't be good.

"Yes, Mrs. Foster?" I said politely as I approached her desk. Students were still piling in when the tardy bell rang and she didn't seem to care. Old people.

"Meet me after class, OK?" She said sternly and looked at me above her glasses that were perched on the tip of her nose. I nodded slowly and walked back to my desk. A familiar girl walked in with her hair pulled up into a messy ponytail and a sweatshirt on. She also had a pair of glasses on her face that made her look different. I didn't think of who it could be until Mrs. Foster called her to the front, "Miss Belle, see me after class."

The class erupted in ohhh's and a few of the guys directing there's at me. And a lot at Sophia. Her cheeks flushed red as she turned to take her seat. I never knew she wore glasses. But then again, I never really noticed her any other time either.

Adam gave me a knowing look and several questions ran through my head.

Why would Mrs. Foster want to see both of us after class? Especiallylittle miss goody two shoes?

———————————

Sorry this chapter was short!

Ohhhhh what does Mrs. Foster want do you think?

I know. Hehe.

It's not to hard to guess! Duhhh

Chapter Four: Tutors

C hapter Four:Tutors

Sophia's POV

I spent my class period day dreaming about how horrible this day had been already. I woke up late this morning after my mom left for work and never woke me up and my dad had to get to the police station for his job. No one was there to wake me or Matt up. I never set my alarm clock because usually it never wakes me up.

After realizing I was going to be late, I threw a sweatshirt over my tank top and pulled on a pair of my favorite jeans. I pulled my hair up and braided a small part of the front back into the ponytail holder to make myself look a little more presentable. To make matters worse, I didn't have any more contacts left. My glasses were old but I could see out of them. And, to be honest, I liked them more because they were less to worry about for me. Since I worry about everything, that is.

I rushed Matt to school and then practically jogged here only to see that I had to be talked to after class. Since I walked in a few seconds after the tardy bell rang, I had the thought that it would be about that.

I was sadly mistaken.

I found myself standing up with my books clutched in my hands while every other students in the room left. I walked slowly up to Mrs. Foster's desk and waited for her to look up from the book she was reading. When Cameron walked up beside me, I knew something was up. So I might not have been getting in trouble for being late this morning.

"So, I got a call from your mother, Cameron." She began. I looked over at Cameron who seemed emotionless, a way I should get used to seeing him.

"She wants you to have a tutor. I think Miss Belle here is perfect for the job." Mrs. Foster rested her chin on her hands and looked up at is with a faint smile, "Think you can do it?" She directed her gaze to me.

Me? Why would I tutor him? Could I really do it? He doesn't seem like the type to sit and listen.

"I don't know Mrs. Foster. Depends on Cameron here." I looked up at Cameron. He shook his head and looked at me for a moment before mumbling, "Yeah." Lowly.

Cameron walked out the door abruptly with his hands in his pockets. I followed close behind him and tried to catch up. If we were going to study, then we have to meet up somewhere, right?

"Cameron," I called his name. He slowed his pace and allowed me to catch up to him. His eyebrows rose, "What?" "When are we meeting up?" I asked him. His eye widened in alert and farmed all around us to see if anyone had heard me. Before I had a chance to protest, he pulled me into the bear by janitors closet and shut the door behind us. I reached up above us to find the string that turned the light on so I could see Cameron for a chance to yell at him.

"What was that all about?! Why are we in here? Aren't your little girlfriends going to be mad?" I babbled on. Yes, he had girlfriends. Well, he didn't exactly know about them but they were always drooling over him. Especially one girl named Danielle. She used to be my best friend, played on the basketball team with me my entire life. When I quit because of Matt, she ditched me and every once in a while finds the time to pick on me. She's now the MVP and a lot of girls hate her for her snottiness and the way she treats people.

Cameron turned towards me, "No one can know about this tutoring thing." He said sternly. His eyes only flashed up to mine for a quick second before he asked another question, "What do you mean 'girlfriends'?" He used his two fingers to make air quotes.

I shrugged my shoulders, "There's always someone that wants you." Was all I said before walking out if the closet. Cameron walked out behind me and disappeared Into the crowd of students down the hallway.

Just when I thought I was done dealing with everyone's crap for the day, I remembered that Cameron still hadn't told me when to meet up. I shoved through the people in the hallways in attempt to find him again. The sea of teenagers was to thick for me to find anyone.

Suddenly, the girls bathroom door swung open and I was pulled inside. The cold fingers that were wrapped around my arm belonged to the one and only Danielle. I rolled my eyes at her antics and crossed my arms over my ribs while I waited for her to say something. Her face was red from anger as she tried to spill her guts.

"Stay away from Cameron!" Was all she could squeal at me before stomping out into the still crowded hallway. An involuntary smile formed on my lips.

Danielle wouldn't do anything to me. She wouldn't try... Unless I pushed her to far. I've seen her fight with other girls. It was never pretty. So, I'm going to have to avoid Cameron unless we're in tutoring. That's just it, I can't stay out of drama unless I stay out of tutoring him.

Knowing what I need to do and fully aware that I'd be late for my next class, I rushed back to Mrs. Foster's room and found her sitting where she was when I left. She lowered her book when she noticed my presence and took her glasses off her face, gently putting them on her desk.

"What is it, Miss Belle?" She asked me. I walked over to her desk and stood there for a moment, contemplating in my mind what exactly to say. "I can't tutor Cameron, Mrs. Foster. I have... uh... family stuff to deal with." I tried to say it without any hesitation, but I could tell she knew I was lying. "Tell you what, If you tutor Mr. Bridges, I'll write an excellent report on you for your college. Any college you'd like. I know that it's only your junior year, but why not start early?" Her words sunk in. I really could use a good recommendation. I could definitley deal with the drama of Danielle for that. Mrs. Foster noticed the hesitation on my face, "Hun," she began sweetly, "Cameron is really struggling. You're the only would I -even his mother- would trust. Could you do this for him?" She was almost pleading. I sighed heavily.

"Of course. Do I still get the recommendation?" I asked hopefully. Mrs. Foster's face brightened as she nodded, a wide grin stretching across her lips and reaching her eyes. I smiled and left the room quickly so I wouldn't be late for my next class.

Cameron's POV

"There's always someone who wants you," Sophia spat before she walked out of the closet. I huffed like a little kid would after not getting what he wants.

It's kind of like I wasn't, though. If Sophia finds out, or worse, anyone else finds out, then I'm not going to be the same. It could effect everything i've worked for. With my grades falling faster than a free-fall, I won't be able to keep my basketball scholarship I was practically promised to this year. With my little secret or whatever you want to call it out, people would do on me. At least, that's what I feel like would happen. Even if it wouldn't, I feel better having it locked inside my head and my head only.

Only, who knows who could figure it out. Sophia's a smart girl, I'm going to really have to cover it up around her.

I shoved hastily through the crowd of students to get to my next class, gym. It was my favorite class for sure. It didn't involve reading or anything to make me use my mind. I could just run and play basketball.

I walked inside the gym doors only to run into Adam. He turned to meet me and gave me a manly handshake. OK, maybe not as manly as you'd think, but it was for us. I smiled at Adam.

"The game for tomorrow was cancelled. Apparently there was a bad snow storm in that county and they cancelled it." He explained. I sighed heavily, I was really looking forward to that game. The Sea Hawks are like our natural born enemies. My dad even talks about how he used to play against them. They were a tough team with mad skills. Nothing we couldn't handle though.

"When's practice?" I asked Adam. He tapped his chin as if he was thinking and finally replied, "Oh! It's Friday." I rolled my eyes at his dumbness and walked into the boys locker room. Coach Fawley walked past me and nodded before yelling to the rest of us, "We're doing drills so I expect everyone to work their hardest!" He went out of the room and everyone grumbled under their breath.

Heh, this should be fun.

*

I entered through the front door of our tall and well built house to find my mom crawling around on the floor. Yes, crawling. I cleared my throat so she would realize I was there and so she wouldn't make to much of a fool of herself. I stifled a laugh before she saw me and nearly had a heart attack. She quickly got up off her hands and knees and brushed herself off.

"When did you get here?" She attempted to change the subject. I chuckled, "Oh, just long enough to see you crawling on the floor..."

She hit my shoulder and laughed along with me, "I lost my earring." Was her excuse. I nodded in a "Yeah, OK." way and threw my bag down on the kitchen table.

"So, how was school?" My mom asked from inside the kitchen. I knew exactly what she wanted to know. Did I get a tutor? As you wish mother dear. I sighed and sat down at the table.

"Yeah, mom. I got a tutor." I said, the word tutor creeping me out a little bit. I don't want to think of Sophia as tutor. let alone a friend... Did I mean that? Do I want Sophia as a friend? She always seems to be alone, but I assumed that I caught her in the times that her friends were somewhere else. She seems to always be helping with the school in the way, for instance, tutoring me. Obviously she's smart. Or else why would Mrs. Foster put her as my tutor?

"Hello? Cam?" My mom waved a hand in front of my face and knocked me out of my trance. I cleared my throat and looked up at her. She smiled, showing the small wrinkles around the corners of her mouth. She had always told me they were laughing marks from her laughing all the time when she was younger. She's always had a good spirit and I loved that about her.

"What?" I asked her. She went back into the kitchen to make dinner and began talking to me again about how tutoring was going to be so good for me.

Me, being the teenager I was, rolled my eyes and went upstairs to start on unwanted homework. Homework gives me headaches, and I'm serious. I always manage to get one no matter what.

_______________________________Holy crap guys. I had horrible writers block for the last part of this chapter. I know it really sucks but I needed to fill it in quickly. The next chapters are going to be so much better I hope!

Vote/Fan/Smile!

Chapter Five: Concerned

- -

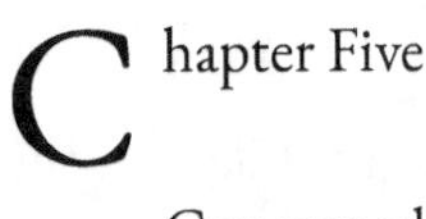

C hapter Five:

Concerned

Sophia's POV

I trudged into school the next day, my glasses still on my face. Mom hasn't really had a chance to get me more contacts. If I decide to not wear my stupid glasses, then I'll be blind. Literally. I can't see like four feet in front of me.

I walked to my locker, tossing everything inside hastily and pulling out my books for Mrs. Foster's class. I loved her class; I also had some business to handle with Cameron in it. It would be better for me to ask him in that class so Mrs. Foster knows we're getting something done.

When I walked into the class, I saw Cameron was here early. That was a little strange considering Adam, his best friend, wasn't even here yet. I thought back to yesterday when he didn't want anyone hearing me talk about tutoring him and decided it'd be best to ask him about it now. Besides, wouldn't want Danielle seeing me around him...

I approached Cameron as he sat in his seat, daydreaming by the looks of it. I chuckled at his dazed face and was about to smack him out of it, but decided against it since I wasn't here to make enemies. "Cameron?" I snapped my fingers in front of his face and laugh when he almost choked on his own spit.

"Huh? What?" He asked me. He almost seemed mad at me for breaking me from his little dream. I chuckled, pulling an empty seat away from a nearby desk and sitting backwards on it, facing him, Aww, did I ruin your dream?" I let my lower lip hang out as he narrowed his eyes at me.

"Anyways, I was wondering if you wanted to study tonight. Like... at the library?" I said, after thinking of where we could go. Cameron simply shrugged his shoulders and leaned back in his seat, placing his hands behind his head. "I need an answer now unless you want your friends to hear our conversation." I warned. If he was gooing to play this game with me, I was going to give it all right back. He sat up quickly when the bell rang, his eyes darting to me as if telling me to leave.

"I'm not leaving until you tell me when we can study, Pretty Boy." I crossed my arms and rose my eyebrow, staring at him. He glared at me mumbling something like "You're so stubborn." I rolled my eyes and didn't move when Adam showed up beside me. I realized I had taken his seat. Not making an attempt to move, Cameron went into almost panic mode and stood up, nearing me an dbending down so he could whisper something in my ear, "Meet me at the library after school."

I smiled triumphantly and stood up, scooting Adam's chair back to his seat. I walked to mine and watched as the rest of the class filed in.

*

I waltzed into the library and nodded to the librarian. I come here often, so I know her name and she knows mine. I found a round table at the back of the building, a few other students doing research or school work. Seeing that Cameron wasn't here yet, I reached into my bag and pulled out the book I had been reading.

Almost an hour passed and Cameron still wasn't here. He said we were meeting here, right? Yes, of course he did. I know he did. I was growing frustrated now as I stood up and shoved the book in my bag. I had finished it and now I was going to grab another before Cameron got here. If he comes.

I walked around the shelf, browsing all the old books. They seemed to be covered in dust from lack of being touched or read. It's a shame all these amazing books were just sitting here, collecting dust, when there was a bunch of people at the high school that would read them. OK, I take that back. They wouldn't. But, I would.

The front doors to the library slammed shut and I heard footsteps approching where I was. I turned to go and see who it was but ended up running into someone. That someone was sweaty and smelled like... Well, sweat. I scrunched my nose and looked up to meet Cameron's gaze. He had a faint smile on his lips from my expression. I swiftly stepped aside and made my way back over to my seat without a word to him.

"I'm sorry I was late, Soph." He said as he carelessly tossed his bag ontot he seat beside his. I was annoyed right now and not in the mood to deal with his sudden up-beat mood. I made myself comfortable in my seat.

"Don't call me Soph," I began. "And where have you been?" I asked, gesturing to his attire. He smiled at me, "Basketball practice." I guess basketball made him happy? Oh, wait, I bet it was some girl. Don't be so Naive, Sophia. The little voice inside my head nagged. I mentally rolled my eyes at it and jerked my english book out of my backpack.

Cameron mimicked my actions. He sat his book beside mine before letting his gaze fall onto the book that I had pulled out of the shelf befor erunning into him. He had a satified look on his face as he examined the cover.

"Do you like reading?" He asked suddenly. I had lost all the venom building up in me, "Yeah. I love it." No eye contact was needed as I flipped through the pages of my english book in attempt to find teh right one. For some reason, I've never been able to hold a grudge. Maybe it was because I witnessed what it was almost like to lose someone so clsoe to you. I don't know, but my heart was to big for that nonsense.

"That's cool." Cameron commented lowly. I realized he was in a mucsle shirt, obviously showing off his strong biceps. His hair was in every direction possible and his green eyes were shining in the light from above his head. When he looked up at me, a smirk played on his pink lips, "Like what you see?" I scoffed, shaking my head dismissively.

I gave him instructions on what page to go to and that he was reading first. Cameron seemed like he didn't want to read. He slowly flipped through the pages as he looked for the right one. I huffed, slightly annoyed by how he was acting suddenly.

"Cameron?" I asked. My voice was calm and collected as if talking to someone who didn't understand what was going on. He glanced up at me with a worried expression before he yawned. If it was possible to look cute while yawning, he did it.

"Sophia?" He mocked my voice. I rolled my eyes and stared at his book until he found the right page.

I read the first line myself, "I had decided to take my dog for a walk this afternoon..." Mrs. Foster never usually assigns us anything in these books because, obviously, they're childish. For the sake of tutoring, she made me take one and assigned me this story. Apparently it will help us get used to each other. Her words, not mine.

"I decided to take my bog for a walk-" Cameron began. I instantly sat up and looked at the sentence once more. That's not what it says. He must've said dog wrong on purpose.

"Cameron, don't be stupid." I scolded, "I have other things to do tonight, to." His eyes hardened at my words and I was taken aback. Why was he seeming so mad now all of a sudden? He looked back down at his book. I watched as his mouth opened and closed like a fish out of water, finding the words to say. Except they were right in front of him. His cheeks looked like they were tinted a light shade of red. I at forward and put my book down with my hands on top of it.

"What's wrong?" I asked him slowly, genuinely concerned. He glanced up at me for a quick second before shutting his book.

"I'm just going to go home. I'm tired from practice and can't focus. Can we re-schedule?" He asked impatienlty. Confused, I stood up and gathered my things. I tucked a piece of my brown locks behind my ear to get it out of my face before looking at Cameron.

"How about I text you?" I was proud of myself. I was being professional about this whole thing. But, you have to remember that I'm used to talking. I always involve myself with stuff at school.

Cameron pulled his phone out of pocket and tapped away until he handed it to me. I swiftly texted my number into his phone and handed it back to him. A slight smile crossed onto his face but was quickly replaced by a smirk.

"You actually have to text me, too. I need to know when we can meet up." I told him sternly as we walked side by side towards the exit. I remembered I still had to check my book out, so I stopped walking. Cameron waved bye and walked away.

As soon as Shay, the librarian, was done checking out my book, I made my outside and back to my house. Mom and Dad and were probably at home with Matt wondering where I was. It wasn't really surprising for me to be away from home, though. I used to be at basketball practice every night and now it's always something like pepp club or honors society. Honestly, that stuff was exhausting.

I entered the house to see the kitchen and living room light was on. Dad and Matt must be in there watching one of the games on TV. I dropped everything in my hands on the floor and took off to my room, eager to lay down. I was completely tired.

Ignoring the calls I got from my mother, I crept into the bathroom and stripped off my clothes. I hopped in the shower and took a hot, relaxing one. Afterwards, I dried myself and put on a pair of shorts along with a baggy t-shirt that used to be my dad's. He didn't care when I took an old shirt of his. I found it to be much more comfortable.

I heard feet patting up the steps and finally caught a glimpse of Matt running past my door towards his. I chuckled and grabbed my laptop and sat it on my desk, turning it on and opening Google Chrome. I had a few questions about what went on today.

Matt flew into my room and I turned around just in time to catch him in my arms. I squeezed him so tight that he began to yelp.

"You're squeezing the poop outta me!" I chuckled at his choice of words and lifted his frail body onto my leg. My eyelids were heavy so I needed to hurry him out of here.

"Have a good day?" I asked him. He nodded his head eagerly before jumping off me and running towards the door. He swiftly turned to me a blew me a kiss before charging down the stairs again.

I turned back to my laptop and typed in, "A disorder that makes it hard to read," before pressing enter. I scrolled down through the suggestions and realized that most of them said Dyslexia. Cameron? Dyslexia? nah. He was probably just tired and couldn't concentrate. He would have told me, right? I did search 'Disorder' but that was only to see what it could've been. I have severe doubts that it's dyslexia.

Or am I wrong?

____

Vote/Comment/Fan!

I follow back :D

Chapter Six: The Boogy Man

C hapter Six:

The Boogy Man

I sat up on my bed on this bright Thursday morning and looked at the snow pouring down outside. It was blanketing everything it possibly could outside including my mom's car that was sitting in the driveway. I sat up and groggily rubbed my eyes. A moan escaped my lips as I stretched my limbs out. Straightening out the shirt I had on, I stood up and shuffled slowly over to the bathroom across the hall.

After brushing my hair and teeth, I shuffled zombie-like back to my desk after noticing the laptop light that was still on. My screen was black, so it must've fallen asleep in the process of me falling asleep as well.

The screen lit up after I pressed the on button and revealed google results. Most were about the reading disorder that some people get called Dyslexia. It baffled me at first to why I had searched it in the first place, but soon realized I looked it up after coming home the other night. I had left on all last night and the night before because I was to busy with homework and everything else.

Cameron and I had went to the library and I tutored him for about 15 minutes before he gave up and wanted to go home. He seemed tired, but in a good mood. When he read, which wasn't much at all, he said his wrods differently. I assumed at first that he just did it by accident and was tired. After much more thinking, I had thought that maybe he had this disorder displayed on my computer screen.

Beside my laptop was my phone. It lit up and vibrated right off the desk. I picked it up and saw it was 20% battery as well as a text from an unknown number that made it vibrate in the first place. I quickly shut down my laptop and plugged it in the charge. A yawn surpised me as I made my back over to my bed which was calling my name.

Unknown Number: school was cancelled. Wanna study?

I racked my brain for a moment in attempt to figure out who it was. I can never function completely when I first wake up so I was a little foggy. Then it hit me, it's Cameron! I gave him my number the last time we were together at the library and he was just now using it.

Before replying, I walked out of my room and downstairs to find my mother fooling around in the kitchen. She had on her work clothes and was messing around with pancake batter when she sqealed, a puff of flour flying everywhere. I held back a giggle as I went to help her. Mom was moving her hands around and dusting the flour off of herself when she saw me. Her movements were frantic and all over the place as she tried so hard to clean herself off.

"What's going on?" I asked her as I dusted the flour out of her hair. It was cascading down down onto her shoulders into soft wavy curls like it usually was.

"School was cancelled becasue of the snow. I still have to go to work and I'm trying to make pancakes for Matt..." She rambled as she hastily continued to pour the pancake batter into a frying pan. I slowly reached forward and grabbed the frying pan handle, "Here, mom. I'll do this. You go get cleane dup for work." I gave her slight shove.

She gave me a grateful cmile before kissing my forehead and setting the bowl down that had batter in it. I wiped off the flour that her lips left on my forehead and continued to make these pancakes for Matt. My mom ruffled his hair as she passed Matt, who was coming to check up on his pancakes.

"Are they done?" He asked me. He stood on his tip-toes so he could see how they were doing in the frying pan. The skeptic look on his face mad eme laugh.

"Almost." I patted his head and shooed him away. As the pancakes cooked, I lifted myself onto the counter and picked up my phone from where I placed it before helping my mom. I swiped it on and tapped on the unknown number.

Me: Cameron?

I didn't want to look stupid for talking about something that only the two of us know about.

Unknown Number: yeah

I quickly added him into my contacts and went back to messages to reply to him.

Me: ok. and isn't the weather bad for us to be going out?

Cameron: i was thinking i could come to your house

I thought about this for a moment. Would my mom mind if I had him over? I know my dad would mind me having a boy over, but he's at work. It would only be for a little while, anyways. Then I had the weather to worry about. Maybe it now being almost 10:00 am the roads wwould be a litle better.

"Mom?" I flipped the pancakes once and ran back the hallway to my mom and dad's room. Mom stood in front of the mirror, adjusting her new outfit and pulling her hair into a ponytail since it was damp after her shower.

"Is it okay if I have a freind over. I'm tutoring them." I was careful not to say it was a he so she didn't flip out. She turned around and had a wide grin on her face.

"Yes! I mean, if the roads aren't bad. I'm happy to see you've made more friends!" My mom gushed. She knew about everything that happened between me and Danielle and the other girls on my basketball tema that I call my friends. I knew she was secretly hoping I wouldn't end up a loner, which is what I've become.

She went back to getting ready and I hurried back to the pancakes, turning tehm off. Matt sat at the table as I cut his up and poured syrup on them. This was his favorite breakfast of all. Matt smiled up at me, his two front teeth missing. I almost forget about him losing both of them. It was one of the most important parts of his life according to him.

I opened my messages again and typed away a response that I was almost happy about. This coul be awkward, or I could let go of all the awkwardness I have in me and act like a normal teenage girl.

Me: you can come over at 10 if you want. do you know where i live?

He replied a few minutes later, which was enough time for me to scarf down two pancakes. My mom also came out and kissed Matt and I, giving us instructions on what to do today. She told me to shovel the sidewalk in front of the house and the one that led from the garage to the front porch and fold the laundry. I didn't mind it since I wouldn't be doing much more today.

I grabbed my phone after she left for work.

Cameron: just give me your address

I typed in my address and rushed up to my room after cleaning up the mess in the kitchen. If I was going to have a friend, a boy for that matter, come over, then I wasn't going to be in pajamas. I pulled on a pair of faded boot-cut jeans and a comfortable blue areopostale long sleeved shirt. Afterwards I allowed my brown locks to be their usual wavy selves and went downstairs.

Matt was in the living room watching morning cartoons. I decided to get a move on with my chores and start shoveling snow. It was still lightly snowing out but the temperature wasn't so low that I'd need a snow suit on. I wrapped my winter coat around me and slig on my gloves as well as a scarf and a hat that covered my ears. Matt didn't seem to notice when I slipped on my boots and out the door.

A shovel was waiting for me propped against the side of the house. I grabbed a hold of it and began shoveling the snow out of the way of the sidewalk.

Just as I reached the middle of the sidewalk that led to our grage, a truck pulled up in my driveway. I pulled the shovel out of a snow pile that it was jabbed in and leaned on it. Cameron stepped out of his truck wearing jeans and his snow stuff. A steelers toboggan covered his fluffy brown hair.

He slammed his door shut and stood there for a moment with his hands stuffed in his jacket pockets.

"Need some help?" He asked me. I snapped myself out of the invisible trance I was in and dropped my shovel in the snow before grabbing another one out of the open garage. I handed it to Cameron without a word, but with a smile.

"Thanks," I said finally. Cameron started to shovel on the opposite side of the sidewalk while i continued from where I was. We slowly met in the middle.

Cameron's shovel was stuck on mine when he tried to get the last little bit of the snow in the middle. A smirk grew on his lips as he stood there, not moving. I leaned on one leg and cleared my throat, trying to play along.

"Eh hem. I believe i'm trying to clear off this snow." I grinned at him and rested my hands on the handle of the shovel, my chin on top of them. Cameron's smirk turned into a cheesy grin and he shoved his shovel so that it took all the snow.

While his back was turned, I bent down to pick up a snowball. I stood up and tossed it at the back of Cameron's head, hitting my mark right on. He froze for a moment before turning around a revealing a chunk of snow of his own. I squealed and took off running around the house. Cameron of course followed me and chucked his snowball at me. It hit my back and I ran faster.

Me being my clumsy self, I slipped in the snow and fell onto my back. I think I was on the patio in out backyard which is what made the ground so slippery. Cameron must not have been able to stop in time because his body came down onto mine, knocking the air of me.

We both burst out laughing and I couldn't help but notice how close our faces were. I continued laughing my butt off as did Cameron, and he helped me up onto my feet. My pants were a little wet frrom the snow so I decided we both had better go inside.

Still laughing, Cameron and I stepped inside the back door. Matt came running in and jumped up and down in front of me. He obviously had to much sugar at some point when I was outside.

"Matt, what did you eat?" I questioned. Cameron joined me after he hung his stuff where I hung mine. I noticed how he looked at Matt, then at me and had a satified look on his face. Yes, Matt and I do look an awfully lot alike. I smiled to myself and turned my ayyention fully to my little brother.

"Yeah! I ate pixy stix that were in the drawer. They were so good! Oh, and the marshmallows and cookies in the cabinet." i clamped my hand over Matt's mouth and picked him up in one scoop into my arms. i carefully walked in to the living room and dropped him on to the couch. He exploded into a fit of laughters and I playfully threw a blanket on him, covering his view from everything.

I turned around and ran straight into someone's hard chest. I felt my cheeks heat up when i realized it Cameron who was smirking down at me. I laugh at myself. Who else would i have ran in to? The boogy man?

I waved Cameron into the kitchen so we could start studying. After grabbing my book out of my bag, I laid it down on the kitchen table so we could start. Cameron seemd as if he was battling his thoughts when I sat down. He snapped himself back into reality and smiled at me.

For the first time in the one week I've been talking to Cameron, I felt butterflies erupt in my stomach. He had a flawless smile. So, I made the decision to hide away all the awkwardness that might come out off what I was about to say.

———————————————

Mwaha! Cliff hanger. Well, I guess that's what you would call it.

Tell me what you think!

Vote/Comment/Fan!

Chapter Seven: I Know a Cute Couple When I See One

C hapter Seven:

I Know a Cute Couple When I See One

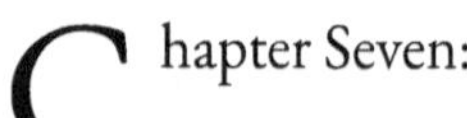

Cameron's POV

I sat up in my seat at Sophia's kitchen table and waited for her to say what she was trying to say. I came here earlier so that she could tutor me a little bit more. Instead, it turned out ot give me some of the most laughs I had in a long time. I also wanted to tell her about my disorder, but seeing that we were having a good time together, I didn't want to ruin it all by her feeling sorry for me. I hated it when people felt sorry for me and I wasn't about to let her do it.

"You know, you should smile more often. It makes you look," She pursed her lips and narrowed her eyes at me as if to find the right word, "Cuter."

Blush crept her neck and rested on her cheeks. It didn't leave for a while, either. I smiled at her as she looked down at the book in front of her. I chuckled at her reaction and opened my book to the right page.

Sophia told me where to start off at and pointed to the paragraph that we ended at. I began to read slowly and tried to process each word so it wouldn't come out wrong. It was hard to do, to be honest. All the letters were jumbling in my head and I couldn't tell if one said dig or big. It was frustrating to no end.

Finally, after about a half an hour of reading and straining my brain, I asked Sophia if we could just stop for a while. She seemed to be studying me. Like she could just tell that's what was wrong with me. It may sound childish, but I honestly have a feeling that if she finds out she'll see me as...well... I don't know, weak? What would she think of me as?

Nothing, now quit being a baby and tell her so there are no more secrets. The voice in my head snapped at me. I mentally smacked myself in the head so it would leave me alone.

"Sure. Do you want to watch a movie or something?" Sophia asked as she stood up from her seat, her book locked in her arms. I arched an eyebrow at her offer, "What kind of movie?" She shifted on her legs nervously and looked around the room, "I have a bunch in my room. Come pick some out and we can watch them down here with Matt." Before I could object, she turned on her heal and was walking up the steps.

I slammed my book shut and followed her up the steps. In her room, I admired the pictures she had of her and her family all in one of those boards girls put there pictures on. They were all of her and Matt when they were younger, along with some of her friends that I recognized from school. I never see her talking to those girls anymore, I wonder what happened to them. Maybe they got in one of those fights girls get into and don't talk to each other for a while. Then again, Sophia isn't the type of girl to hold a grudge.

My mind had a ton of questions floating around in it when I reached a picture that just about made my jaw drop. I turned around to see if Sophia was looking at me, she was digging around in her back pack with her book still her hands, mumbling to herself.

The picture was her -a little younger looking than now- sitting on a hospital bed with Matt against her. She had her arm slung around his frail shoulders while he was slumping down under her arm. Sophia was dressed in regular clothes, but Matt was in a hospital gown. He looked really different with no hair and a bandana wrapped around his skull. Did Matt have cancer? Does he still have it?

I plucked the picture from the board and turned to Sophia. I sat down beside her, making the bed sink under my weight. When she looked up to see what was in my hands, her whole body tensed from beside me. I felt a pang of guilt run through my veins when her face became wary.

"Is this, uh, Matt?" I asked, unsure of how to approach it. Sure, it wasn't really my business, but I don't think Sophia will push me away from this.

"No," She said a little to quickly, "That's my, uh, Cousin. Yeah, he had leukemia." For some odd reason, I could sense she was lying. It was practically etched all over her facial features. I decided not to push the subject since she obviously didn't seem to want to talk about it.

"Over there are the movies." She broke the comfortable silence that fell over us. I followed her finger until I laid my eyes on a stack of movies that were all lined up in a crate acting as a shelf. There was another crate sitting on top of the movies loaded with chapter books. They looked like they had been read. Gosh, Sophia must really like reading.

"How about Harry Potter?" I asked her, pulling it out of the shelf. She took her eyes away from the photo she was putting back on the board. I stood up when she nodded, walking over to her and standing behind her in grit of the board.

"Who's this?" I pointed to the girl standing beside a younger Sophia. They were both in our high school's basketball uniforms and making a Number one sign with their fingers. The girl beside of Sophia had blonde hair that was pulled back into a ponytail and light Blue eyes with freckles sprinkled across her nose and cheek bones. Sophia smiled for a moment.

"That's Amber. She sits at my lunch table and we used to play basketball together," She pursed her lips, "We don't talk as much anymore." Before I could ask more questions, Sophia turned and began walking out the door. I clamped my hand around the DVD in my hands and followed her downstairs and to the living room. Matt was staring at the TV watching Tom and Jerry while he was sprawled out on the floor. Sophia suddenly stopped in front of me and held her pointer finger up as if to say hold on a minute. I stopped and waited for her turn around and tell me what was up.

"Would you mind helping me with one more thing before we turn the movie on?" She asked me eerily. I stared at for a second before nodding my head and following her to wherever she needed me. We ended up in the laundry room, grabbing clothes out of the dryer and tossing them into a basket. Sophia propped them up onto her hip and walked out of the room and back to the living room. She dumped them on the love seat and dropped the basket to her side, catching Matt's attention.

"Whatcha up to, sis?" He bounced up on his feet and wrapped his arms around her waist. A smile spread across her face from ear to ear and she patted his back, "Folding clothes. Cameron here is going to help me." She gave me a pointed look and I smiled down at the dark haired boy. He had a frown on his face before tugging on his sister's shirt gently.

"I thought I was your helper?" He pouted, his bottom lip flopping out. His Blue eyes grew wider and made me almost melt- Wait. I'm not a softie. I simply grabbed a pair of jeans that looked like might be her dad's and began to fold them. My mom used to make me help her fold our clothes, so I wasn't new to this kind of thing.

"You are! Just... Why don't you clean up your little mess here," She gestured to his the blankets and pillows spewed out on the floor, "and we'll make a big bed so we can all watch Harry Potter?" Matt's face immediately lit up and he flung himself towards his things, gathering them up in his small arms and carrying them up the steps.

"I guess he likes Harry Potter?" I asked Sophia as she began to fold some clothes as well.

"Yeah. That's why we have the movies." She said matter-of-factly. I nodded my head, wanting to know why she liked them, like I did.

"Which one is your favorite?" I picked up a t-shirt and folded it while I waited for her to respond.

"Probably The Chamber of Secrets. I've read all the books, but I've never watched the movies." She told me. She's never watched them, yet she has the movies?

"Of course you've read them. You're like a little bookworm." I joked and smiled at her. When she giggled, it was like music to my ears. Corny, yes. Sophia smacked my arm with the shirt she had in her hands playfully.

I kept my eyes on her red face as I picked up something else, only to look down and see a pair of pink zebra-print underwear in my hands. I kept my laugh down which was most likely making my face red, "Hey Soph, look what I have."

"I told you not to call me- OH MY GOSH!" Her face began to burn red as she snatched them out of my fingers and waded them up, placing them under another t-shirt that must've been hers. I let out an enormous amount of chuckles that made me feel like I was going to have abs on top of the abs I already had.

"Your pretty pink panties!" I said through laughs. Sophia scowled at me. I could tell she was holding back a laugh.

"They aren't panties," She scolded me, "They are underwear." I saw the blush continue to color her face beet red as she explained it to me.

"Whatever you say. Everyone else calls them panties at school." I told her with no shame what-so-ever. I'm serious, the guys are always talking about how they can see a girls "panties" at the parties they go to. I only go to them occasionally. Plus, the girls in my gym class are always talking about it. It's almost annoying, but, then again, I'm a guy, so it doesn't bother me to much.

Yet, I was kind of relieved to hear that at least one girl doesn't obsess over that type of thing.

"Well do I look like everyone else?" Sophia's blue eyes looked directly at mine for a second before she tore them away, a triumphant smile forming on her plump pink lips.

"Nope," I pressed my lips into a thin line to keep from laughing again while the two of us hurriedly finished folding the clothes. When we were done, Sophia went to put the piles of clothes where they belonged while Matt came back downstairs.

"Wanna help me make some popcorn?" I asked Matt. He looked at me with a wide grin before nodding his head eagerly. I followed him into the kitchen and waited for him to get the bags of popcorn out of the cabinet beneath the counter. He handed me two of them and i gave him a questioning look.

"One bag is for me and the other is for you and Sissy to share." He instructed me, "You two are really cute together." He added. My eyes went wide at his words, a 7-year-old? At least, I'm pretty sure he was seven. Maybe he wasn't, but he looked like it.

"What? Sophia and I aren't-" I was cut off when Matt cleared his throat.

"I know a cute couple when I see one." He said sophisticated. I stifled a laugh as I continued to help him with the popcorn.

This has turned out to be the weirdest tutoring session ever.

Sophia came back into the kitchen, "Want to help me lay some blankets out, Matt?" She pointed her thumb towards the living room and sent a small smile to me. I didn't take my eyes off her even when her and Matt went to the living room. What Matt said...

Wait, no.

I could never and would never feel that way about Sophia Belle. How could I? What would the guys think? She's only my tutor and that's all she'll ever be. Besides, I haven't know her for that long. Sure, I've been through almost all of high school up to now, our 11th grade year, but I've never talked to her as much as I have now. That's the end of these thoughts now.

That's what you think. The stupid voice in the back of my head spoke up. I shook my head violently and heard a beeping noise that indicated the popcorn was done. I aggressively popped the microwave door open and took the bag out, opening it up and setting it on the counter.

I searched the the few cupboards above the counters to find a bowl and finally found two, one blue and one yellow, and sat them down. After the other bag of popcorn was done popping, I poured both bags into the bowls and sprinkled salt on them both before trotting into the living room.

"Looks like me and you have the whole floor to ourselves. Matt snuggled up ot his favorite ninja turtles pillow and passed out." Sophia giggled as she looked at Matt. He was lightly snoring as his chest moved up and down. I smiled at him and turned my attention to Sophia who was looking at me expectantly.

Oh, I have the popcorn.

I handed her a bowl and sat down beside her on the large unzipped sleeping bag she had laid out on the floor, "Guess we have our own bowl of popcorn." I told her.

I leaned my head back on the couch as the movie began, the two of us instantly became glued to the TV.

———————————————

Give me your feedback! What do you think?

Vote/Comment/Fan!

Hope you liked it!

Chapter Eight: A Bit of Heart Break

Chapter Eight:

A Bit of Heart Break

Sophia's POV

I felt my eyelids trying to slide shut as my head leaned against something hard. Something that I opened my eyes to see was Cameron's shoulder that I was leaning on. A blush warmed my cheeks, but I pushed it away.

I wasn't in the mood to pick up my head and move it. Plus, his shoulder was more comforting than I thought it was at first. That is, until I could practically feel his eyes burning a hole in the side of my skull. I felt my eyes try to slide shut again, but the movie was almost over and I didn't want to miss the rest. We were right at the part where Harry is about to fight a gigantic snake.

Quite like the book, if you ask me.

I felt myself begin to fall but soon realized that Cameron was lowering himself down so that he could lie down on his back. My head fell forwards and stayed on his chest while he cautiously rested his arm -the one I was laying on- on my torso. I felt tingles on the skin that my shirt wasn't covering on my waist.

I could feel Cameron's heart beating in his chest, faster than you'd expect it to be right now.

I brought my hand up to the side of my face and rested it on his chest beside my head. My eyes slowly began to flutter shut but I already felt like I was in dreamland, having a boy this close to me. it's never happened before. Like, ever. This was new to me.

I glanced up at the mirror my mom had hung above the TV set and caught a glimpse of Cameron's face. It was emotionless. His eyes were on the top of my head and he had his -emotionless- thinking face on, eyebrows furrowed. I felt awkward for a minute. His hand lightly played with the tips of my silky brown hair as his face stayed the same.

Right as I was about to fall asleep and brush this feeling of sadness I got from just an expression on Cameron's face, the phone's ringer burst through out the house. I shot up so quick I was sure I would have whiplash when this was all over.

I grumbled under my breath as I stood up quickly, not having time to look at Cameron. I wanted to get to the phone before it woke up Matt. My hand wrapped around the phone and I read daddy across the screen. Mom put his name in the land phone so if he called, we'd know who it was.

I mentally groaned before pressing the answer button and holding the cold object to my ear. I noticed that my contacts were getting a little blurry on me and that I was about to fall asleep with them in -not a good idea. I allowed my fathers deep voice take over my attention.

"Hello?" I answered.

"Sophia? Hey, I'm working late and I need you to tell your mother when she gets home. She's not answering her phone because she's at work." He paused for a moment before realized that I got all that, "Are you guys doing OK? How's the weather at the house?"

"It's fine. We're fine. Can I go now? I was just about to fall asleep. And you almost woke Matt up." I scolded him. My dad knows I'm protective over Matt, so anything that rubs me the wrong way that has to do with him, I'll step up and take someone's head off if I have to.

My dad chuckled which made me smile, "OK, Soph. I'll talk to you guys later. Love ya."

"Love you too. See you in a while." I told him before hanging up the phone. When I looked back over at where I had been laying at, I saw it was empty. Cameron was up and moving around at the backdoor area.

I stepped into the small corridor that allowed me to see the doors and him. I crossed my arms over my ribs and leaned against the wall, sleep was calling my name.

"Where are you going?" I asked innocently. I was secretly hoping he wouldn't leave right now. Mom wasn't going to be home for another three hours and dad was coming in late which means -since he's a cop- he'll be home at around 8:00 tonight. It was going to be boring around here since Matt was conked out.

Cameron's face went back to it's usual frown that I always saw plastered on his face at school when he turned to me. He was pulling his heavy coat over his shoulders and pushing his feet into his boots.

"I have to go home, my mom'll be wondering where I'm at." I knew it was more than that. What, was he to shy to tell me the real reason why he was leaving? Maybe that was slightly true, but it wasn't the whole truth. I was used to telling the truth from a lie. When Matt first got sick, my parents tried to tell me it was just the stomach flu.

I wasn't stupid; I knew that a little kid like him puking up blood wasn't just the stomach flu.

I felt like what I did when that moment happened in my life; Lied to for my own good. Then again, I was probably pushing it to far on the subject like I was earlier and pushed it away, looking back up at Cameron. I just now noticed that he was probably a half a head taller than me. If I was to hug him, which won't happen, my head would be perfectly under his chin for him to rest it on the top of my head.

Pshh, a weirdo? Me? Nahh.

"OK, sure." I gave Cameron a reassuring smile. Regret flashed over his facial features before he dashed out the door, closing it behind him. I dropped my arms to my sides and walked into the dining room to see the book we've been studying out of laying on it. I sighed and grabbed it quickly before running towards the front door, hoping to catch Cameron before he left.

The only thing I caught was the sight of the back of his truck speeding off down the street. I groaned and tossed it back on the table, making a mental note ot take it to school with my tomorrow morning to give it to him.

I walked into the living room and collapsed on the floor where I once was laying -with Cameron. I couldn't tell if I was just acting all zombie like because I was tired, or pouting because I didn't have a cuddle buddy. I slapped myself mentally for saying "Cuddle Buddy".

I laid my head down on the warm pillow that still had Cameron's and mine's heat on it. In less than a second I was out like a light.

I woke up to the sound of a door opening and shutting. My eyes were burning slightly and I hopped up, realizing my contacts were still in. I rushed into the downstairs bathroom and plucked one of my other contact cases out from under the bathroom sink. I sighe heavily, still feeling a little sleepy. I walked out into the dining room to find my mom carrying in a few grocery bags. Catching glimpse of my glasses on the kitchen counter, I pushed them onto my face, wondering how they got down here.

"Hey," My mom began as she emptied the bags and put the contents away, "Where's Matt? And your dad?" I fixed myself onto a bar stool and leaned my elbows on it while I watched her. This would be the moment where she turned around and scolded me for not helping her, but I was still slightly in dreamland since I just woke up and didn't really care.

"Oh, uh, Matt's asleep and Dad has to work late." I informed her. She looked at me with frustration written all over her face. She groaned loudly, "Why can't he just call me and tell me that next time? I brought home some hamburger helper for dinner; his favorite." She said as she clutched the box in her hands.

"He said he did but your phone was off," I took up for a dad, "You can still make that. Me and Matt love it." I chuckled at her frustration and hoped off the stool I was sitting on and walking towards her.

"OK, I'll make it for my babies." She cooed as she enveloped me into a hug. I was as tall as my mom, her heels made her an inch or two taller this time, though.

"Mom, I'm not a baby." I reminded her as she released me from her half-death grip. She laughed and turned towards the stove where she would start to cook our dinner, "You'll always be my baby no matter how old you get."

I faked a choking sound, "Mom," I held my throat like I was actually choking, "Stop it, you're choking me with your kindness." I rolled my eyes playfully as she scowled. I sat down at the bar again and watched her bustle around the kitchen and make her magic on the stove like she always did.

"So, I was thinking, for Matt's birthday-" I jumped up at the reminder of his birthday.

"When's his birthday? I totally forgot. Oh my gosh, how could I forget Matt's birthday?!" I rambled on to myself. I paced back and forth frantically, racking my brain for something that I could get my baby brother. What all does he like? I asked myself.

my ranting was cut off by the sound of a spatula slamming into the counter. I whipped my head around, my hair smacking me in the face in the process. Mom had an amused grin on her face from my actions. I narrowed my eyes at her while I pulled up the sleeves on my long sleeved shirt before sitting back down.

"It's OK, Soph. We can go shopping soon and get him something for his birthday. I was thinking about having him a surprise party. Like right here in our backyard. When it clears up that is." She mumbled as she cooked up the food.

That;s right, Matt's birthday was in the beginning of March. Although it was still January, mom and I like to plan ahead when it comes to Matt. You never know what to expect with that boy.

After dinner was over, I slipped upstairs and took a shower so I wouldn't have to rush in the morning. Dad told me that the roads were cleared up pretty well and I was supposed to start getting warm so we most likely would have school tomorrow. That was OK, I wanted to go to school. In a way, I mean. In another way, I kind of wanted to avoid it.

After a shower, I put on the same pajamas I had on the night before and laid down in my bed, pulling out a book and beginning to read it. It feels nice to be able to read after so long. I wasn't as tired since I had a nice long nap so I will be able to stay awake for a while longer.

I stared at the book that was laying on top of my back pack. It was the one that Cameron left and I had carried it up here after dinner so I would remember to give it to him. I felt the urge to tell him that, so maybe he'll reply and I won't feel so gulity. I feel like I did something to make him leave. There's only one way to find out.

Me: hey. I have your book that you left. i'll give it to you tomorrow

I quickly texted and sent it to him. After not getting anything back, I slowly began to fall asleep, my phone in my hand. I plugged my headphones into it and let the song Secrets by OneRepublic, my favorite singers, put me to sleep.

Video to the side of the song.

Secrets by OneRepublic.

I love that song and OneRepublic so... anyways, sorry for a bit of a boring chapter. It kinda needed to be there.

Vote/Comment/Fan!

Chapter Nine: Three-Pointers & Rambling

C hapter Nine:

Three-Pointers & Rambling

____

I stepped foot off the stinky bus that I was forced to take today because of all the ice and adjusted my backpack, letting my hands hang from the straps I held on to. My dad decided that I wasn't walking today since ice was covering the sidewalks. He thinks I would fall and die. Well said dad, well said.

Just as I opened the front doors to the school, the bell was ringing for everyone to get to class. I immediately sped down the hallway towards Mrs. Foster's classroom. Being late was one of my fears; I had managed to keep a perfect attendance these last few years of high school. I still have my senior year to keep it up, nothing's impossible.

I charged through the door and realized I still had my backpack. Oh well, now was not the time to worry about that. I quickly took my seat before Mrs. Foster could enter the room and realize I was late. As I went to sit down, my chair was pulled out from under me and I busted my butt on the hardwood floors of the classroom. I groaned aloud and let my head fall back to see who the culprit was. Of course.

I was staring into the dark Brown eyes of Danielle Pierce. She had an evil smirk growing on her face as she tapped her fingers on the chair. If it wasn't basketball season, she'd have long, french tipped, fake nails on her real ones. That's just how she was.

I grumbled to myself and stood up, dusting off the dark jeans I had on today. Danielle seemed more confident now than she did in the bathroom the other day when she told me to stay away from Cameron. Which reminds me, where is he? He wasn't in here right now...

I hastily took my chair from her grip and ignored all the giggles and laughs I was getting out of this class. Danielle stepped closer to me before I sat down. She fixed her white scarf that was wrapped around her neck, "I told you to stay away from Cameron." I rolled my eyes at her and sat down.

I have nothing to worry about. Besides, how did she know I hung out with him yesterday? Did he say something and she overheard? He doesn't want anyone to know he's being tutored, though, I imagined the only person that knows is Adam, his best friend.

Mrs. Foster came into the room finally and sat down at her desk. Today seemed like it was going to be boring.

Once class was over, I stuffed Cameron's book back in my locker since I had the feeling I wouldn't see him soon today. As I began to walk away and to my next class, I ran right into him. I am good at jinxing myself. I smiled up at him and barely noticed he had his friends with him. Wesley, Zach, Cody and Adam all looked at me in confusion. Adam's face was less confused than the rest, though.

"Hey, Cameron. I have your book in my locker-" I jabbed my thumb in the direction of my locker and narrowed my eyes at him when he interrupted me, "I don't know what you're talking about." He said nervously. I slowly caught on to what he was doing. Snickers sounded from the boys behind him while Adam just stood there, looking disappointingly at Cameron.

I crossed my arms and stood there for a minute, letting the frown on my face become a natural thing. "Okay, whatever you say, jock." I spat at him before walking right between all his friends, purposely bumping into his shoulder. He never budged, but I heard his friends continue to carry on.

I was beginning to think that this kid is bipolar. One minute he's sweet and funny, the next he's either looking confused or mad about something. I will never understand why popular people did that. You know, dust a new un-popular friend off like they were nothing. Oh Cameron, no, I wasn't helping you learn or anything.

That's it. The next time I find him alone, I'm bringing up the dyslexia thing. It doesn't matter if he gets mad or not. I need to know, and he needs to get help on it or else he won't get his grades up. I have a feeling his parents had something to with it all, too.

A few classes later and it was time to eat lunch. I was overly excited about eating since I forgot to eat this morning. I know what you're thinking, how could someone forget to eat? Well, you see, my brain is always jumbled together. You never know what to expect with my brain. If that makes any sense what-so-ever.

I quickly grabbed my tray, passing all the lunch table that held a lot of popular people. The only person I didn't see was Cameron. i saw all of his friends, his jock-jerk friends. All of them played sports. Wesley and

Zach, the twins, play football. Cody plays baseball and soccer and Adam plays basketball with Cameron. The two of them are best friends and seem completely dedicated to playing basketball.

I sat down at the end of my table, a few girls sitting at the other end. Amber, who usually sat between the group of girls and me, scooted down and sat directly in front of me.

"What's up?" She asked, smiling brightly. I cocked an eyebrow as my jaw almost fell to the floor. I haven't to my ex-best friend since I quit basketball. She knows why I quit yet she left me all alone when Danielle decided that I was a waste of time to talk to. No more basketball = no more friends.

"Hi?" My answer came out more like a question. Amber's smile didn't fade as she began to take a bite of her sub we were served today for lunch. I hesitantly took my eyes off of her and took a few bites of my own food, my stomach growling in the process.

"So, how's life been?" I could tell that Amber was trying her best to keep a conversation going. She used to be my best friend. She know everything about me. How could I not talk to her?

I know that she hasn't exactly been there for me and all, but I didn't want her to feel the way I have been for past while. She doesn't seem to hang with as many people as she used to. Maybe I should just give her a chance...

"It's been good. Matt's healthy," I remembered telling her everything after what happened to him, "everything else seems to be going good." I finished. I didn't even think about what just happened in the hall. Cameron's in denial and I'm just going to have to accept it until find him and talk him out of it.

"Awesome. Uh..." Amber trailed off as she thought of what to say, "They are having try-outs for the girls All-Star team. Are you doing it?" She took a bite of her sub and waited for my answer.

"I doubt it." I replied. Of course I wouldn't. The reason I stopped playing in the first place was because I was dedicated to staying at the hospital with Matt and also my parents couldn't afford to keep me in it. Now that my dad can spend more time for his job, things have gotten a lot better. I still didn't feel comfortable playing the sport, for some reason.

"C'mon, Soph. You are a great player and I know you miss it." Amber told me excitedly. Why does she not understand that I just don't want to. I won't like any of the girls on the team.

"You know, I think the reason that Danielle doesn't like you that much is because you were the best on the team. Honestly. I always thought you were," She paused for a minute after realizing I wasn't as interested, "Just think about trying out, OK? I'll tryout with you?" I didn't respond as I took more bites of my food. I didn't really have anything to say. Finally, Amber sighed heavily and tapped her finger on her tray.

"I'm really sorry, Soph. I was a horrible friend." My eyes widened at her words. Amber wouldn't make eye contact with me at all for a minute. She stared down at her tray and awaited my answer once again, "I should've stuck by you like a great best friend would do. But I didn't and I'm so sorry. I really miss you." Her voice was full of regret as well as her eyes when they finally met mine.

"I really missed you, to. Amber, don't feel bad, OK?" I rested my hand on hers to give her reassurance. I was never one to hold a grudge against anyone. Even if she did leave me hanging, I can't stay mad at her. Especially since we'd been best friends for years before basketball was even in the picture.

Amber stood up with an empty tray and hugged me. I hugged her back, happy to have my best friend back.

I scurried out of the lunch room and down the hall before the bell even rang. I was aware that we had about 15 to 10 minutes left before the next class started but I was hoping to clean my locker out. It was a little messy and I don't have time to clean it out between classes. After school isn't any good either because I have to run to catch the bus.

As I twisted the combination, I heard the faint sounds coming from the gym that I had a good view of from my locker. The doors were propped open and the smell that I had grown used to was in the air. When I saw Cameron move in front of the basket that was visible to me, I knew now was my chance to get him alone.

I reached in my locker and pulled out the book he'd left at my house and walked up to gym, cautiously stepping inside. Lucky for me, only a few kids were sitting on the far end of the gym with textbooks in their hands most likely studying, They were the over achievers in all our classes.

Cameron had on his gym clothes; a pair of dark blue basketball shorts and a muscle shirt that showed off his sides, and his unbelievably buff stomach. I kept my eye glued to the back of his ruffled brown hair to keep myself contained. It's so weird saying that...

Cameron shot, the ball hit the back board and bounced onto the floor. He kept his eyes trained on the basketball hoop, most likely swearing at it. The ball slowly rolled to a stop right at my feet.

I debated between picking up and shooting it and kicking it back to him. I went with the first choice and picked it, the surface of it feeling foreign to me. With Cameron's book stuffed in my sweatshirt pocket, I made the shot, swishing it and watching Cameron slowly turn around. I had just made a three-pointer and I was feeling pretty proud.

Cameron's eyes went wide when he noticed it was me. His hands placed on his sides and his foot stuck out so he was only leaning on one. I did a very sad attempt at wiping the triumphant smile that was growing larger by the minute. I couldn't help it; I hadn't shot a basketball in what seems like forever.

Seeing that Cameron was to stunned to move his feet, I walked up to him and tugged the book out of my pocket, practically throwing it at him. I wasn't trying to be mean about it, it just kind of came off like that. The smile on my face made it less mean.

"Why were you late today?" I asked him as I put both my arms behind my back and held them there. I always did that when I was standing up, I'll never know why it's a comfortable position.

"I woke up late. Got here after 1st period." He told me. His fingers ran over the pages and fanned his hair softly. I waited a minute before I finally decided that now I should ask him what i really wanted to, putting the earlier events behind us. Like I said, I don't hold grudges and I'm not going to start.

"Um, can I ask you something?" That caught his attention as he nodded his head. I followed him over to the bleachers and sat down beside him. The kids that were studying got up and left, probably because the bell was going to ring in a little bit. Cameron propped his elbows on his thighs and leaned on them, playing with the book still in his hands.

"If it's about earlier today, I'm really sorry. I was being a jerk and-" He said suddenly, throwing me off guard. I didn't really expect him to apologize.

"No, no. It's not about that. I'm not mad over that, I understand." I replied honestly. Cameron looked over his shoulder at me and raised an eyebrow, probably expecting a different response from me.

"What is it then?" He asked as he turned himself sideways so his legs were straddling the bleachers we were on. I cleared my throat because I knew this conversation could go two ways. He could blow his top or he could just let me help him and stay calm. I'm hoping for the second one.

"I've noticed how you kind of, uh, have trouble reading sometimes. It frustrates you. I can just tell." I began. Cameron's facial expression went emotionless as I continued to talk, only making eye contact a few times since his eyes were glued to the gym floor. He propped his Jordan's up on the seat and put his arms around his leg.

"I was wondering... do you have Dyslexia? Well, you don't have to tell me. I was just wondering because I could not put so much pressure on you to read and I could, you, know help you or something. Isn't that why you needed help in the first place?" I rambled on about it until Cameron's face started to get red. I felt my heartbeat quicken as he sat on the seat in a regular style, feet on the floor.

"Sophia, I don't need or want help. This is why I didn't tell you in the first place! I don't want your pity." He slightly raised his voice, making me cringe at the sound of it. I wasn't used to that coming from him.

"I wasn't pitying you, Cameron. I am trying to help which is what I'm supposed to be doing as your tutor!" I shot back. I was careful not to raise my voice like he did. No, I'm not going to stoop to the level of arguing over something like this.

Cameron looked at me and his face softened, "Well, now you know. I don't want people knowing my weaknesses. So don't think you can run off and tell your little friend that the jock can't read to save his life." He referred to what I had called him earlier. OK, that hit me in the heart. I can't believe he would think I'd do that. I racked my brain to try and think of a good reason he'd say that. I am not like the others. The only reason I can think of is that he's only known me -besides just knowing who I am or if I exist- for a little more than a week.

"For one thing, I am offended that you think I'm that cold. And for another," I paused and just pure rage was wanting to come out as my face reddened, "What friends would I tell it to? Cameron, that is something I would never do and you have to understand that!" I practically yelled at him. I had a feeling the veins in my neck were standing out like they used to when I yelled. It was never often, mostly during basketball games or something, but I never yelled.

Cameron put his head in his hands and ran his fingers through his tousled hair. It took all I had not to get up and walk away. My dad always told me not to run away from my problems, they only got bigger. Right now, I feeling it couldn't be bigger than it is.

"I'm sorry, Soph." Cameron's blue eyes met mine and they were filled with worry. I scanned his facial features. From his light spread freckles to the button nose and his perfect lips.

"I don't want your pity, Cam." I said softly. It was almost mockingly to what he said a minute ago, but I tried to not make it be since I was trying to be the mature one here.

A light smile tugged at his lips when I called him Cam. You'd think we had been friends forever just by what we call each other. I sunk down on the bleachers, leaning my back on the seat behind me. It takes a lot to hold all the anger I've got in me to settle it down. I never express my feelings in anger because I was taught it was bad to that way, but after all i've been through with Matt, almost losing him, and just everything like basketball girls, I could scream at the top of my lungs and it still wouldn't be fine.

Cameron could tell all this. I had the feeling he could by the way he was looking at my furious face. Amazing how you could know a person by spending such little time with them.

"Let's shoot some hoops before the bell rings." Cameron smiled down at me as he held a hand out to me, standing in front of me. I blinked a few times to keep the hot tears from spilling over and looked up at him. I uncrossed my arms and let them fall to my sides.

"Don't make me do something you'll regret." He teased and shook his hand anxiously. I kept my face straight as I stared at his shaking figure. He grinned down at me and did something I didn't see coming.

———————————————————

Ohemmgeeeeee!

Whatdoyouthinkhedid?*Wiggleseyebrows*

Letmeknowinthecomments!

Vote/Fan/Comment!

Gotabooksuggestionformetoread?Orevenyourown?Tellme!I'lltrymybest-tocheckitout!

Thanksforreading!Hopeyoulikedit(:

Chapter Ten: Detention? Ugh.

C hapter Ten:

Detention? Ugh.

My heart rate accelerated when Cameron got closer and closer to me. His arms were outstretched and a smirk was plastered on his face. I had a feeling I looked completely stupid sitting there. My eyes were huge in confusion and I gulped.

Before I could run away from him, Cameron wrapped his strong arms around me and lifted me up over his shoulder. I screamed at first and felt all the blood rush to my face when I realized I had the perfect view of his butt. Well....

"Cameron! Put me down!" I shouted as I pounded my fists on his waist. It wasn't long before he did and I found myself in the middle of the gym floor. A few basketball's were still scattered on the floor and I watched Cameron pick one up. He tossed it right at my head, most likely trying to get me in the face with the ball. My reflexes kicked in when the ball was literally an inch away from my face so my hands caught it.

I peeked at Cameron past the ball and saw him gawking at me. One of his stupid smirks came along and made me drop the ball to rest at my side. I narrowed my eyes at him, knowing he was up to something.

"Let's see how well you can play a game." He told me, shooting the ball in his hands at the basket. I rolled around the rim before falling through the net and bouncing to the floor. Cameron jogged up to get it and put it on the tip of his finger, spinning it around cockily. I rolled my eyes and tossed the ball I had over my shoulders before agreeing to his challenge.

"Your on. First one to 20 wins." I said. Of course, at the time, I never even thought about us having to get back to our next class because by the time Cameron shot the the basket that allowed him to win th game, the tardy bell rang. Kids filled in the gym for their gym class and I about fainted. My French class was on the opposite end of the school and I had less than a minute to get to it. I glanced up at Cameron who I realized still needed to change into his regular clothes.

He dropped the ball in his hands on the floor and darted to the locker room. This was better, in a way, because now he can't gloat to me about how he won. He only won by two points! I had 18 and he got 20 right before the bell rang. I guess I still have a little pizzazz left in me.

I took off down the hallway, walking swiftly to my locker. Not having time to grab the correct books out of my locker, I looped my arm through the strap of my backpack and slammed my locker door shut swiftly.

I caught a glimpse of Cameron dashing out of the gym. He must have me to because he winked and took off down the hall. I blushed and glanced behind me, wondering if that was meant for me.

It totally was.

I am turning into such a girl. Ugh.

I continued down the hall until I reached the door to my French teachers room, Monsieur Parks, and stopped for a moment. He was going to explode. That's what he did to the other kids every time they came in late. You know, I'm always there on time so maybe he'll go easy on me.

I reluctantly knocked on the door and it was opened immediately by a student with the hall pass in there hands. My eyes widened in shock when I saw Monsieur Parks staring at me with his icy cold glare. I mentally groaned and dropped the hand I had knocked with to my side.

"Quel plaisir de vous joindre à nous, Miss Belle." He spoke to me. Of course, being an A+ student in his class, I knew that meant, "How nice of you to join us, Miiss Belle." I gave him an apologetic smile before scurrying to my seat. I was completely aware of all the pairs of eyes on me as I sat down.

"You'll serve an hour of detention after school," Monsieur Parks said in English to me as he wrote it on a slip and laid it on my desk. I ran my fingers over the pink sticky note and felt my cheeks redden. I had never gotten detention before and I didn't want start now. This is just great. Since I was sitting in the back and Monsieur Parks was sat up front at his desk that was facing towards the door, I reached for my phone in my pocket. I tapped on the message app and pulled it up, tapping on Cameron's name. Hoping that his phone was on silent, I quickly texted a "I'm going to kill you." And put my phone away. That's right, it was all his fault that we were both late. If we had detention together, I was going to strangle him on the spot.

Before the bell rang for the next class, out vice principal came across the intercom with a message. I grinned my backpack straps in my hands and waited for her to continue.

"During 8th period, I would like all students to report to the gym for a pep rally. The occasion is for the girls' basketball team who are leaving for championships this evening after school. Hope to see you there!" Mrs. Rodriguez spoke. The bell rang and everyone cleared out of the classroom, I still had my detention slip clamped in my hand. As sweaty as my hands were, I was sure that it was going to dissolve from the liquid. I was still a little hot from playing that basketball game earlier.

All through French class, I couldn't get my mind off of Cameron. How he reacted in our last conversation. I wanted to pretend like it didn't happen. Because let's face it, it didn't go near as planned.

I neared my locker to see Amber waiting for me. She had a giddy smile on her face which -if I remember correctly- meant that she had good news. I felt the corners of my lips twitch upwards at her as I approached her. Since I already had my books and junk stuffed in my backpack, I didn't need in my locker.

"Hey," I greeted her, a small smile to go with it. Amber's grin widened even more, "Hey, Soph! I have great news. It's so exciting." She was practically jumping up and down while her backpack was banging against her spine.

I laughed at her, "What is it?" Amber looped her arm through mine as we trudged towards the gym doors. Eighth period was about to start so we were going to get some good seats to the pep rally. It was best not to get the ones close to the band because they would blow our eardrums out. At any other pep rally, we'd sit near the top of the bleachers so we could see good, hear fine, and stay out of anyone elses way.

When Amber and I entered the gym, I saw that Cameron and Adam had thought of the same thing. Cameron was sitting on his hands looking around anxiously as his legs bounced up down. I gave him a weird look even though he couldn't see me.

"Anyways, It's Adam. Remember how I used to have a crush on him during basketball season? Well he asked me to go with him and his friend to this indoor mini-golf thing this weekend." She explained way over excitedly. Wait a second...

"What friend?" I asked her, trying not to sound to suspicious. We had both stopped at the doors of the gym as we talked.

"Cameron, I think." Amber tapped her chin and looked up at the ceiling as if in thought. Danielle had an evil smirk as she walked by us, obviously hearing everything Amber had just told me. I growled under my breath which only made her cackle. I grabbed Amber's arm and followed behind Danielle into the gym completely.

I was planning on sitting with Cameron and Adam until Danielle stalked her way up to them. Stuck in the crowd of kids filling the gym quickly, I watched as Cameron gave her small-unsure smile. She was asking about something, I could tell. Adam smiled at her as she talked and nodded his head while Cameron simply had a confused expression on his face but nodded anyway.

Danielle turned around towards our direction, smirking. She strutted down off the bleachers and walked past us, finally getting Amber's attention.

"Oh no." Amber muttered under her breath. I turned to her but kept moving us through the crowd. Her eyes were locked on the same place that Danielle was just at. She must've seen what happened and knew what was going on. I sure didn't.

"What?" I asked anxiously as we stepped up on top the first bleacher.

"I bet I know exactly what Amber just asked them." Eyes wide, she looked at me with a frightening look.

Yes, Amber didn't like Danielle as much as I did. During basketball, I happened to be the Captain since I was level headed -seriously, not tooting my own horn, here- and a good player. Danielle was obviously jealous and pulled the stupidest pranks as well as faked injuries when Amber and I were around.

Needless to say, she made basketball horrible for us.

I followed Amber closely as she shoved through people, cussing under her breath as she did so. Typical Amber. She wasn't scared to do anything unless it got her in big trouble. Like pushing through people, she just wasn't embarrassed by, well, anything really.

I grunted when someone accidentally elbowed me in the side. It was a girl that seemed to be a freshman by how young she looked. She automatically shook her hands and said sorry at least five times. I told her it was fine and continued after Amber again. She finally stopped, a smile on her lips. She was looking at Adam before she crossed in front of them to sit beside him. Cameron stopped acting like a nervous wreck when his eyes met mine. A goofy smile on his lips made me chuckle and sit beside him. I was still clutching the pick detention slip and it reminded me that i was going to kill Cameron.

"So, did you get detention?" I asked him. He shook his head and smiled while pulling out his phone. He checked the message that i had sent him a while ago in French class.

"According to this, you must have." He showed me the screen of his phone. I couldn't help but notice that my name was Soph in his phone. That's what it said across the top of the screen, anyway. I scoffed at his reply, "Are you telling me that you don't have it?" I was shocked! How could not get it but I did? Is Monsieur Parks that evil? Is he the only teacher that would give a student detention for coming in late?

Cameron let out a light chuckle, "Nah. I got it. For an hour after school." He told me, leaning back against the bleachers behind him. I thought about how funny it was that just a little bit ago he didn't want his friends seeing me with him yet here I am. I also caught a glimpse of the rest of his friends sitting at the bottom of the bleachers gawking at the girls about to come out of the locker room in their basketball uniforms. No, they didn't really reveal any cleavage, but they'd find something to stare at I'm sure.

"Me too." I told Cameron absent mindedly. I glanced over at Amber who was giggling every second as Adam flirted with her. It doesn't even seem like he was flirting on purpose, it just came to him when he was around Amber.

"I thought you said you didn't have any friends," Cameron cautiously asked me. I could tell he wasn't trying to strike a nerve so I answered nicely.

"We actually made up today. It surprised me, to be honest. I didn't see it coming. I mean there was a little conversation between us every once in a while but today she actually apologized to me. That's big." I crossed my arms and leaned back like Cameron was. I stared off at whatever caught my eye in front of me and waited for Cameron to reply. He just nodded and we waited for the pep rally to begin.

My mind drifted to Danielle when she came running out of the locker room, leading the team. She was also the oldest on the team, being a senior this year. Her and I had one class together which was one that she failed; Mrs. Foster's. Yet somehow, her rich daddy must have bribed the coach to allow her on the team.

Coach Fawley, the boys' coach stood on the sidelines and watched everything happen before him.

I turned to Cameron who was watching the gym floor and all that was happening, "I saw Danielle talking to you," I forced a smirk to not look to jealous, "Was she bugging you?"

Wait. Did I just say I was jealous? No! Of course not! I simply wanted to know if he was bugged by her presence.

Cameron groaned, "She's annoying. It'll be great when she graduates and we never have to see her again." He grinned up at me. I couldn't help but smile back, that crooked grin getting to me.

Oh lord, what is this boy doing to me?

____

Heh heh. What do you think Cameron will do about the mini-golf thing?

Vote/Comment/Fan!

I follow back, remember that ;)

Thanks for reading!

Chapter Eleven: Stuck In The Storm

C hapter Eleven:

Stuck In The Storm

Is this ever going be over? Detention was definitely the worst. Ms. Wiggins, the 56-year-old woman who was our guardian during detention, fell asleep on the desk in front of her. Ever since her eyes fluttered shut i wondered if she was still breathing. That woman needed to either retire or go home and never come back. Same thing, really.

I had to endure Cameron throwing paper balls at the back of my head for the rest of the hour. It was torturous not being able to turn around and choke him to death. I had a feeling that would just get me detention again. That was the last thing I wanted. So, I glared at the chalk board in the front of the room and allowed the hundreds of paper balls bounce off the back of my head.

I fixed the glasses on my face, wishing I had my contacts in instead. These stupid glasses were making it hard for me to put my head down and come back up without a mark on my nose. Of course, I had the option to take them off but that would involve me possibly losing them to Cameron or a paper ball.

As soon as we were allowed out of the school, I made my way towards the student parking lot. Then it hit me, literally. Cameron hit me with yet another paper ball while he was walking to his truck. I didn't have a ride home and guess what? The clouds in the sky only proved that it would start snowing soon. Feeling defeated, I trudged over to Cameron's truck just as he was getting in. When his eyes landed on me he rolled down his window and rested his elbow on it.

"As much as I don't want to," I jokingly lied, "I need a ride home." I faked an annoyed look and watched as he put his truck in drive.

"Well, I guess I could give a pretty lady a ride home." He said with a sly grin. My cheeks heated up when he called me pretty and I smiled, running to the other side of his truck. I tugged on the door and got it open before I jumped into it. Cameron started driving down the road.

I watched the sides of the road how snow was piled up along them, covering the ditches. There was still a good bit of snow on the ground but in empty corn fields you could see the remaining corn stalks sticking up from the snow. it looked like a lot of fun to just run and jump into.

"What's the deal with you and basketball?" Cameron suddenly asked, bringing me out of my train of thought. His face was serious now and I could tell he really wanted to know. I just shrugged my shoulders, not wanting to tell him about Matt. Besides, it wasn't his business, right?

"I just kind of... stopped." I lied. i would have never just stopped playing basketball. I lived that sport. Heck, it was all I ever did. When I had free time, I was outside shooting hoops in our paved driveway no matter what the weather was. Raining, I had a rain coat on. Snowing, I had boots and a warm coat on. I gave it up for my little brother, to spend time with him and because I just couldn't play when we were so low on money.

Cameron stared at me for a long moment as if trying to place something. I bit my bottom lip and stared at the yellow line in the middle of the road. Snow was beginning to fall, and fast to. You almost couldn't see in front of you. Cameron finally decided to keep his eyes on the road and left the subject be for a while. Hopefully he wouldn't bring it back up for a while.

I leaned forward a turned the radio on, Rebecca Black's "Friday" was playing. I thought this song already had its days? This song got so annoying. How could it still be playing on the radio? Oh yeah, it's Friday! That still doesn't matter. I reached forward again to change the station but Cameron smacked my hand. I winced and pulled it back, staring at him in shock. He was to busy singing along with the song to notice he left a red mark on my hand.

"So, this is what you do in free time?" I laughed as he moved around in dramatic ways. I had a feeling he was pretending to like it just to make me laugh, but there was a little bit of doubt in that. I found myself laughing so hard at him that a few tears came out of my eyes and my stomach muscles were killing me. Cameron himself ended up laughing to. The song changed to something I didn't recognize and our laughs died down.

"You're an amazing singer," I told Cameron sarcastically. He just bowed in his seat, "Why, thank you, ma lady." I giggled at his silliness and looked in front of us. Holy crap, you couldn't even see the road in front of us. Panic suddenly rose up in me.

"Uh, Cameron..." I sat back in my seat further. He glanced at me and a worried expression crossed his angelic features, "Yeah? What's wrong?" He asked.

"Can we pull over or something? This is caring me. We could wreck!" I babbled. I didn't even realize what I was doing until I did it. I had unbuckled my seat belt and was scooting myself into the middle seat of his truck. I quickly buckled myself right back up and unconsciously put my back against his side. I couldn't help it; I cuddled next to anything possible when I was scared.

When I touched Cameron, I felt his muscles tense. They slowly went back to normal and I was able to concentrate on how we were going to get out of this safely. Cameron pulled over onto a gravel pull-over area where he must've known was going to be there. I sat up against the seat and watched his as he pulled his phone out of pocket, dialing a local number. He tapped his fingers impatiently on his knee as he waited for the person on the other end to pick up the phone. His face brightened a slight bit when a voice rang through. I could hear mumbling as the other guy spoke.

"Hey dad," Cameron began, "Can you come get us? I'm pulled over on the side of the road because I can't see the road." I looked out the window to see a few cars go by very slowly. It's a good thing that it's Friday or else there would be no school tomorrow. I have things to do, like my sports article in the school newspaper. That was very important to me.

"Yeah... OK. We'll be here." Cameron said after giving his dad directions to the place we were at. I would've never known where we at, I was horrible at directions.

Cameron slipped his phone into his pocket and turned the heat off. I knew he was trying to get the truck warm because we'd have to turn it off soon. We'd run out of gas and/or get poisoned by the gas. I sighed heavily, feeling tired right now. It was a long day at school.

I unbuckled my seat belt and scooted my butt towards the other seat so I could lay down. Cameron tensed up when I laid my head on his lap. I looked up at him with a ginormous grin on my face as he stared at me with no expression. "Now would be a good time to explain that I get loopy when I'm tired. And then I get grouchy. So watch out." I giggled as I made a makeshift gun with my fingers and pointed it at him. A smile broke out onto his face and I laughed. Suddenly, a hiccup escaped my mouth and I quickly placed my hand over it. I couldn't help but laugh even more, my whole body shaking with laughter. Cameron's booming laugh erupted after mine and I knew I wasn't going to stop laughing any time soon. This was to funny to me! I turned my head to the left so I was facing the steering wheel, my forehead touching it barely. Under my head was Cameron's knee.

"You're comfy," I told Cameron as I yawned. He chuckled and ran a hand through my silky hair. "Well, thanks. Your hair is soft." He replied in a low voice. I laughed and turned on my back so I was staring up at the ceiling of the truck, glancing at Cameron every other second. He reached for the keys to turn the truck off without breaking the gaze between our eyes. I felt my lips stretch in a smile and slowly fade when my eyes were becoming heavy. Cameron continued to play with my hair which only made me even more sleepier since that's what happened to me when someone played with my hair. He slowly became blurry as my eyes fluttered shut, never taking his eyes off mine.

*

I woke up by the sound of a loud motor roaring by. My head was in the same position on Cameron's lap and he was softly snoring while sitting up. I felt a little guilty for making him sit up and sleep while I got to take up the rest of seat. A coat was blanketed over top of me as I flipped it off to reach for my phone in my pocket. We had only been asleep for 15 minutes. I looked at all my missed calls, all from my mother. Well, that's not good. I quickly sat up and dialed her number, knowing I was in for it.

"Hello?" She answered frantically.

"Uh...hey mom." I said hesitantly. I knew she was going to yell at me... I could prepare myself..

"Sophia?! Where are you? Are you OK?" Her voice was filled with worry as she rambled so many questions on. I bit my lip and waited for her to finish, peeking over at Cameron to make sure I didn't wake him up.

"I'm fine, mom. Cameron and I got stuck in the snow storm so we pulled over and his dad is coming to get us to take us home; safely." I told her. Then I realized, I never told her about Cameron. Or that he was the friend I'd been hanging out with, or that he was a he.

"What? Who is Cameron? Where are you?" I could hear my dad in the background laughing along with Matt's adorable laugh.

"Calm down. I'm tutoring him. He was giving me a ride home after-" I stopped myself before I went on saying I got detention. That was another story for another time, "school." I finished Cooley. I crossed my fingers in hopes she wouldn't ban him from my life since I didn't tell her about my friend being a guy.

"So that's the 'Cam' Matt hasn't stopped talking about? Well... As long as you get home safely. I don't care. I expect to meet this 'Cameron' the next time he's with you, understood?" Mom's voice was stern but I could tell that she wasn't to scared of me being with him. I had good judgment, which meant that I would never take a ride or invite someone to our house unless I knew them.

"Yes ma'am." I replied with a light chuckle. I never called her ma'am but it seemed appropriate. Cameron moaned from beside me and I jumped, holding my hand to my heart. I said a quick 'goodbye' and 'love you' to her before hanging up and pushing the phone back into my pocket.

Cameron rubbed his eyes and did a double take when he saw me out of the corner of his eye. I giggled at his shocked expression.

"What? Did you expect to see a model sitting here?" I asked jokingly, crossing my arms loosely over my lap. Cameron just made a weird expression that meant he was still trying to wake up, "No, I didn't know if you were really here." My heartbeat quickened as I tried to figure out what that meant, but was distracted when I saw a Ford Explorer pull up in front of us. Cameron became even more awake as he checked his pockets quickly for his phone. He pulled out and murmured the 'S' word under his breath.

"I forgot about practise tonight. Coach Fawley is gonna kill me." He ran a hand over his face and groaned as he hastily shoved it back in his pocket. A man that looked an awfully lot like Cameron knocked on the window. Cameron didn't hesitate to roll the window down as greeted the man with a, "Hey Dad." I smiled at Cameron's dad when he waved at me.

"Let's get going, kids. I still can't see the roads so we need to get back to the house quickly." He told Cameron and I. We grabbed all our things and hopped out into the snow before we both climbed into the backseat of the Ford Explorer. I didn't question it when Cameron hopped in beside me, though.

Cam's dad got it the driver's seat, "I'm Dale, by the way. That's what you can call me." Dale said as he looked at me through the rear view mirror. I couldn't help but notice how much him and his son looked alike. Same brown eyes and everything.

"I'm Sophia, nice to meet you." I replied with a genuine smile on my face. Dale sighed heavily as he started driving, "Looks like you'll be staying over tonight, Sophia."

———————————————————

Chapter Twelve: Perfect

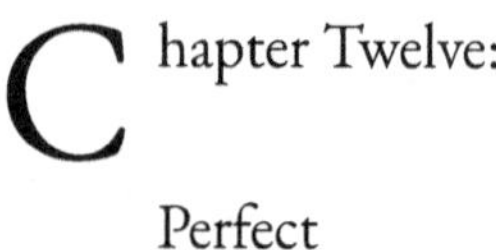

C hapter Twelve:

Perfect

We pulled into Cameron's drive way and parked, all of us hurrying into the house because it was so cold outside. Dale had called my mom and explained everything to her also telling my dad that he would keep and eye on us. My dad always managed to embarass me in anyway possible, most of the time not on purpose.

I met Andy, Cameron's mom, when we entered. She fussed at Cameron for wearing his shoes onto the hardwood floor and leaving wet snow where he stepped. Andy quickly turned her head to me and smiled as she stuck her hand out, "You must be Sophia, Cameron's tutor," I shook her hand na dnodded my head as if to say 'yes'. Cameron sighed at the word Tutor and gradually tried to pry me from his mother's conversations about him when he was little. Evidently he used to run around the house in cowboy boots, underwear, and a cowboy hat while yelling "Yee Haw!". I was never letting him live that one down, that's for sure.

Andy shooed us off so Cameron could give me something to sleep in.

I followed Cameron into his bedroom, taking in the Navy Blue walls and the random posters of basketball players on them. Like he did to me, I looked at a few framed pictures that were sat on his dresser. Only one caught my eye, Danielle. I almost gagged on my spit when I looked at the picture. It had several people in it including a Shirtless Cameron and his parents along Danielle, and older girl who looked like Danielle and two other older people that must've been Danielle's parents. They all stood on a sandy beach with the waves in background.

"I thought you didn't like Danielle?" I asked Cameron as I pointed to the picture frame in my hands. He glanced up from digging in the drawers of his dresser, a pair of grey sweatpants in his hands. He shook his head at me.

"I don't. She's a stalker. You'd think her being a year older she'd not want to mess with me, but she does," He stood up and walked over to me with the sweatpants in his hands, "Our families are kind of close. We go to the beach house her parent's own every summer. That's her big sister," He pointed to the older girl that I thought looked like Danielle. I nodded and waited for Cameron to go on with his story.

"I guess Danielle thinks she owns me or something because of that. It's not like I want to go to the beach with her. I like going to beach, just without her. I'm forced to go every year." He said matter-of-factly. I placed the frame back on the dresser and faced him, "Well that sucks. I mean, the Danielle part, not the Beach part. I like the beach too." I smiled triumphantly at the one thing we had in common. Cameron smirked as he stepped closer to me, our chests almost touching.

"We'll have to go there together sometime, then." I could have shrieked under his stare when my heart began to beat out of my chest. Could he hear that? The self-consious side of me was screaming. I freaked out, right then and there.

"I-I, um, are these for me? Thanks! Hey, can I borrow this sweatshirt to? I can just wear my cami underneath it and that'll be fine. I'll be right back!" I rambled nervously as I jerked Cameron's team basketball sweatshirt off his door knob and rushed out of the room. I turned left, hoping to find the bathroom on my own.

"Other way, Soph," Cameron chuckled at me. I gulped as my face turned red, turning the other way and heading towards the bathroom I could now see clearly. I avoided his stare while I walked past his bedroom again. I quickly went into the bathroom and shut the door behind me, locking it. What did I get myself into? It's not like I could refuse to stay here. For one thing, it wouldn't have been polite of me to say no to an offer of a nice warm house. For another, It's dangerous for them to take me home in this weather.

After dressing myself in the sweatpants which were very baggy, I took my shirt off and left myself in my cami, a spaghetti strapped tank top. I slipped the over sized sweatshirt on myself and cozier right into it. I pulled my hair into a low messy side bun to keep it out if my face. When I get back to my backpack, i'll have to get my skinny black head band to keep the stray strands out of my face.

Cautiously, I opened the door with my jeans and shirt in my hands, looking both ways as if making sure no one was there. I tiptoed over to Cameron's room and peeked in and saw him facing toward his dresser, searching for a shirt. He was shirtless. The muscles in his back flexed as he moved around and he finally pull a dark blue Nike shirt out to go with his black shorts. I stepped inside and sat my clothes on his bed near my backpack.

"Um, I'm sorry I made you miss practice." I told Cameron as he grabbed blankets and pillows from his closet and bed. He completely tore off his thick bed spread and in the process knocking all our stuff on it off onto the floor. I groaned and picked up all my crap before setting by the door. Cameron chuckled.

"It's not your fault. I shouldn't have got detention and I wouldn't have missed it. Besides, this is more fun than running the halls a million times," He rolled his eyes as he exaggerated. I smiled at this, no one ever likes spending time with me.

"Well, they should." Cameron smirked. My cheeks got red when I realized I said that out loud. Trying to avoid the awkwardness I was bringing on myself, I helped Cameron lay out the blankets and pillows that we would be laying on. He got up from where we was adjusting the blankets and opened up the cabinets under the TV stand that his small flat screen was sitting on. I sat down on the bed we made on the floor and sat Indian-style. The sleeves of the blue sweatshirt I had on came down over my hands and I clenched the ends in my fists.

"Okay, so how about the movie... Armageddon?" Cameron queried as he held up the movie case. I grinned wide before nodding my head excitedly, "Yes! I love that movie." Cameron chuckled at me and put the movie is before grabbing his remote and sat back beside me, his elbows brushing mine. I felt that spot tingle but ignored it. Of course it would, he has been saying the sweetest to me. Why me? I'd like to know that. I wasn't the type of girl people just take a liking to. Sure, I was friendly and all at school, but most boys don't see friendly as anything compared to "Skimpy" or whatever else.

I stared at the side of Cameron's face for a moment as I contradicted the thoughts in my head. What was wrong with him? Did someone put him up to being nice to me or is he doing it because he felt guilty for being a jerk earlier today? So many questions... I could just ask him, but that would be to easy. There's the possibility of him being nice because I'm his tutor but that won't last forever. Would our friendship last forever? this is the only set of questions that I don't know the answer to.

"Take a picture, it lasts longer," Cameron smirked as he turned his head towards me. I blushed and silently thanked the heavens it was dark in here so he couldn't see me blush. I laid back on my pillow and crossed my arms. The blanket on top of me was soft and comforting as I held on to it. The part where Harry is chasing after A.J with his gun was in and I giggled, this part always made me laugh. Cameron laughed from beside me and I shivered, his laugh was really cute.

I mean that in the manliest way possible.

*

I felt a tear slip out of my eye while they were glued to the TV screen. A.J was telling the other guys that Harry forced him to come back and go to earth to take good care of his daughter, Grace. It really got me when Harry shoved A.J into the tune to go back to their space ship. I had to continuously tell myself, "It's just a movie". Cameron was lying on his back with both of his arms behind his head. His eyes were closed but they fluttered open a few times before they shut again. I could tell he was trying to stay awake for my sake.

When the credits came on, I laid back onto my fluffy, Cameron-smelling pillows and snuggled into them as he turned the TV off. I adjusted myself to rest on the side of my hip and tucked my hand under the pillow, something I did every night to fall asleep. My eyes had been closed and oblivious to how close my face was to Cameron's. The creepy part was, his eyes were slightly open.

I held breath as I scooted away a small amount to that I wasn't breathing in his face. Cameron chuckled lightly as he turned on his back. I suddenly wasn't as tired as I was a moment ago and was wanting to talk. Even Cameron was sleeping, I'm definitely not letting him sleep.

"Hey, Cam?" I asked as I propped my head onto my hand, my elbow on my pillow.

"Hmm?" Cameron mumbled. He was clearly tired.

"What's it like?" I murmured. He turned on his side so he was facing me, his eyes partly closed as he adjusted himself.

"What's what like?" He replied.

"Dyslexia," I answered reluctantly. Maybe I shouldn't ask about that...

"It just makes it difficult to read and write sometimes. I didn't like reading in front of you because I only embarrassed myself." Cameron answered. I could tell it was truthful by the way he said it. I sighed.

"You don't have to be embarrassed to do anything in front if me, you know that, right?" I said quietly. Cameron's eyes bored into mine.

"I feel like I do. And I don't usually get that way around anyone," He replied. I'm pretty sure my heart skipped a beat.

"Well, I am embarrassed to do stuff in front if you," I told him matter-of-factly.

"Really? Like what?" He questioned like he knew I was lying. Which I wasn't.

"I don't know, anything."

"You don't have to worry about anything, Soph."

"Why not?"

"You're perfect. Every inch of you. Your personality and your adorable looks are just a bonus. Nobody wants to take the time to know you like I do, now, anyways. Don't ever be embarrassed in front of me." Cameron reached down for my hand, took a hold of it and squeezed it, not taking his eyes off mine.

I felt a smile on my face and it was impossible to wipe it off. With a heart beating a thousand miles a minute, my eyes gradually closed as did Cameron's.

———————————————

Chapter Thirteen: Snow & Ice

- -

C hapter Thirteen:

Snow & Ice

Sunshine came through the bedroom window and pierced my eyelids. I groaned and raised my hands to run my sleepy eyes. My left hand was laying on my side, intertwined with another hand. That hand wasn't mine, either.

My eyes shot open and I was completely aware of my surroundings now. The boyish decorations, messy floor, not to mention the boy snoring so quietly beside me that you wouldn't know he was snoring unless you were as close as I was. Cameron's hair was messily thrown around on the top of his head, his mouth slightly open. I looked down at our laced fingers and stared. Is this real life? I shrugged my arm in attempt to get my hand back, but Cameron's fingers tightened. He was still asleep with no other motion from his body.

When his grip released, I swiftly pulled my sweaty hand from his and cracked my fingers. They were sore from staying like that all night long. I quickly got up and tiptoed over top of Cameron to get to his window. Outside the snow was blinding when the sun reflected off it. The houses surrounding Cameron's were limited. Only one or two were scattered here and there. I noticed that we were back farther from the road, but it was still visible. I turned around from the window and saw Cameron wasn't where I left him. He was retreating to the bathroom, I caught a glimpse of his shirtless back while he zombie-walked out of the room.

This was going to be awkward.

Once Cameron came back in, he explained that we should go to my house, pick up Matt, then come back here and sled ride. I agreed, since I wanted to get some clothes as well. As we climbed into Cameron's truck (his mom and dad got it for him early this morning) I remembered what my mom said last night. She wants to meet Cameron the next time he's with me, which is now. I just hope my dad doesn't make a fool out of me or himself.

We approached my house and I sighed. The roads on the way here had been much better than they were last night. Considering it was 12:00pm, the state road workers really got their jobs done.

Cameron followed behind me as we went inside the house. Matt's footsteps came running down the stairs in front of the door and jumped in Cameron's arms. Cameron swung him around in a circle as Matt giggled.

"What am I? Chopped liver?" I joked as I placed my hands on my hips. Matt climbed out of Cameron's arms and got into mine. I kissed all over his face and neck, mi\aking him giggle and try to hide his face on my shoulder. I rested my head on his and squeezed him tight, happy to see his smiling face.

"Sophia?" My mom's voice rang throughout the house. I gently put Matt back on the floor and told him to get some clothes ready to go play in the snow. I followed my mom's voice into the kitchen with Cameron behind me.

"Hey mom," I greeted when I saw her cooking grilled cheese. Yum... That's my favorite lunch.

"Oh! Is this Cameron?" Mom wiped her hands on a dish towel and stuck her hand out for Cameron to shake. He had a wide grin on his face as he shook her hand. I scoffed, he was putting on his good boy act.

"Nice to meet you, Mrs. Belle." Cameron said. I never knew he could be a gentleman.

"You too! Do you guys want some grilled cheese? I can make more," Mom offered as she turned back to the stove. Cameron looked at me expectantly with a raised eyebrow. Something told me that he really did want a grilled cheese. Wait, no, it was him nodding his head up and down eagerly that told me that he wanted to stay and eat. I rolled my eyes, "Yeah sure. I'm going to take a shower and grab some clothes to take with us," I said more to Cameron than to my mom. Cameron nodded and my mom turned to me with a surprised yet happy expression.

"Where are you going?" I could tell she was trying not to get to into my business.

"We're going back to my house to sled ride, if that's okay with you, Mrs. Belle. We'd like to take Matt with us." Cameron piped in before I could. My mom's eyebrow rose before a smile took place on her face.

"Sure! That's sounds fun," She chirped. I groaned. If I would've asked that or said that, it'd be an automatic no. Stupid Cameron.

I stomped up the steps, passing Matt with his arms full of snow clothes, and went to my room. After grabbing all my clothes I needed, I went to the bathroom and took a quick shower. I blow dried my hair and pulled it into a ponytail before dressing myself in jeans, a big t-shirt from my basketball years, and a hoodie. Grabbing my bag of snow clothes, I skipped down the steps.

Matt and Cameron were sitting at our bar on the stools my dad had made as they stuffed their faces with grilled cheese. I immediately dropped my bag and waddled over to the stool next to Matt, putting him between Cameron and I. Mom placed a plate with two grilled cheese in front of me. I grabbed one and shoved it in my mouth not-so-gracefully.

Cameron snickered from the other side of Matt.

"I love grilled cheese," I said defensively. It wasn't as effective since my words were muffled with the food in my mouth. Matt giggled while my mom leaned on the counter in front of me, "We know you do honey." I grinned and kept the food in my mouth the best that I could.

A car pulled up into our garage from what I could see through the window of the door that led from the kitchen to the garage. Cameron's eyes widened, "Why is there a cop in your garage?" He asked casually. I giggled a little bit. There was a cop car in our garage, but it was my dad's patrol car.

"That's my dad, Cam." I told him. He gave me small worried smile before taking the last bite of his sandwich. My dad got out of the car and slammed his door shut.

"Where was he?" I asked my mom as I took up mine and Cameron's plate and placed them in the sink.

"He was called into town for a wreck. I guess everything went well because he's back early." My mom replied as she started to wash those two dishes. Matt added his dish to the sink.

The door suddenly burst open and my dad came in, obviously not in the best mood. I smiled and went towards him wrapping my arms around his neck, "Hi, daddy," I told him as I kissed his cheek. My dad smiled at me and caught a glimpse of Cameron and did a double take. I felt my cheeks redden in embarrassment for Cameron. It had to be kind of awkward for him.

"Hi, Mr. Belle." Cameron grinned. He was actually acting like the kind of guy my dad would want me to be with, a gentleman but not to fancy. My dad slowly took his shoes off and walked over to Cameron, without taking his eyes off Cameron's. Everyone in the kitchen was so quiet that you could hear a pin drop. My heart rate increased when I thought he was going to blow. I mean, he can't just jump to conclusions! He doesn't even know Cameron!

Wait, Cameron's only a friend. What do I have to worry about?

The expression on my dad's face was hard. His stare was hard and cold and i swore I saw Cameron step back when he got closer to him. Out of no where, my dad burst into laughter as he clutched his stomach. I found myself smiling at Cameron's reaction, plain out confused.

"Oh, son, it's nice to meet you!" Dad shook his hand roughly and walked past him into the living room.

The second we all three climbed into Cameron's truck, I burst out laughing with no way of stopping myself.

"You should've seen your face!" I laughed as he started driving off towards his house. Matt, who sat between us, laughed along with me. I turned the radio on so we wouldn't have to be so silent after my laughing seizure.

*

"So, Matty," I called to Matt as he wrestled with the snow to get up with his sled, "what do you want for your birthday?" I stepped into Cameron's footsteps so it wouldn't be as hard for me to walk in the deep snow. We were about to go down the giant hill behind Cameron's house when the subject of birthdays came up. I learned that Cam's is sometime in July, which already past and he turned 17 on his last one, I told them mine was in June and I had yet to turn 17. That means I'll be 17 when I graduate high school.

"I want a tree house!" Matt told me cheerfully. I laughed, "A tree house? Like a big one?"

"No, Soph. He wants one for his action figures," Cameron said sarcastically from in front of me. I punched his arm which didn't take any effect on him since he had layers of clothes on.

"I want to build one in our backyard. Will you do it for me, Cam?" Matt tapped his shoulder. Cameron turned towards me, "Of course. Sophia and I will definitely get right on that, buddy." Cameron smiled at me. I grinned, of course I'd help. To be honest, I'd like to have a tree house in my backyard. It'd be fun to hang out in.

"Okay! Everyone ready?" I asked. We were all on one sled, piled together. Cameron sat in the back and I had to sit between his legs while Matt sat on my criss-crossed legs. Cameron used his strong arms to give us a push down the hill. We glided along the path we'd already made as the cold wind pierced our skin. I let out a small squeal when we reached the bottom. I had a feeling that Cameron did it on purpose; he flipped us over and made all three of us tumble down the rest of the way. Matt was giggling like crazy as was I. I landed at the bottom of the hill and snow fell down the back of my pants.

I jumped up and started dancing around like a crazy person, "Oh my gosh! That's so cold!!" I yelled as I pulled the fabric off my legs so the snow could fall out of the bottom of my pant leg. Cameron and Matt were occupied by wrestling around. When the snow was finally out of my pants and giving me cold chills, I took off walking towards a forested area. A glimmer was what caught my eye when the sun reflected off a shiny surface.

"Hey, guy, what's this?" I waved them over to me as I kept walking toward it. I can't help it, shiny things always catch my attention. Unless it's jewelry, then, not so much.

The boys reached me finally and we all looked at the snow covered area. In a large circle, tall grass was sticking up out of the snow.

"Oh, this is our pond. It was here when my mom and dad bought this place before I was born. It's on our land, so my dad used to take me fishing in it," Cameron smiled at me, "I bet it's frozen." He wiggled his eyebrows at me and Matt before taking off towards the pond.

"Let's go ice skating!" Matt called. Cameron and I followed after him and got to the pond, stepping onto it. My foot automatically came out from under me and I fell onto my butt on the ice. Cameron laughed as he put a hand out for me to grab. Instead of letting him pull me up, I pulled him down.

That may have been a mistake.

Cameron's heavily muscled body fell right on top of mine, knocking the air of me. I coughed between laughs and smelled his minty breath on my face. Cameron let his head fall onto my face while the rest of his body went limp.

"Matt! Help!" I yelled as deafening as I could so Cameron would go deaf. Matt came sliding towards us and fell right on top of Cameron.

"Guys! My ribs and lungs are going to be broken!"

They both slowly but surely got off me, Cameron picking me so I could stand on my feet. He snickered, "A broken lung, huh?"

I threw my head back and laughed as his arms went around my waist to give me balance and keep me from falling on my butt again. My arms instinctively wrapped around Cameron's neck and we slowly slid along the ice with Matt.

This moment couldn't be more perfect.

Ugh, I know right. So lovey dovey. Sorry guys that don't like that kinda thing, I had to make this chapter at least a Little bit more interesting!

Thanks for reading!

Chapter Fourteen: Everlasting Smiles

- -

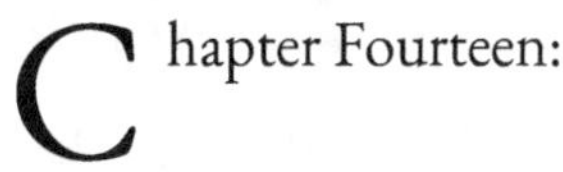

C hapter Fourteen:

Everlasting Smiles

____

It's crazy how time flies when you're having fun.

For the past few weeks, whether Cameron was at my house studying or I was at his, we always had fun. There were laughs and tears of joy.

Now I'm school, heading towards my journalism class which will allow me to be part of the school paper. I couldn't wait to start writing again after taking a break from that class. I had to, to get my credits to graduate next year. On the bright side, Mrs. Foster is sending in a good report on me for the college I want to go to. It's exciting for me, and all I had to do was tutor Cameron. That so far was the best choice I made because now, Cameron is like my best friend. Since I started tutoring him, I got Amber back somehow, which was very unexpected at first. She later explained to me that she just wanted to stop ignoring each other and get back to the way we used to be.

Speaking of the blonde, she was walking right towards me since we had journalism together.

"Hey, Amber." I waved and grinned at her. I still had my glasses on since I keep forgetting to tell my mom to get me some contacts. She hasn't been out towards the direction of where my eye doctor's building is in forever. Who knows when I'll get more...

"Hey," Amber chirped. Her hair looked like a professional beautician did it this morning compared to mine. I had mine pulled up into a ponytail since I didn't feel like doing anything with it this morning.

We walked side by side into the classroom and took our seats near the front of the room. Mrs. Reid smiled at me when she looked up from her computer. Mrs. Reid was a young woman probably in her late twenties. She had shoulder length red hair and warm brown eyes along with a heart made of gold. Many students think she's a push-over but those students have never been in her class. She can light someone's attitude on fire if they give it to her, which is why I don't giver her any.

"OK, class," She put her hands together and stood in front of us all. I gave Mrs. Reid all of my attention as she assigned certain students to certain columns for the paper. She finally came to me, "Sophia, I want you to do the sports." I smiled at her. This is great! I think this is actually a good one for me since I do like to watch the sports. The boys' basketball championships are coming up soon and I'll get a free pass to watch them as well as write about it.

"Can I help her?" Amber asked from beside me. I was surprised that she offered to help me write something since she didn't like reading or writing. She always tried to avoid it at all costs. Then again, maybe she's doing this so she doesn't have to be with anyone else. Besides, I don't think she really knows anyone else in this class that's not in our grade.

"OK. Both of you work together on this. Now, go to the gym because I heard the girls were starting practice for the all star team." Mrs. Reid explained and shooed us off.

"So, you wanna help me, huh?" I asked Amber as we walked towards the gym. She gave me an uneasy smile, "Yeah." There was something about the way she wouldn't look me in the eyes that made me a little on edge. I'd have to ignore it now, I have business to take care of.

We sat at the top of the bleachers and watched the girls' basketball team run back and forth while in a scrimmage against each other. I missed this so much; running and fighting for the ball to win for my team. It was so much fun and even more fun when we won the games. Now, I don't know if i'll ever get that awesome feeling back. Amber must have read my mind.

"You still have a week to decide if you're trying out for the All Star team. This is just for girls that are wanting to practice before the tryouts. I'll do it if you do." She gestured towards the court. We were currently waiting for them to stop so we could ask a select few if they want and interview for the sports column. Danielle was down there, and I was not asking her.

I looked over at Amber's hopeful face, "I don't yet, Amber. I mean... it don't have anything else on my schedule that I can't handle," I thought about tutoring, the tree house we're supposed to build soon - that is, if we are actually building it- and now All Star's. I chewed on my bottom lip.

"Just think about it. Call me or text me tonight and give me your decision." She replied. I nodded my head at her, "Oh yeah, how was your trip mini golfing with Adam and Cameron? And Danielle..." I added distastefully. Amber chuckled.

"It was pretty good, actually. Adam is awesome and Cameron is hilarious. And Danielle, well, she's Danielle." She told me. I smiled at the Cameron part. I knew he was hilarious. I was around him almost all the time.

"Cam is funny, isn't he?" I said almost dreamily. I quickly snapped out of that state and mentally slapped myself. Amber gave me a weird look and for a moment, I thought she was going to take back what she said. There was no reason for that, though, right?

"Yeah," She chuckled, "Danielle was kind of all over him. She tried to get his attention every minute. I actually kind of thought that he-" Amber looked at me with a guilty expression on her face. It's like she was having a battle in her head with herself between what she was going to say to me. I looked at her expectantly as I waited for her to finish what she was saying.

"I actually kind of thought he was going to punch, for real." Her usual smile surfaced and I knew she was being honest. For some reason, I felt like I couldn't trust Amber like I used to. We used to be inseparable until, well you know, and I could tell her anything. Even now I still do, but later on I feel like I made a mistake by telling her. It's just that I have it stuck in my head that her and I are back to the way we used to be. Maybe I'm wearing my heart on my sleeve, but usually my gut feeling is right.

"I bet she was fun to have along with you guys. I would've come, to be honest. Cam even asked me. I just... I don't know. I didn't want to intrude." I said more to myself so i convince myself that's why I didn't go. The real reason? Danielle is the one who continues to warn me to stay away from Cameron (Which I obviously haven't done) so why would I go with Cameron if I knew Danielle was going to be there? That would be like adding gas to the fire -deathly. Knowing that she spends her summers with Cameron doesn't help my situation. Who knows how she's going to torture me. Danielle has been known to publicly humiliate people just because of the smallest things. I'd be lying if I said I wasn't a little frightened at what she may do.

Do you want to hear the weird part? She hasn't paid me any mind since... Well, since the day she went mini golfing with Cameron. That was also near when Amber and I became best friends again and when I got my first detention. Did something happen on that mini golfing trip that made her change her mind about me? I can only wonder...

*

Cameron's POV

The bell rang for school's dismissal and I bolted out the door. With my backpack hanging from my shoulders, my eyes searched around the hallway to find one familiar face. I was way to excited for my own good to see her. Why? Because I love whenever she laughs, no matter how girly that may sound. I couldn't help it. Everything about her was just amazing. The way she understands me and doesn't get frustrated with me like most people do. She takes her time to get to the bottom of what could be bothering me. I know I shouldn't have these feelings wrapped up inside me, but they were there. The questions like "What will my friends think?" and "What would happen to my social status?" didn't even matter anymore. I could only concentrate on her.

Finally, my eyes landed on her short figure standing in front of her locker, Amber by her side. She listened contently as Amber rambled on about whatever it was she was rambling on about. Speaking of Amber, she doesn't shut up when she's hyper. A few weeks ago at our mini golfing trip, she proved that. A smile never left her face while Adam was there. The same for him to, he couldn't keep his eyes off the girl. Then you had Danielle who pulled Amber away a few times to whisper something to her. She wouldn't stay two feet away from me the entire time. To be honest, I was ready to punch that girl, Danielle. I didn't know if it showed or not but

Amber gave me curious looks that were mixed with guilty ones. I didn't really pat attention to them, though.

"Hey," I said cooly as I leaned against the locker beside Sophia's. Adam came along and stopped in front of Amber. She immediately stopped talking and grinned at him before walking towards the parking lot. I scoffed playfully, "OK, see you later to man!" I called after Adam. He put his hand up in the air and gave me a small wave without looking back. Sophia shut her locker and smiled up at me, adjusting her backpack on her back. She seemed happy about something and i had a feeling she was going to gush about it any second.

There's another thing that happened, she practically tells me everything. She made me promise that if one of us needed to tell the other something, that we would keep it a secret. And so that we wouldn't keep any secrets between the two of us. I agreed, I didn't have any secrets to keep from her anyway.

"I have great news!" She broke out in a smile as we walked towards my truck. Although the weather was warmer now and there was no snow, I insisted on giving her rides home. Even if we spent almost every second together, it was nice to have her around all the time.

"What?" I asked, interested.

"I got the sports column in the school's paper!" She squealed and hopped into my truck, "That means I get to come to your games and not pay to get in since I'm writing and taking pictures for the paper. It's so cool." I laughed at her giddiness and started driving towards her house.

"That's great, Soph. You'll be able to come to the championships next month. I'll have a cheerleader for me!" I squealed playfully like a little girl would after getting a new doll. Sophia threw her head back and laughed,

"Yeah right! I am not a cheerleader. There are actual cheerleaders for that purpose." I expected that answer.

I glanced at her through the corner of my eyes when we stopped in front of her house. It didn't take us long to get here.

"Remember, we are building the floor of the tree house, OK? How about we go to the lumber mill around... 5? Sound good?" She asked me. I remembered telling her earlier we could start building today, "Yep!"

She gave me one last smile before disappearing in her house.

The smile on my face never left.

Chapter Fifteen: Mickey D's at Midnight

C hapter Fifteen:

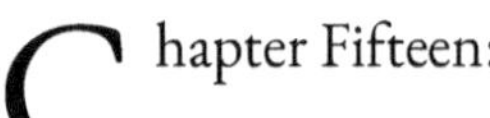

Mickey D's at Midnight

Sophia's POV

"Thanks, Mom!" I called over my shoulder as Cameron and I walked out my sliding back door. I heard my mom yell a "you're welcome" before I sealed the door behind me. In my hands was a plastic bowl filled with green juicy grapes. Cameron picked a few out and dropped them in his mouth while we made our way closer to the tree house.

After we got all our supplies, the two of us got started immediately. Now, with it being 10:30 at night, I could definitely say that we deserved a break. We haven't even eaten yet so we decided on grapes for now. With all the hard work we did, we got done with the floor of the tree house. Amazing right?

I'm not tooting my horn or anything...

I handed Cameron the bowl of grapes while I climbed up the rope ladder we hung off the floor. He tossed them up to me and surprisingly didn't spill them. I caught them with ease and relaxed back on my hands as I looked up at the sky sprinkled with stars. Cameron sat on the other side of the bowl and sat criss-crossed on his butt.

"What do you think about me?" Cameron asked so suddenly. I turned my head to him and stared at the side of his face for a moment before pursing my lips.

Why would he ask me that question? How in the world was I supposed to answer it? I think you are so cute, Cam. I think I like you. No, you can't just tell somebody that. Or could you? I quickly shook my head to clear those thoughts as my mind flooded with images of us together. What would people at school say? They'd pick on me and give Cameron crap for just about everything they could think of. Not to mention Danielle. Even if she has been backing off, something bad would happen. Something bad always happens to me.

"W-What do you mean?" I asked him nervously. I kept my blush to a minimum and thanked the lord it was dark outside so he couldn't see it creeping up my neck.

"I mean, what do you think of me?" His question repeated itself inside my head until I got so nervous that I thought I was going to pass out.

"I think that, um..." I trailed off as my eyes caught glimose of the bowl of grapes, "I think you're amazing. And my best friend ever." I told him as I crawled closer. If only he knew I wasn't trying friendzone him. If only he knew I wanted him as more than a friend. That was a big dream of mine.

"Best friend, huh?" Cameron said. I heard the small ounce of saddness in his voice as he said it. A pang of guilt ran through me right then. That's when I grabbed a handul of grapes and plopped one in my mouth. He had no idea what was about to happen.

"Forever," I murmured before chucking my handful of grapes at his head. He was taken off guard and his face was priceless. Before I knew it, Cameron was picking up handfuls of grapes, standing to his feet and throwing them at my head. I dodged a few, but the others just his my face and bounced off it and landed on the floor of the tree house.

I grabbed a handful myself and threw them at them, most of them completely missing his head or any part of him. In my defense, I could barely see! I kept closing my eyes and shielding my face so that the grapes wouldn't hit me. It cut off my way of aiming.

Cameron stepped towards me with a lot more grapes in my palms. I stood there and prepared for what he was going to do. Instead, his foot landed in the bowl of grapes. He lunged forward -into me- and grabbed my shoulders so he wouldn't lose his balance or so I wouldn't either. I laughed so much I thought I was going to have abs for a moment there. Cameron laughed along with me and didn't bother to move away from me. Not that I mattered, though. In fact, I liked being this close. Even if the butterflies were about to bust out of my stomach at any moment, I liked it.

Cameron eventually composed himself and unintentionally leaned his forehead against mine. I didn't notice exactly how awkward this would've been several weeks ago when we sorta hated each other's guts.

"Do you still like me as a best friend?" Cameron squeaked out in a raspy voice. I was about to ask him what that meant but instead he pressed his lips to mine.

I melted right into the kiss as my eyes fluttered shut and my arms went around his neck. No way in heck was I about to stop him. My lips were on fire from all the fireworks going off inside me. Not to mention my churning stomach. Cameron's hands went to my back and held onto me. It was like he thought I was going to fly away at any moment and he didn't want to let go. I felt the same right now.

Sadly, we both needed to catch a breath so he went back to leaning his forehead agaisnt mine. I still had my eyes closed, trying to figure out if this was a dream or not.

"Soph? Sophia? I'm so sorry. I shouldn't have done that and-" I cut him off by pressing myself agaisnt him tightly and my lips to his. Just for a brief moment, though.

"Don't ever apologize for doing that." I said breathlessly, not wanting to move from this spot. Ever.

The biggest and happiest smile spread across Cameron's face as he picked me up and spun me in a circle before kissing my lips again. Once my feet were on the ground, Cameron grabbed my hand and laced our fingers together. I squeezed his hand, letting the foreign feeling take its place.

"Are you hungry? Not for grapes, though." Cameron snickered. I laughed as well and nodded my head at him.

"Where are we going to eat though? It's getting close to midnight on a school night. My parents are going to freak that I'm even up this late and-" Cameron covered my mouth with his hand to stop me from rambling on.

"It'll be OK, Sophia. C'mon." He pulled me forward with him and we both got down off the tree house. It was probably a good thing that my dad helped us as well earlier or else we wouldn't it anywhere close to how it is now.

I followed Cameron out to the driveway in front of my house. He hopped in the driver's side of his truck and I climbed into the passenger side. My first instinct was to be nervous because I haven't exactly had a real boyfriend in my life. And even though he's not my boyfriend, I'm scared to death. He only kissed me and I shouldn't be freaking out because technically, a kiss could mean anything. I felt my heartbeat pick up as I tightened the seat belt around me.

"Do you like McDonald's?" He suddenly asked, bringing me out of my trance. I looked over at him and saw he was giving me a small smile. I had a feeling that my face was red.

"Yeah," Was all I could get out. Cameron pursed his lips and reached over the middle seat of the truck with his right arm. His fingers reached mine and they intertwined with each other, my fingers curled around his. For a moment I felt like I wasn't going to breath. Then he squeezed my hand and I came back to reality, tearing my gaze away from our hands and staring up at the side of his face. He glanced at me from the corner of his eye and a smirk formed on his lips. I smiled.

Cameron pulled into the parking lot and we both hopped out. I was eager to get some food but also to ask Cameron why he kissed me -of all the girls he could kiss, which he probably already has done. It seems crazy to me that somebody would actually like me. Cameron waved me over beside him and we walked towards the door of McDonald's.

Besides all those crazy thoughts running through my mind, a flyer for the girls' All Star basketball team was tapped to the front of the door. The soft breeze was blowing it up so I flattened it out with my hand. Cameron hadn't noticed as he opened the door. I quickly took my hand off the flyer and followed after him.

"What do you want?" Cameron asked, "I'll pay-" A loud growling sound erupted from my stomach and I burst into fits of giggles, my cheeks getting hot from laughing and embarrassment. Cameron laughed with me and I realized we had the very few people that were in here staring at us. I quieted myself down and told Cameron I wanted a Big Mac. He didn't question me on my big appetite, either. And I was happy that he didn't.

The woman at the register smiled at the two of us politely and gave us our orders without question. Cameron so kindly carried the tray over to an empty booth and sat it down, sliding into the booth as well. I slid into the one across from him and grabbed my sweet tea off the tray, poking my straw through the top of it. Cameron handed me my Big Mac and French Fries and he took his chicken sandwich and fries.

"So..." I hesitated. Instead of saying what I had to, I panicked and shoved the sandwich in my mouth. I probably looked like a slob right there with my cheeks puffing out from being stuffed with a burger. Cameron looked at me and waited for me to answer. I finally chewed down my bite and cleared my throat, taking a big gulp of tea.

I knew I would do this. I'm just going to change the subject and ask him why he kissed me later. Yeah, that sounds good.

"So," I started again, "Amber wants me to try out for the All Star team with her." I sputtered out. Cameron chewed on his food for a moment then smiled at me.

"You should." He told me. I gave a small and hopefully reassuring smile. But I don't think the smile reached my eyes. Should I tell him why I quit basketball in the first place? Why wouldn't he know? Well, it seemed like a lot of people didn't know that Matt once had cancer. Even though he collapsed in public, people don't act like they know it happened. We weren't really public about it, anyways. We never put it on Facebook or in the newspaper or anywhere else in social media so there's a reason people might have no clue about it.

And you want to know something? I think I need to get that off my chest. Since I don't like people in my business, I never told anyone. Should I tell

Cam? Can I trust him? He may have just kissed me and that might have not meant anything to him, but it did to me. And I have to not forget about how long he has been my friend. Not as long as a best friend should be, but I feel like I could trust him with my life.

"I don't know if I should, though." I shoved a fry in my mouth. "I mean, I quit for a reason." My eyes shifted to anything but his face. I'm having a war in my mind of whether to tell him or not. Why is this so difficult to tell people about? I sit because I want to protect my little brother's privacy? Or is it because I feel like telling people might just jinx me?

"What did you quit in the first place? You know, I remember watching you once, now that I recall. You were like... a ninja out there, Soph." He had an amazed expression on his face as he looked at me. I knew it was real; he wasn't just telling me that to make me feel better about myself. My cheeks still felt warm and were probably tinged pink. I bowed my head and looked up at him through my lashes.

"I stopes because," I cleared my throat and kept my head down, "my parents needed money for Matt and his..Leukemia treatments." My voice was low but, judging by the fact that he wasn't asking "what?", he must've heard me.

"It's OK, Sophia. You can look up at me now." He said softly. I forced my head up and looked at his eyes. They were kind and filled with something unexplainable. To my surprise, he doesn't seem completely shocked that I just told him my brother had cancer. It's like he already knew it, but how?

"He's OK now isn't he?" Cameron started as he laced our fingers together over the table. "You shouldn't have a weight like that on your shoulders."

"I know, Cameron. But Matt... what if it happens again and my mom and dad are all out of money? I just-" I choked on my own saliva and felt tears welling up in my eyes. No, I refused to let them fall. I didn't want to seem weak in front Cameron.

"It's not going to happen again. Yes, it could. You can't let that hold you back. I know you're only thinking of your family, but isn't that what you always do?" His fingers tightened around mine and gave me a surge of hope. A small smile made it's way onto my face. Cameron grinned wide, "That's my girl. And her beautiful smile." He leaned pressed his palms onto the table and leaned forward on the table, connecting his lips to mine.

*

Cameron drove me home that night at about 12:30. I definitely wasn't tired now since I had this crazy energy running through me like a wildfire.

I held tight to his hand as we walked as slowly as possible towards the front door of my house. Reluctantly, I slid my hand out of his and reached for the key to the door above the door frame. My dad always locked the doors at night which was a very smart idea.

Right as I turned to unlock the door, Cameron's arms snaked around my waist from behind and he rested his chin on my shoulder. My skin tingled from his touch, as weird as that sounds. I froze in my spot, hand in the air with the key dangling from it. I'm surprised that I hadn't dropped it. Suddenly I was being turned around in his arms. The key fell out and dropped onto the welcome mat in front of the door. Cameron pressed his forehead to mine and stared at me for a long moment, just smiling.

"I never actually asked you officially yet." He said, " Will you be my girl-friend?"

I felt my body tense. I've never been asked that question in person. Whenever someone asked me over text message or social media, I always said no. Either from them being to scared to ask in person or me being to scared to be in a relationship.

The words were on the tip of my tongue right then. I wanted to spit them out but they were frozen in their place. I raised myself on my tip toes and kissed him lightly and sweetly, taking my time removing them from his and whispered to him while my lips were barely off of his,

"Yes."

———————————————

For anyone who's reading or cares (Lol) Sorry I took so long updating! I've been reading the Divergent series and writing my other stories on top of school work. Thanks for reading everyone! I love writing for you people :D

Chapter Sixteen: Being Helpful

(I just wanted to let you see what Cameron was thinking at this moment! Sorry for such the short POV!)

Chapter Sixteen:

Being Helpful

Cameron's POV

A smile stretched across my face so wide when I heard the word "Yes" come out of Sophia's mouth. I wrapped my arms around her and picked her up, spinning around so she was on the edge of the porch. A giggle erupted from her mouth and she smiled up at me.

"I'll see you later?" I said in a low voice, resting my forehead against her's. She nodded her head and beamed at me. I leaned down and kissed her softly on the lips before stepping to the side and letting her unlock her front door. She stepped inside and waved goodbye to me before shutting the door completely.

With a warm, fuzzy, feeling swirling around inside me, I walked away reluctantly. There is nothing I'd like more than to just go lay down with her. Stare at the ceiling and talk. It sounds so good right now that I'm having trouble walking in the opposite direction towards my truck.

There is nothing that could make me happier right now.

*

Sophia's POV

I woke up with a smile on my face the next morning. I'm usually a morning person, but today I am definitely am. My mom and dad are going to think I'm going crazy or something from all the happiness coming from just my smile.

I reached school just a little bit after leaving the house and made my way straight for my locker where I hoped Amber would be waiting. I texted her last night about what had happened. It kind of seems crazy for me to do that, but she really has proved herself to be my best friend again and be trustworthy.

But now, seeing her whispering to Danielle, I'm having regrets.

Slowly, I approached Amber after Danielle walked away with a mean expression on her face. Amber went about her way towards my locker. She jumped and held her hand to heart when she laid her eyes on me, obviously startled that I saw her with Danielle. I thought she didn't like her.

"So, what did she want?" I asked her as I twisted my combination and opened my locker.

"She was just ya know..." Her voice faded when she looked the other direction. I had my own suspicions but right now I was in to good of a mood to ask her crazy questions about why she was talking to the enemy. That sounds more childish than I thought it would. Just as I shut my locker a pair of arms covered my eyes. My back was suddenly pressed up against another's and my hands automatically lifted to the person's hands covering my eyes. The smell of someone familiar floated through air and I knew who it was.

"Guess who," Cameron said in a high pitched girly voice. I couldn't hold back the smile stretching on my face.

"Gee, I don't know." I played along. Through his fingers I could see Amber with an astonished look on her face. It was like she was seeing me for the first time. Then another figure which could only be the blonde that calls himself Cameron's best friend, Adam.

"Cameron I know it's you." I twisted myself around and was now trapped in his arms and pressed up against his chest. I could hear my heartbeat in my chest beating a million times in one second, my breath hitched in my throat when I saw his face. He looked just so... handsome. I always knew he was cute, but now he's all mine. And I can call him handsome if I want to.

He leaned down and kissed me right on the lips, staying there for a short moment before dramatically pulling away from my face. I had a feeling my cheeks were burning red from embarrassment.

"PDA," I whispered to him. His smile didn't fade as he let loose on me and let me turn around, lacing his fingers with mine. Butterflies were still fluttering around in my stomach and I had a feeling there was a dazed look on my face. Amber and Adam stared at the two if us with their jaws almost touching the ground. I'm kidding, of course.

"This is what you wanted to show me?" Adam asked, his eyes flickering between Cameron and me. A smile made it's way onto his face and he smirked at Cameron. I giggled and looked at Amber expectantly.

"Wow..." Was all she could muster. I was a little scared of her reaction since her lip didn't even twitch up into a fake smile. Does she not like Cameron, or what? Is there something my so called best friend isn't telling me?

I mentally wiped the dumbfounded look on my face and replaced with a half fake grin, since there was already one half way there. Amber's expression turned cold as she said her goodbye's and hurried off down the hallway. Cameron's chest vibrated against my back and brought me back to reality. He tugged at my hand, pulling me toward first period.

"Do we have test in here today?" He asked me before we took our seats in the classroom.

"Yes. And we studied for it so you better do good. Remember; concentrate." I made the motion that meant "I'm watching you" and watched the boyish grin on Cameron's face take it's place. Mrs. Foster walked into the room and announced the test.

I glanced at Cameron and saw his eyes widen once the test was placed in front of him. I wanted to tell him to just take his time and don't worry about anything, but that would mean talking and talking would get me in trouble. Then again, my support to him probably means more. I leaned over and whispered-yelled, "Take your time, OK?" I smiled at him and he nodded to me. My eyes flickered towards Danielle giving me the stare down. Why was my life so important to her? I will never understand what she envies so much about my life. Her's seems perfect. What the heck, it is perfect. I've been to her house before after basketball practice every now and then when I played. She's an angel at home. You know, to have her parents on her side.

I fixed my eyes on my test and took a deep breath -not a nervous one, just one to put some breath in my lungs- and began writing answers done immediately. I've always thought that if you know the answers, you need to hurry up and write them down so you don't forget them in that short time frame. So, I was the first to finish my test.

My eyes scanned the room to see all my other classmates working hard on their tests. Cameron had squinted eyes as he contracted hard on his test. It was so hard for him, and although neither of is like sympathy, I felt a smudge of it for him.

I hesitantly got up and took my test to Mrs. Foster who was grading another classes papers, her glasses perched low on her nose. She looked up at me and pursed her lips, "Meet me at lunch here? I need some help with something." She said. I nodded my head swiftly and took my seat again. Thoughts ran through my head about what it could be about, but I'll never know until after class.

Everyone had turned in their tests eventually. Cameron was the third from last to turn his in, slipping a folded piece of notebook paper under my binder. He never glanced at me to make his action look casual just in case Mrs. Foster saw him. After he sat down I took the paper and held lose to my lap, unfolding it and reading his sloppy and boyish handwriting.

It said for me to meet him by the bleacher outside at the football field before 7th period. That was the second to last class of the day. What in the world would he want me to meet him there for?

Soon enough my endless train of questions going through my brain about what Mrs. Foster wanted ended. The bell rang and I walked up to the front desk while the other kids filed out. Cameron gave me a questioning look as he exited the room. I returned a shrug of my shoulder.

"Um, so after lunch?" I asked Mrs. Foster. She looked up at me with a startled look on her face as if she didn't expect to have someone talk to her at the time. I gave her a small and weak smile.

"Oh yes! I need help organizing my files and you seem like the one to do it. Is that alright?" She had gestured to the file cabinet in the corner of her room. My eyes widened when I saw there were files sitting sloppily on top of the cabinet, sitting on the floor around it, and jammed in the top of it like it was a junk drawer.

"Dang..." I mumbled on accident.

"I'm a little bit in a tizzy with all this grading I'm behind in and this isn't acceptable for a classroom. I'm glad you agreed to help with it." Mrs. Foster smiled at me. I nodded my head and told her I'd meet her after lunch to help with her mess then left the classroom.

I ran in to someone as soon as I stepped out if the room and turned towards my next class. Cameron was staring down at me with a blank face, eyelashes batting. I cocked an eyebrow and unbent my arms from between the two of us.

"What's up?" I asked. He turned so he was right beside me and laced out fingers together. I felt my body tense at his touch -I loved his touch. Did that sound creepy? Sorry.

"So I heard you might try out for the All Star team. What's up with not telling me?" He actually seemed hurt by the fact that I didn't tell him about it.

"I actually was going to, ya know. It's just that... I didn't want to get you excited and then get myself excited if I didn't make it." I explained as we walked slowly towards my next class hand in hand. The last thing I wanted to do was let go of his hand but my grades are very important. I feel like I'm not a normal teenage girl that would rather make out with her boyfriend than go to class. But hey, I was made differently.

"You'd make it, I know you would. I've seen you play and you're amazing. The way Amber put it was that you were trying out next week." He told me. I stayed quiet for a moment. I didn't think it was that important of a thing to tell your boyfriend that you were trying out for a sports team. Then again, I'm kind of new at this whole dating thing and I don't know what the heck I'm doing.

"What's this whole thing with you wanting me to skip 7th period to meet you outside?" I asked with a grin that I couldn't make disappear. I also wanted to change the subject. Talking about tryouts made me nervous. Cameron smiled and chuckled, glancing down at me then back in front of him.

"I don't know. I just want to spend some time with my girl." He pulled his hand out of mine and slung it over my shoulders. I grabbed his hand over my shoulder with my left hand so that it was bent and my fingers were laced with his once again.

"Sounds good. You do realize that's against school rules. Skipping class?" I asked when we stopped in front of my classroom. Cameron grabbed both my shoulders with his hands and got so close to my face that his forehead was pressed against mine, "Rules were meant to be broken," He said quickly and kissed the tip of my nose before running down the hall like a maniac. A teacher yelled at him, too, but he kept going with a giddy laugh coming from his mouth. That moment was so Cliché it's not even funny. OK, it was. I laughed a lot at it.

Time passed quickly and by the time the lunch bell rang, I was already in the cafeteria and getting a tray to take back to Mrs. Fosters' room. I wasn't that hungry but I decided that it wouldn't be bad if I had a snack to munch on while doing all that hard work for her. I told Cameron and Amber what I was doing and told than I'd see than later.

Mrs. Foster was bent over in the back of the room on a desktop computer typing away when I entered the room. I dropped my tray on her desk a little roughly so she'd know I was here. She jumped a little when the tray banged and turned to greet me.

"Can you organize these files here for me? I am just such a mess." Mrs. Foster clicked her heels as she mobbed her small, old body over to the file cabinets in the corner of her room. I stood back while she pointed to a few of the stray files and told me exactly how they needed to go. She informed me that they were all her classes' files and that she needed them for our important papers. None of it was so confidential that I couldn't help her place them in alphabetical order. So, she went on doing her business at the computer and I did mine at the file cabinets.

I grabbed a bunch of them in my arms in attempt to sit them on her desk so that I could organize the files that were already sitting in the drawers. One flopped right off the top of the tall stack in my arms and fell to the ground. I quickly sat the stack down on the desk and bent over to pick up the fallen one. My eyes latched on to a name that I recognized.

Danielle Pierce. I could have choked right then and there when I saw that her GPA was higher than mine by a few points. What is going on here? Only one question ran through my head at that point. Why was I chosen for Cameron's tutor if Danielle is smarter than me? Not that I was complaining about being introduced to him. It was fate. But why?

"Mrs. Foster?" I asked as I walked towards her, eyes trained on the folder.

"Hmm?" She voiced.

"Why did you pick me as Cameron's tutor?"

My question must've caught Mrs. Foster off guard since she stopped moving her fingers in the middle if the keyboard. She spun around on her chair and looked at me, a faint smile playing on her lips.

"Because you had good grades and understood what we were doing." Was her simple answer. I dropped my hands to my side with the file still clutched in one hand.

"No, I don't have the best grades. Danielle does. Why didn't you pick her?" I asked. It was like an interrogation in court right now.

"Sophia," she began, "I picked you because I knew you'd be the perfect one to help him."

"What?"

"You have patience, you have the kind heart that would help him even if he was mean to you. I think you two are a cute couple."

I let out a disgruntled laugh and followed behind Mrs. Foster as we walked up to her desk and she took a seat in her rolly chair.

"So you paired us together because you thought we'd make a cute couple? Not that I' complaining, I really like him. But... why?" I asked her.

"Cameron obviously has dyslexia. I have known Danielle longer than I should have from her years in this class and we all know what she would do with that information if he'd have broken her heart. I could tell he struggled with letting that information out. I figured you'd be the perfect one for the job." She told me.

"Yeah, but-"

"Miss Belle, must you know the answer to everything? I know you have excellent grades and all but... Anyways, I don't just pair my students that need help with the best student in my class. I take their situation in to mind first." Mrs. Foster explained further. I leaned on her desk and smiled brightly at her. I couldn't be mad at her for that. There wasn't anything to be mad about anyway.

"Did I ever mention that you are my favorite teacher of all time?" I asked her. She just gave me a small grin, "Why no. No you have not."

____

Chapter Seventeen: Bruises

C hapter Seventeen:

Bruises

The bell rang for Seventh period by the time I had reached the exit doors that lead outside. I looked for any teacher in sight before I used my ninja skills to slip through the doors without a trace.

A puff of air escaped my mouth after I was out of the school. I have never done anything like skip a class -it just wasn't me.

The sidewalk led me up to the fenced in football field in front of our school. A shadow of a boy was made by the sun as he sat under the bleachers. Cameron sat on one of the beams that helped hold up the bleachers.

"Hey skipper," I smiled as I neared him. He slowly turned himself around on the beam and smiled at me, offering a hand to me.

I gladly took it and allowed him to help me up onto the beam so that I was sitting right across from him. He laced our fingers together and pulled me into him, kissing me lightly in the lips. I smiled at him.

"So, what was so important that you wanted me to skip class?" I asked.

"I just wanted to talk to you and see you." He replied as he played with my fingers. I nodded before saying, "Well let's talk."

I couldn't help but realize how weird this actually was. Just the other day we were friends. Now suddenly we were dating. How did this happen so fast? It seems so foreign, like a new subject I have to learn in school. I guess it's a good thing that I like to learn.

"Tell me about your day," Cameron said as he scooted to sit right beside me on the beam, dangling his feet beside mine, his fingers still intertwined with mine.

"You know how I had to help Mrs. Foster clean out her file cabinet? Well I did and you'll never guess what I found out." I almost wanted to burst out laughing right then. It just seemed so funny to me for some reason.

"I dropped Danielle's folder on the floor and guess what?! She has a higher grade than me in that class." I wasn't finished with my story, but Cameron's chuckling stopped me.

"That's her what? Second year in that class? She should be getting used to the work by now-" I pushed my finger roughly against his lips to shush him. He smirked undertaken finger and I removed it, feeling the blush rising to my cheeks.

"No! That's not what I meant. Would you shut up so I can finish my story?"

"Of course, your majesty."

"Anyways, I asked Mrs. Foster why she made me your tutor. Since, when she asked me to do the job, she told me I had good grades -but not as good as Danielle's. Well that and a college recommendation. That's not what's important here. Do you wanna know what she told me?" I asked, a mischievous smile slipping onto my face. Cameron simply nodded his head.

"She said, and I quote, 'You have patience, you have the kind heart that would help him even if he was mean to you. I think you two are a cute couple.'" I watched his expression closely to see if he would be horrified that our teacher set us up together.

"All I can do is go in there and kiss Mrs. Foster right on the forehead and thank her." Was what he said. I started laughing at him and his weirdness.

"So, what are we doing after school?" I asked him.

"How about working on the tree house? Matt would like that." Cameron chuckled and twisted my fingers with his more.

"Sounds like a plan." I grinned at him and he helped me off the beam so we could go ahead to my house.

It didn't take long for us to arrive there. After we had grabbed all of our stuff out of our lockers, we ditched again and went to Cameron's car. We drove to my house and got a bite to eat before we started working on anything.

It was during that little time that I realized how much of a blessing this kid was. Instead of my first real boyfriend being a complete jerk and everything, he was Cameron. My Cameron. He was imperfectly perfect and that what was so special about him. At first I will admit that he had a hard she'll to crack and I had to use my own hard head to break into it. All that work and frustration was worth it.

I found myself sitting on the patio with Cameron eating our hamburgers that he and I fried up. I took my last bite and leaned on my hands while I waited for Cameron to finish.

"You wanna know something?" I asked as I looked at the side of his face. He was chewing and the vein in his temple popped out when he did. Sometimes the littlest things satisfy me.

"What?" His voice was muffled from the burger he just stuffed in his mouth.

My heartbeat picked up for a money and butterflies erupted in my stomach, alerting me that I could be on the verge of saying those three words that I could either regret or totally score a big kiss.

"I'm really happy Mrs. Foster paired us together. We would have been strangers for the rest of school," I told him. My face was burning from embarrassment because I wasn't used to telling people how I felt. Cameron stopped eating, his mouth froze mid-chomp on his burger. He looked at me through the corner of his eyes with a blank expression. My eyes widened and I felt even more embarrassed that I had just what I felt. Then I realized: why should I be embarrassed? Yeah, no matter how many time I tell myself not to be, I am. I looked away.

"Well," Cameron swallowed his bite and sat his burger down a safe distance from us, "I want you to know something too." He continued in a disappointed sounding voice. My heart immediately sank.

Then, out of nowhere, he tackled me into the grass.

I let out a squeal and felt him poke at my sides, finding amusement in my squirming under his touch. He was no straddling my body as I laid flat on the ground and was tickling me all over, making burst into fits of giggles. It wasn't until our faces were centimeters apart that I was pulled back to reality. My laughing slowly died down and I held my breath. The last thing I wanted was for him to say I have nasty breath.

"You're just so darn beautiful," He said with a grin.

I pressed my lips to his in a rough kiss. I smiled and laughed in the middle of the kiss, totally ruined the whole moment but he kept kissing me in silly places on my face, and wrapped my arms around his neck loosely to keep him close to me. He had a small smile playing in his lips as he remained in his straddling position and stared at me as if waiting for me to reply. But I already knew my answer. I've known it for a long time.

I grinned like a maniac and pulled him back down for one last kiss. Finally realizing that we had stuff to do, he rolled off of me and settled in the grass beside me. Cameron stood up a second later without a word and held his hand out to me to help me up. I took it gratefully and he hoisted me up without any problem.

I followed him over to where we had stacks of the boards we were using to build the walls and roof. He instructed me to pick up one of the other boards since we would need to put them all up on the platform we already made. As Cameron picked up one board, I bent down to pick up another and when I stood up, he turned around and accidentally smacked me in the jaw with the board he was holding. To my surprise, all I did was drop the board I was holding and my hands flew up to my face. Cameron's eyes got as big a saucers and he tossed his board to the side to come to my aid. I looked up at him and warned him with my eyes not to touch it.

Pain was shooting through the side of my face and mostly my jaw. I had a feeling it would be bruised within an hour and I needed some ice for it. Maybe I should stop being to accident prone.

Cameron grabbed my elbow for support and led me into my house and into the kitchen. He knew I needed ice. Him being an athlete and all, he knew what being hit in the face was like and what treatment it needed. I smiled softly at him when he handed me a bag of ice covered up with a dish towel.

He chuckled, "One minute I'm telling you you're beautiful and the next I'm hitting you in the jaw with a piece of wood. What kind of boyfriend am I?" I laughed at him and slumped as I sat on a barstool, "You're still gorgeous." He made up for it. Cameron put one hand on the counter and one hand on the bar so that he was standing directly in front of me with a smirk on his face.

"Even if you did hit me in the face and give me a what will probably be a big bruise on my jaw, I love you no less." I smiled and tipped his chin down with my finger so I could kiss his lips. While occupying me with his kiss on my lips, he put his hand over mine and pulled the bag of ice away from my face. He swooped over and planted a soft kiss on my jaw. I winced a little; it hurt like I had just been smacked with a piece of wood. Oh wait, I did.

"You are too funny," He faked a very unattractive laugh and began picking me up bridal style. I kicked my legs so he would drop me on my feet but he had his grip to firm.

"What do you think you're doing?" I queried as we made our way to the living room. He didn't say a word as he dropped me on the couch and then sat down beside me. I still held the ice securely to my jaw.

"I have to make it up to you. You're going to have people staring at you for the big bruise that's in the making right there," He pointed at the spot he hit me, "So how about a movie and popcorn and foot rubbing date?"

The adorable smirk on his face was keeping me from answering, I snapped back to reality once more.

"Uh, I agree on the movie and popcorn but don't you dare touch my feet." I held up a finger and had a threatening look on my face.

"Why, are you ticklish down there?" He said in an excellent British accent. I slapped his arm and pointed my finger at him, "You touch them and I'll touch my foot to your face."

I couldn't hold back the smile creeping onto my face.

"Actually, once when Matt tried to tickle my feet, I kicked him in the face with my heel. Do you want me to kick you in the face?" I asked with a hint of amusement. Cameron shook his head dismissively and got up to make some popcorn.

This reminded me of the time he first came over for tutoring and we watched a movie. It seemed like forever ago but it wasn't.

"When are tryouts?" Cameron asked me once we were in the middle of the movie and running out if popcorn.

"I think next week." I said kind of quietly, not wanting to talk about it. Cameron sensed this and sat up straight. My legs that I had earlier stretched out on his lap fell to the ground and I looked at him like he was deranged.

"How about we practice together? I need to do some- oh, shit." Cameron suddenly stood straight up and darted out of the room. When I heard the back door open and close loudly, I stood up as well and marched out side in a tizzy. What was going on with him? I held the ice to my face still as I watched Cameron hurry for things.

"What's wrong?" I strained.

"I'm going to miss practice and then I won't be able to play in the game that's coming up - the championship game." He cut it. I still stood there in shock until he turned around abruptly from where he was walking towards his truck and kissed me on the lips, his hand on the back of my neck to hold me in place.

"I'll call you later, okay?" He smiled and kissed the tip of my nose before running off to his truck.

———————

Stick around things are going to start getting exciting!

How do you think Sophia's tryouts will go?

Let me know!

Chapter Eighteen: So Many Kisses

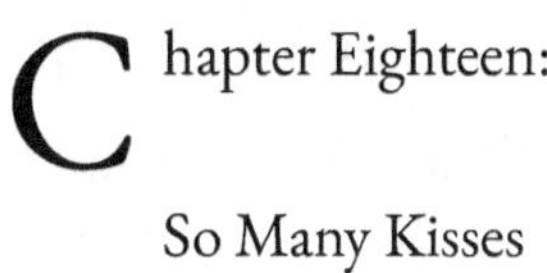

C hapter Eighteen:

So Many Kisses

____

Cameron's POV

I smiled down at Sophia's sleeping face as she rested her head on my chest. We were supposed to be working on the tree house, but someone get the idea to just lay down for a little bit. Last night was Friday night and since Matt's birthday party is tomorrow evening after church services.

I sucked in a breath and pushed a few strands of hair out of Sophia's face. She didn't even flinch as I touched her skin. She was fast asleep now and it's the middle of the day. We finally managed to get the roof and the walls up these past couple of weeks. All we really had to do was put the rope ladder down and also fix the door. I accidentally put the hinges on the wrong side of the door and the handle is on the same side of them. Yeah, I don't know why I did that. Sophia didn't even notice until we realized we had to get the door open somehow.

So that was a major blonde moment for me. No offense to all the smart blonde's out there or anything.

Sophia slowly stirring around and her eyes opened slowly. She looked up through her eye lashes at me and smiled, her cheeks turning pink.

"Sorry I fell asleep on you," She mumbled sleepily. I chuckled and kept running my fingers over her hair, "It's fine. Don't take this in a creepy way, but I like looking at you when you sleep. You make these faces and it's really cute." I said quietly. It sounds extremely corny of me to say that but it was true.

She blushed even harder and sat up so I could only see her back and her messy hair. She pulled it back into a loose ponytail and got to her feet.

Sophia put her hands out for me and I grabbed them as she helped me up to my feet.

"We're almost done," She smiled gratefully at me. I returned a smile and placed both of my hands on the sides of her face.

"I think Matt is going to love it." I said as I leaned down and kissed her softly. Sophia was such a shy person sometimes. But every time I kiss her, she kisses me back and all I want to do is deepen the kiss. Since I really want this to work between the two of us, I won't go to far.

This time, I deepened the kiss. Sophia went right along with it and then I got the feeling that she was only going with it because O was doing it to her. I broke our kiss but didn't move and inch away from her.

"You don't have to kiss me like that, Soph. I'm serious." I told her seriously although inside I was wanting more.

"No, I want to. I promise." And she's the one that kissed me. I felt her lips from a smile in the middle of our kiss and I once again deepened it. I allowed her to jump up and wrap her legs around my waist so I could just be as close as possible to her. She tangled her slim fingers in my hair as I held tight to her and spun around once to make her laugh.

I put her back down on her feet and she broke out kiss so she could wrap her arms around my torso as I did to her.

"How about that ladder?" She said aloud and I chuckled.

"Ah, I guess we should do that shouldn't we?" I said in a playful yet disappointed tone.

"Well I wouldn't have a problem doing all that again, but my little brother is inside along with my parents and I don't think they'd appreciate us making out in here." She smirked at me before walking out of the door to the tree house. I picked up the rope ladder and followed her out the door, a permanent smile on my face now.

Adam would totally call me whipped.

I helped Sophia nail the ladder to the ledge of the floor boards and we climbed down. She grabbed the wooden ladder we were using to get up there and placed it back down beside the shed outside.

We walked into the sliding doors of Sophia's house and I wishes we were still alone up her brother's tree house.

"Matt!" Sophia called throughout the house. I raised my eyebrows, "I thought we were showing him tomorrow?"

"Yeah but I thought he might want to put some things in it. I know how he is. He won't show any of his little friends his bedroom unless it has his favorite car posters in it." She told me. Matt came running down the stairs suddenly and jumped up into me. I held tightly onto him and laughed at his eagerness. Such a little boy with so much energy.

"Wanna see your tree house now?" Sophia asked him with excitement.

"Duh," Matt said as if it was obvious he wanted to, "I have been watching you guys build it for a long time and I want to play in it! That was torture, sissy!" He exclaimed.

"Gosh, Sophia! You made the poor boy wait forever!" I said sarcastically as Sophia rolled her eyes playfully.

"Let's go." She walked passed us to open the sliding doors and Matt immediately jumped out of my arms. He ran lighting speed over to the rope ladder and up inside the tree house. I slung my arm over Sophia's shoulder once she stands right beside me. She laces our fingers together with her other hand and we stand there just looking at Matt enjoy his new tree house.

"I didn't think you guys would actually build me a tree house!" Matt yelled from the open window. He had a grin that reached from ear to ear.

"I'd do anything for you," Sophia whispered to herself. Matt couldn't hear it, but he should've. I pulled her close to me and wrapped my arms around her. She nuzzled her head into my chest and I held her tighter. I know her little brother is the most important thing to her in this world and I was happy that I could help her make him happy.

"Tomorrow is his birthday." Sophia suddenly said. "He's going to be eight years old." It almost sounded like she was about to cry so I pushed her away the slightest but so I could see her face. Her eyes wouldn't meet mine. They only stayed on her baby brother as he moved and jumped around in the tree house we just finished.

"Yeah, you're gonna be so old." I joked in attempt to make her feel better. She only smiled and chuckled a little as she looked down and then back up at me. Her blue eyes were glistening as the sun hit them.

"I know it. I'm just really happy that he's still here." She said. I smiled at her even though she didn't see it from looking at Matt again and pulled into a hug once more.

*

The next morning I drove straight over to Sophia's house to help decorate for Matt's birthday party. The theme was supposed to be Cars from the Disney movie. Just as Sophia had told me, Matt had taken a few posters from when he saw the premiere of Cars and hung them up in his tree house.

Now that we had decorations and food ready, the only thing we needed was a cake. Sophia's mom ran into town to grab it and arrived just a minute before the mom's and Matt's friends arrived.

They were all a little bigger than him with more meat on their bones. For some reason, Matt looked a little pale today. It was easy to tell because Sophia and Matt were usually tan. No one else seemed to notice, so I let it go and didn't bring it up.

"Happy Birthday Matty!" Sophia sang out as she wrapped her arms around his small body and picked him up. She planted a big kiss right on his cheek and he groaned while wiping it off in disgust. She only grinned back at him.

It soon came time to sing happy birthday, eat some cake and ice cream, and then open his gifts. He had at least something from everyone. Whether it was a card with money in it or a gift wrapped in Cars wrapping paper. Mine and Sophia's gift was the biggest, and it was built into the tree in their backyard.

"Thank you, guys." Matt came up to us while we were sitting together on a chair. He tried to give us both a hug and only managed to fit his arms mostly around Sophia. I ruffled his hair and watched him run off into the kitchen with his mom.

Sophia turned her head to talk to a few relatives that showed up to celebrate with Matt. She was laughing at something one of them said while I turned my head towards the kitchen. You could see through the glass window doors and right into the kitchen. Most of the other kids were playing in the tree house or on the swings they had in their backyard.

I smiled when I saw Mrs. Belle reach down to talk to her son, until I noticed why.

He was crying and had blood pouring out of his nose. He coughed and some sprayed down the front of his shirt.

My heart started to beat faster and the only thing I could think of was that I couldn't let Sophia see that. I just couldn't.

____

Sorry for the wait! I finally wrote this chapter and I know it's short, but I kind of needed it to end like this.

Thank you for reading!

I still have a good bit more planned for this story so don't give up!

I'd seriously appreciate feed back! Vote and comment what you think because it matters to me. I want you to like this story, okay? Thanks!

Chapter Nineteen: Again

Chapter Ninteen:

Again

Sophia'sPOV

Everyone left about a half an hour ago and Cameron and I helped my mom clean everything up. It didn't take long at all, but I couldn't help but see that there was something wrong with her. Matt went to take a bath not long after everyone left and now it's just my mom, Cameron and I. She's being awfully quiet until I decided to speak up.

"So, did it turn out how you wanted, mom?" I asked her. We were all seated in the living room, her on the recliner and Cameron on the love seat with me stretched out on the couch.

She gave me a small smile that didn't reach her eyes, "Yeah it did. I'm happy Aunt Jen could show up with the little one." She told me. By "little one" she means Aunt Jen's baby girl named Nevaeh. Jen had her baby not to long ago and we just got to see her since she lives in Winchester, Virginia. That's not too long away from us but it's far enough to not have frequent visits. I grinned at my mom even though she couldn't see, "I know. Nevaeh is really cute. She likes it when you tickle her stomach. Cameron did that." Cameron smiled a little bit at my comment.

"Are you planning on staying home the rest of the evening?" Mom suddenly asked me. I shrugged my shoulders.

"I don't know. I guess I can if you want me to. Cameron never said anything about going anywhere..." I glanced at him and he shrugged his shoulders.

"No, no. I was just wondering." She looked extremely tired at the moment.

"Do you wanna go practice for your tryouts, Sophia?" Cameron stood up and crossed over to me. I looked up at his hand he had outstretched for me to grab and took it with a smile, "Sure."

We went outside and I grabbed a faded yellow basketball that had a smiley face on it, like Walmart had as their logo a few years back. Or maybe it's still the same... I don't know.

Cameron practiced with me on dribbling, passing, and shooting. He even challenged me to a game that I won. We played one more and the loser had to buy the other ice cream tomorrow evening after school. I agreed of course.

"Be prepared to buy me ice cream tomorrow!" I laughed at him. He only smiled triumphantly, "Yeah right. Did you forget that I'm MVP on the team?"

I jumped in the air and pretended to shoot as Cameron jumped too. He would've blocked it, too, if I wouldn't have ducked under his arm and made a layup. I stuck my tongue out at him as he shook his head in disappointment. We were now tied, 14-14. The next point wins and we were both aware of that.

I smirked at him but he didn't look up at me. He kept his eyes on the ball and was in his game zone.

Since he wasn't looking at where I was looking, I quickly dodged him and ran past him but he was fast for me. He stuck his muscly arms out and took the ball right out of my hands. I didn't even have time to think before he ran up to the basket as fast as he could and jumped, doing a slam dunk and holding onto the rim. Since the hoop wasn't held down by anything, it started to come down with Cameron. He landed on his feet and pushed the hoop back up and it landed perfectly. He turned to me with a triumphant smile.

"You have got to be kidding me," I said in monotone. My jaw probably hit the floor just now.

"Nope. Bring your money tomorrow, little girl. You owe me a chocolate fudge sundae." He poked the end of my nose as he started walking away, towards his truck.

"At least don't make me spend my money on that nasty sundae thing!" I yelled back at him since he was farther away. I hated chocolate fudge sundae's. I don't know why I always have, but I have. Cameron turned around and started walking backwards as I started walking towards him.

"A bet's a bet." He held his hands up as if to say "deal with it".

He climbed inside his truck and slammed the door shut, putting his elbow half way out the window. I leaned against the door and touched his arm as he smiled at me.

"You're a butthole." I pouted, hoping he would give in.

"That puppy dog face doesn't work on me." He told me quietly before leaning his forehead on mine. I smiled and my nose crinkled from him being so close to me. He lightly pecked the end of my nose with his lips, "See you tomorrow, Soph." And he was gone.

*

I glanced over at Adam and Cameron walking down the hallway as I leaned against my locker with my books pressed tightly to my chest. Adam had his arm locked around a girl's shoulder and it took me a minute to figure out who she was. She was in my journalism class but I barely spoke to her. Mostly because I barely spoke to anyone in there. Emma Jones was her name. She had dark brown hair that reached her shoulders and dark brown eyes. Emma was small and petite, but she seemed perfect for Adam. He wasn't majorly muscly and that made look kind of smaller than the rest of the boys that practically lived at the gym. Emma and Adam looked really cute together.

Cameron's eyes were searching the hallways and when they landed on me, he smiled. It was more of a goofy grin that I couldn't help but giggle at.

"Hey," He said cooly once he reached me.

"Hey," I replied back. Adam was quietly talking up a storm with Emma at the moment. I looked passed Cameron and at Emma who smiled when she saw me looking.

"Hey, Emma." I said politely and waved at her. She grinned at me, "Hi, Sophia." I waited in front of Cameron while Emma made her way over to me. She had to slip out from under Adam's arm leaving him with a pouty face.

"How are you?" She asked me as we walked to class together. We had journalism right now. Amber also has that class.

"I'm okay. Do you want to help me take pictures of the try outs today? Amber and I are in the tryouts so I can't exactly take pictures of it." I asked her. She shrugged her shoulders, "Sure. I don't see why not."

Before we walked into the classroom, I stopped and narrowed my eyes at her jokingly because joking around was the best way to make good friends, "Are and Adam... a thing?"

Her cheeks turned a shade of pink and she looked down at her feet. Emma and I were alike in many ways. Being shy about talking about this personal stuff is one of the many similarities.

"Yeah. we started talking over maybe a month or two ago and he asked me to be his girlfriend the other night. I don't why I'm telling you this..." She rambled on. I chuckled under my breath and patted her shoulder, "It's okay. I think you guys are perfect for each other."

And I think I just made a new friend.

*

It wasn't long before lunch rolled around and I was sitting at a table with Cameron, Adam, Emma, and Amber.

Amber brought up tryouts and Cameron immediately started on how good I was and how he thought I was going to get on the team with all his heart.

"I really, really, think you're going to make it." He told me while everyone else around us listened. I smiled at him and felt my cheeks warm since all the attention was on me.

"Amber will too. I know she will." I stated and took a bite of my food. Amber warily looking up at me then smiled.

"You're really good though. So good, that you have to buy me ice cream after school." Cameron smirked and poked my side with his fore finger causing me to flinch.

"Yeah yeah. Don't rub it in. You just got lucky the other night." I told him as Adam cleared his throat quite loudly, "Um, what's this I hear about the 'other night' and 'getting lucky'?" He said with a raised eyebrow. My jaw dropped to the floor while Cameron just burst out laughing. I elbowed him under the table with force which only made him laugh harder.

"No! we played a basketball game against each other and he won. He got lucky that way." I could feel the bright red blush creeping up my neck all the way to my ears as everyone around laughed.

"Cameron! Stop it!" I punched him hard on the shoulder, that got a reaction out of him. He rubbed his arm and stopped laughing long enough to say, "You have an arm on you, girl!" But he slowly stopped laughing. He glanced over at me after a moment and his face grew sad or guilty in a way. He didn't know that I noticed, though.

This is one way Cameron and I are good for each other. We're both good at hiding our emotions.

*

Tryouts started right after school and Cameron planned on taking me to an ice cream shop in town so I could buy his sundae. I didn't argue because I just wanted to be with him for a while instead of going home and doing homework all night. How unusual of me, right?

With my hair pulled back into a ponytail, my black knee-length basketball shorts, and my baggy t-shirt that had rips on the side so you could see my black sports bra on, I stepped into the gym ready for a sweaty practice. I spotted Danielle and Amber on the other side of the gym standing close to each other but not acknowledging the other. I waved at Amber and smiled at me before walking across the gym to meet me half ways. Danielle glared at Amber's retrieving figure.

"What's her problem?" I asked Amber once she reached me. I crossed my arms over my chest as we both looked back at Danielle to see her keeping herself busy while shooting.

Amber shrugged, "I don't know. She's been acting weird all day. I mean, from what I could see." She rushed out. I didn't take note to the way she seemed nervous all of a sudden and turned towards the gym doors just as coach walked in.

"Alright ladies, give me five laps around the gym!"

Insert frowny face.

Another ten laps and basketball routines later, I was ready to pass out. We had practiced layups, shooting from different angles, and defense. All of this was for coach to see how well we did. I couldn't help but think every time she looked at me that she was admiring what I did. Was that self-centered of me to think? Coach told us she'd call at around 6:30 tomorrow night to let us know the final decisions.

After rubbing cold water over my hands and splashing my face clean of sweat until I'm able to get a hot shower and relax my tired muscles, I made my way outside to the parking lot. Cameron was waiting on the back of his truck with a math book out on his lap, a calculator on the truck bed, and a piece of paper and pencil laying beside him. Since the tailgate was down, I ran up to it and stopped abruptly right in front of it. Cameron didn't even flinch at my sudden appearance. He looked up and looked back down as if nothing happened. This made a frown form on my face.

After hopping onto the tailgate and getting to my feet, I walked carefully over to him and sat down.

"What's up with you? Aren't you ready to get some ice cream that I'm paying for?" I nudged him on the side and he turned to me with a small smile. I had the hunch that something was wrong. I made one quick decision on whether to interrogate him or not. No, I'll give him his space. If he wants to tell me then he can when he's ready. He unexpectedly rested his head on my shoulder and made an adorable pouty face, "I freakin' hate math." Was all he said. I giggled and patted the top of his silky hair before standing up to my feet and pulling my basketball shorts back to my knees instead of my mid thighs. I held my hand out for him to grab and he took it. We both grabbed up his supplies he had out and put them in the truck before we both got in and took off towards the ice cream parlor in town.

"You know, you should wear that more often." Cameron said from beside me. i had a feeling he had been looking over at me but I had no clue why.

"What, basketball shorts and sweat?" I joked and scooted over to the middle so I could sit beside him. His radio has been going on and then completely back off again, something he said he needed to fix. This problem gave us quietness to talk.

"No, a ripped shirt and sports bra." He told me. I felt my cheeks warm as I rolled my eyes, he's such a guy.

We finally arrived at the parlor and Cameron was able to park up front. He climbed out on his side and left his door open for me to slide out. Right as I was about to jump off myself, he put his one arm around my waist and lifted me down. I simply rolled my blue eyes, "Oh, so romantic."

Cameron laced our fingers together while we walked towards the entrance, placing a lingering kiss on the side of my head which made my stomach do flips.

Once inside I ordered what we both wanted and Cameron tried to pay for both. I guess he was feeling guilty. Ha.

"No, no. A bet's a bet, right?" I pushed his money out of the way and handed it to the cashier. Cameron grabbed our orders and walked outside with them to sit down at a picnic table that happened to be placed right in front of the truck.

"So, what about tryouts? When do you find out?" Cameron asked before taking a big lick of his sundae.

"Coach said she'd call around 6:30 tomorrow night. I gave her my cell phone number so she could call me on it. I didn't know if we'd be at home then." I told him honestly. I licked a big chunk of chocolate chip into my mouth and Cameron chuckled under his breath while looking at me. I froze, knowing something was funny.

"What?" I asked in a defensive tone.

"You have a cute tongue, that's all." He smirked at me.

"Tongue? Really?" I scoffed playfully. He went back to eating his sundae and had a deep thoughtful look on his face. I remembered the way he looked at me in the cafeteria and the way he acted on the back of his truck not even twenty minutes ago.

"Cam?" I asked. He didn't answer. I reached over and nudged his shoulder, "Cameron." I said a little louder.

He snapped his head back over to me, "Hmm?"

"What's up with you today? You've been acting weird and I can tell that you're trying really hard to hide something." I narrowed my eyes at him in a sort of playful yet serious tone, but he looked as if he was doomed in that moment. He looked down at his ice cream for a moment.

I knew it must be something bad. He wouldn't be acting like this.

"What? What is it?" I reached across the table and lifted his hand so I could link our fingers together. I squeezed them to let him know that I'm here and I'm listening to whatever he's got to say.

"Cameron, you can tell me anything. Remember? I already told you you could. And I promise it'll always stay that way." I practically pleaded. I hated seeing him look like he was about to be ripped to shreds.

"It's about last night, at Matt's party..." He started and I was confused as soon as he said that.

"Did someone tell you something? What-" He cut me off. What could have gone wrong last night? Everyone seemed to be perfectly fine and happy. What happened that he knew and I didn't? I was with him the whole entire night.

"Before I tell you, you have to know that I only kept it from you because I know you would have freaked." He locked his eyes with mine and they seemed so worried.

"If you don't tell me right now, I swear..." I choked out. I wasn't about to cry, but when I get scared, my throat tightens and I have a hard time controlling my breathing. Which is happening right in this moment.

"I saw Matt bleeding out of his nose. He coughed and it spewed everywhere and your mom was flipping out. I had to keep it from you, Sophia. I had to..."

The rest of that sentence was a blur to me because the only thing I could think of was that my whole world was crashing down.

Again.

———————

Hey! I hope you liked this chapter as much as I liked writing it! The story is coming to it's climax right now but it's not the end just yet. I have plenty more ideas that still need to be used!

Also:: I want any of you to feel free to correct me on my spelling so that I can go back and fix it. I write on a computer sometimes and I don't always catch the mistakes like I do on my iPod. Thank you in advance!

Questions:

What do you think Sophia's reaction will be to Cameron keeping this from her? **Remember, she is a very calm person about bad situations!

Do you think Matt's nose bleed was just a coincidence or was it a dangerous one?

Let me know!

Chapter Twenty: Just Not A Good Day

ChapterTwenty:Just Not A Good Day

My grip on Cameron's hand grew limp and felt as if I was spinning in circles. Calm down, I tried to tell myself as Cameron continued to talk, but his voice was muffled by the ringing in my ears.

It's not like he just told you Matt's dead, And I shook my head when that came across my mind. It's practically the same thing! How could he keep something like this away from me? Even if it was just one night that he didn't tell me, how could he?

Finally getting a grip on myself, I stood up abruptly and dropped my ice cream to the ground. I no longer cared for ice cream at this point. I grew even angrier by the second because I left the house this morning. I didn't tell Matt I loved him, I had no idea. Why didn't my mother tell me? She knows I worry about that stuff!

When I looked back down at Cameron's face, the anger faded a tad bit. I've always been level headed about everything. But for some reason, I couldn't get anything besides screaming at the top of my lungs out of my head.

"Why didn't you tell me?" I raised my voice. It had so much venom in it that I was even a little scared. This was so unlike me to lose my cool. I guess when it came to my baby brother, nothing mattered. Cameron stood to his feet and rushed over to my side. He tried to hug me or comfort me in anyway possible, I could see how hard he was trying to make it right, but I wouldn't let him. One thing mattered right now; I needed to get to Matt.

I may be overreacting a little. Am I, though? I get that he was trying to protect me from being so brokenhearted. I think it hurt more finding out like this than seeing it myself like the first time.

"Matt," I whispered more to myself. I wasn't even crying. How could I not be crying? I learned a few years back not to cry. I can't show how weak I really am.

I stiffened my back and looked at Cameron sternly. His face was the definition of sad.

"I have to go," I mumbled and pushed passed him. My house was only three or four miles from here and I was for sure I could run that distance. I took off down the road and almost ran out in front of a car. I scolded myself the minute I heard the horn blare. I needed to get a grip, run back to the house, and and later I'll yell at myself for being so careless and for acting like this.

Not long after I had been running, Cameron's truck pulled up beside me on the main road. I slowed to a walk because I was out f breath from already have been hyperventilating. Cameron rolled down his window and spoke quietly, "Let me take you home. You'll get there a lot faster." His tone sounded depressed and when I looked over at him, he was looking towards in front of him, at the road. I nodded my head.

Cameron drove me home in complete silence. With the radio going on, playing a few seconds of a song and then going back off for the next couple seconds of the same song, the atmosphere didn't get awkward.

My hand paused on the door handle once we got to my house. I looked over at Cameron to see if maybe he'd say anything. Yes, I was feeling a little guilty about reacting like I did. I bit down on my bottom lip nervously, not wanting the word sorry to come out of my mouth. Should I be acting this way?

Cameron kept his eyes on the road in front of him even though he wasn't driving.

Instead of saying anything, I hopped out of the truck with my stuff in hand and practically ran up to the house. They should be home by now if i know their schedules correctly. Mom got off at five everyday and it's six now. Dad works until seven so he wouldn't be home.

Mom and Dad's cars were parked in the driveway. My dad must've brought home his sheriff scar since it's sitting in the driveway. He usually only brings that home when he has no time to stop back at the police station. That must mean he had to rush home.

I dropped my stuff as soon as I walked in the door and jogged up the steps since the downstairs was silent.

"Mom? Dad? Matt?" I called out once I got to the top of the steps. My mom came rushing out of the bathroom and left the light on. I could hear voices from inside of it and new it was my dad and brother. Mom came out with a forced smile on her face and stopped me from going any further. She wrapped her arm around my shoulders and we started walking the opposite way of the bathroom.

"Sophia! How was your tryouts?" She asked a little too chirpily. I stopped my feet from moving and looked at her straight in the eye, "Fine. Now where's Matt?" Her face dropped and my heart started to pound.

"Matt?" I said and raced to the bathroom. The sight terrified me.

My dad was bent over rubbing Matt's back while Matt puked up his guts by the sound of it. Before I could run forward to see if he was puking up blood or what, my mom grabbed my shoulders and pulled my out of the bathroom.

"Sophia, honey," She cooed. "Matt, I'm sure, just has the flu. He was running a fever and has an upset stomach. He's fine, okay? I'm making him a doctors appointment on Friday." I really believed her. My mother had this sense to her that whenever she told me something, I knew she was telling me the truth. I took a deep breath and threw my arms around my mom. She hugged me back and for that brief moment, I felt like everything was going to be okay.

*

I slept much better knowing that Matt only had the flu. It was still awful knowing he's suffering from that now, but it's also calming to know that it's not what I thought it was. If his cancer came back, I don't know what I'd do. We have everything so good now. It's been fine, Matt's been healthy and everything has been going so perfect.

I sat up in bed and grabbed my glasses off my bedside table. Today we had off of school because of parent-teacher conferences. I don't know why they always had to take off a whole day of school just for meetings, but I didn't want to argue with them. I like having a day off every now and then.

Mom stayed home with Matt today and I was sure that Matt was going to be in his bed all day long. Mom was probably still sleeping as well since she loved sleeping in when she could. I glanced at my phone to see it was only

7:30 in the morning. Not one message or call from Cameron. Not that I expected him to apologize, but I was looking forward to hearing his voice.

I quickly got dressed in a pair of jogging pants and a tight Hollister shirt. I pulled my hair up into a messy bun before walking down the stairs quietly so I wouldn't wake anyone up.

There was a knock on the door and I walked over to it, not thinking about whether to check if it was a stranger that would murder me.

Cameron stood in front of me in a pair of dark jeans and a Nike t-shirt and light zip-up jacket. He hand his hands stuffed in his pockets and was looking at me apologetically. My heart warmed a little bit at the sight of him.

"Hi," Was all I could think to say.

"Hey, can we talk?" He asked me. I nodded my head and stepped outside on the porch with him. Dark clouds gathered in the sky and it looked like it would rain any minute. I wrapped my arms around myself to keep the chilly breeze from giving me goosebumps, but it didn't work.

"Here," Cameron said before handing me his jacket. I took it thankfully and wrapped it around myself and i instantly became warm. Cameron's smell lingered on the jacket.

"I'm really sorry I didn't tell you. It wasn't my business to keep from you. I'm really, really sorry." He rushed out. I locked my eyes with his for a moment before I lurched forward and hugged him tight, my arms going around his waist. It didn't even take him a second to hug me back. My face was pressed against his chest and my voice was muffled when I talked, "I'm sorry, too. I shouldn't have freaked out like that. I never lose my cool."

He tangled his hand in the tips of my hair and rested his chin on the top of my head, "You don't always have to be so strong, you know."

I pulled my head back to look up at him. My eyes roamed around his facial features one by one until finally he leaned down and kissed me on the lips. I kissed him right back and snuggled up against him so that the breeze couldn't freeze me.

"Wanna come inside?" I asked him after a moment. He nodded his head and we went into the living room and sat down on the couch. I turned the TV on and we sat back with a plush blanket covering our legs. Cameron propped his legs up on the coffee table and I sunk back into his side.

"Mom says that Matt only has the flu. Nothing big." I said, more to reassure myself.

"He'll be fine." He said in a almost a whisper, "We'll be fine."

My phone started buzzing in my sweatpants pocket which totally ruined the moment. I groaned and reached for it, pulling it out to see it was coach. I sat straight up probably scaring the crap out of Cameron. I pressed answer, "Hello?"

"Sophia?" I heard coach's voice through the phone and waited for her to tell me whether I did or didn't make the team. It only took a minute to make polite talk with her before we finally got down to business.

"I'm sorry, Sophia. You didn't make the cut."

I told her thank you and hung up. Cameron sat up beside me and smiled, "What did she say?" He asked excitedly. He knew it was her because I said coach a few times during our polite conversation.

"I didn't make it." I sighed heavily and fell back onto the couch. Cameron sat back with me and hugged me close to him without saying a word which I was grateful for.

"Do you want to go out for some breakfast?" He asked me.

"Sure." I replied since I really didn't want to stay here and drown in my sorrows.

I got up and wrote a note for my mom to let her know I'm going out with Cameron for breakfast and I'll be back soon. We had to run to the truck because it was pouring the rain down and we didn't want to get soaked. We drove into town until we got to McDonald's. Cameron parked and he slid out his door into the pouring rain. I swear it's been raining for an half hour straight. He ran over to my side of the truck holding his jacket over his head. He opened the door and hopped out as he slammed it. We both ran to the door of McDonald's with Cameron holding his jacket over both our heads.

Once inside, Cameron followed me over to the front counter so we could order. A bunch of older people were here having breakfast and there was a line that seemed like a mile long. Eventually I grew tired of waiting and told Cameron I had to pee. I walked back to back of the restaurant and spotted the bathroom. But sitting right in front of me was Danielle.

With Amber right beside her.

They were chowing down on their salads and drinking orange juice and didn't even notice me standing there behind them. It's not that I have a problem with Amber talking to other friends because, hey, I've dealt with her not even talking to me at all for the past several months. It's just shocking to see her with Danielle of all people. She always talks about how she can't stand her and everything, what is this?

"I can't believe that actually worked." Danielle suddenly said. It caught my attention for some reason. I'm usually not nosy, "Sophia will never want to play again. More room for us, huh Amber?"

Amber shrugged her shoulders as if she didn't exactly agree, "Yeah, I guess."

"You aren't feeling guilty, are you? Now you could be the second best player! Coach's list was sitting there all vulnerable and we only touched it once. It was one little tweak. Don't feel guilty." Danielle reassured Amber.

"She used to be my best friend and... I just... I don't know." Amber said.

"Used to," I replied loud enough so they could hear me. Amber turned around and looked like she was about to cry while Danielle only looked shocked. In a pretend kind of way.

I turned and walked away from them, passing Cameron on my way out the door. I heard Cameron following after me as I fast walked towards his truck.

"What's wrong? Sophia! What happened?" He got right in front of me and tilted my chin up so I could look him in the eye. I wanted to tell him that nothing was wrong. That I was fine.

Why are there so many bad things happening? Everything happens for a reason... What reason could this bring?

"It was Danielle and Amber. They took my name off the list. They said that coach was letting me on the team!" I practically yelled. I did not want to take it out on him, I wanted to take it out on them. But I couldn't because what would people think of me then? They'd think I was a brat just trying to get her way, right? Because that's how people are. They judge you as soon as they set their eyes on you. They judge you by your mistakes and not the right things you've done.

Which is why I've never stepped out of line. Until now.

Cameron came close to me with his arms held out for me to hug him, no words even spoken. I flinched away when he touched me and dropped his arms.

Sophia, you can't let them get to you. Let Karma handle this one." He told me. I kept my gaze on the ground. I knew what he was saying was completely true. But why do I not want to believe it?

"I can't believe she did that! Why would Amber do that? What did I do to her? Or Danielle for that matter?" I paced back and forth in the spot in front of the truck while Cameron leaned against the front of it.

"C'mon. Let's go get some food." He said and pushed himself off the truck. I shook my head at him and finally made eye contact.

"I don't want to go back in there." I said just as I felt a rain drop land on the end of my nose. Cameron stepped forward and gently wiped the rain drop off the end of my nose.

"If you don't want to get wet, I'd advise you to go inside with me," He whispered with humor laced in his voice. I shook my head, just wanting to think about this. There was a part of me that was happy that I didn't get on the team, the other part of me was wondering what the reason for this was.

"Can we just leave?" I asked with no emotion. Although, it felt like I was begging him. The small smile on his face faded and he slightly nodded.

The rain was pouring by the time we got to my house. Cameron parked out front and would have to dart across the yard to get to the front door. I turned to look at Cameron. He was focused on his key chain in his hand instead of looking at me. I sighed, he must be upset that I didn't go back in there and pretend like it didn't bother me.

I opened the truck door and hopped out, standing there for a moment longer. I got soaked in the process. I slammed the truck door shut and took off to the house. It was silent inside.

My note I left for my mom had been replaced by a note for me from her.

Took Matt to the store with me. He doesn't feel too bad anymore. Love, Mom.

I crumpled the note up and held tight in my hand. With all the anger I had inside from just everything, knowing that Matt was sick and I had a feeling my mom only told me he was fine to save me from being upset, and the fact that amber just ruined my basketball experience. I threw the piece of paper as far and hard as I could and watched it land on the couch in the living room.

I walked upstairs to my room and was about to strip down into dry clothes when I heard taps on my window. Someone was throwing little pebbles at my window.

Cameron was standing at the base of my house, tossing tiny pebbles up here to get my attention. I smiled at him, hoping he wasn't annoyed with me anymore.

"What, no goodbye?" He called out to me with a smile playing on his lips. I leaned against my window pane.

"I thought you were mad at me," I told him honestly. He just shook his head and put his hand up to block his eyes from the rain drops getting in them.

"Come up here." I waved him up and watched him disappear to the front of the house.

Chapter Twenty-One: Surprise Surprise

C hapter Twenty-One:

Surprise, Surprise

Cameron's POV

I laid on the other side of Sophia's bed with her head resting on my chest and my arms wrapped around her protectively. Her chest rose and fell and I listened to the small breaths leaving her mouth. She was so even more innocent when she slept than when she was awake.

I heard footsteps coming towards her door and closed my eyes. I was already still pretty tired so it wasn't

hard for me to fake sleep.

"Sophia?" I heard Mrs. Belle say as she creaked the door open lightly. I couldn't see what her facial expression was when she saw me, but I didn't hear any bad kind of reaction. She lightly shook Sophia.

Sophia yawned loudly an sat up, leaving my chest cold from where her head was. I opened my eyes the slightest bit so I could see what was happening. Sophia's fave was blood red as she stared up at her mother. Mrs. Belle had an unreadable expression on her face.

"Um... we fell asleep. Sorry, mom." Sophia said nervously. If she was nervous, I probably should be too.

"It's okay, Sophia. Dinner is almost ready. Cameron can stay if he'd like." She told us before exiting the room. Sophia turned to look at me with and embarrassed smile on her face. Smug, in a way. I fluttered my eyes open and held myself up on my elbows, smirking at her.

"I thought she was going to chew me out right then and there in front of you." She said. I put my arm around neck and pulled down against me again, our heart beating together.

"I would love to stay for dinner." I said quietly. She instantly sat up and hit my chest playfully. "You were listening!" I just shook my head at her and sat up all the way, attempting to get up and go downstairs.

Sophia followed me to the door and caught my hand in hers, intertwining our fingers together.

"What's for dinner?" I heard Matt say as he crossed in front of the stairs. His eyes met mine and they lit up with excitement. Matt charged up the steps and clung onto me. I propped him up on my side and smiled at him. Sophia's smile faded. I knew she was still upset about the whole bloody nose thing. I don't blame her.

"We're having barbecue chicken and baked potatoes. Sound good?" Mrs. Belle smiled at Matt once I out him down and he ran into the kitchen to bring some plates out. I looked at Sophia and noticed she still looked tired. How long did we sleep? We went out for breakfast, came right back and I came up to her room. Her mom must've came home while we were sleeping. Sophia and I got showers to wash the rain water off of us and she dried my clothes for me. It must be around five o'clock now.

"This looks good, mom. Where's dad?" Sophia asked as we took our seats next to each other.

"He had to work late at the station. He'll be home later." She answered. We ate in silence with small jokes from Matt every once in a while. After dinner, I helped Sophia and her mom carry all the dishes into the kitchen. Mrs. Belle told me that I should be getting home because my parents were going to wonder where I was. So, I decided something right then and there. The brilliant idea popped into my mind just before I reached the door to leave. For one thing, I actually did leave my truck keys up in Sophia's room so I had an excuse to go up there. So this plan was going. To work perfectly while Sophia was helping clean up the dinner table and wash dishes.

"I have to go get my keys. Be right back," I told Sophia before sprinting up the steps. Once inside her bedroom, I grabbed my keys and shoved them in my pocket. Then I walked over to her closet and opened it up, releasing this amazing smell that smelled just like her. I stepped inside and went through the hangers until I found a yellow spaghetti strapped sundress. I lived with my older sister and my mom since for ever, of course I know what the dress is called. I'd never seen Sophia wear this before, and it would be beautiful on her.

I then slung it over my shoulder and grabbed a pair of her sandals before laying them on her messy bed. I walked over to her dressed and found a sparkly necklace that she could wear and laid it with the other things.

After everything was put together and I was feeling more girly than ever (having to go through girls clothes and actually match them together was hard for me), I grabbed a piece of notebook paper off her bedside table and jotted down a quick note:

Wear this tomorrow night. I'll pick you up at 5:30. Love, Cam

P.s. You have no choice ;)

I walked down the steps casually and wiped the grin off my face at my brilliant idea. I had the perfect date for us, and she'd just have to find out tomorrow.

Sophia was standing at the bottom of the steps, saying something to Matt with her parental voice. She turned to look up at me and jumped, obviously not expecting me to be right there. I grabbed her shoulders to steady her as she held her hand to her heart.

"You scared the crap out of me," she said breathlessly. I didn't think I scared her that bad. I smiled a crooked smile at her leaned my forehead on hers for a moment, my hands still holding her shoulders barely a foot away from me.

"See you tomorrow," I kissed her lips for more than a few seconds and dropped my hands, stepping past her to get to the door. She stopped me by hugging me for a moment. I hugged her back and squeezed her tight before finally leaving.

I could only think about what her reaction would be to the things I laid on her bed.

*

I spotted Sophia by her locker the next morning talking up a storm with Adam's new girlfriend, Emma. I thought those two were really good together. They have a... playful relationship. If they have a disagreement, they end up laughing about it and forget they ever disagreed.

"Hello, ladies." I said and Sophia's head shot around to look at me. She smiled and hugged me, kissing me quickly before turning back around to look at Emma. Adam strutted down the hall towards us with another group of guys from the team. He walked right out of the group to stand beside Emma and hold her hand. Such puppy love.

"So," Sophia started as we walked through the halls on our way to class, "what's the sundress for? Where are we going?" She asked as casually as she could. I smirked at her curiosity.

"You'll have to find out when I pick you up at five thirty." I winked at her and we were on our way to class.

By lunch time, everything was good. Instead of Amber sitting with us at lunch, she sat with Danielle for the first time insuring the whole year. I could tell she was avoiding Sophia, giving her curious looks probably to see how she's doing. I know that Amber used to be a good friend to Sophia, so her curious and apologetic looks were for real. Even if she did do this one horrible thing, she had some good left in her somewhere.

"So, how are you going to cope with this whole beach house thing this summer with Danielle and her family?" Adam asked me while we all crowed down on our half decent school lunches. I shrugged my shoulders and could feel Sophia sigh heavily at the subject at hand.

"Well, I could either ditch and stay home to a house to myself, or spend the summer with Sophia and you two." I gave a look down at Sophia and saw her blushing. I knew it meant something to her. I still remembered when I told her we'd go to the beach together when she came to my house for the first time. The memory makes me even more excited for tonight.

"Are you sure your mom and dad would let you ditch family fun time?" Adam asked and the girls giggled softly. It really surprised me at how well they get along. Well, not as much considering how much alike they are, in certain ways.

"I guess I'll have to do some begging and proving my maturity." I shrugged my shoulders.

"Yeah... what maturity?" Adam joked. I laughed and shook my head at him.

"What about Friday? Do you think we have a good chance at winning?" Emma asked. She would be there for two reasons: she's Adam's girlfriend and she and Sophia and part of the school paper.

Sophia eagerly nodded her head. "They are going make the Cougars eat dust." I laughed at her choice of words and smiled down at her.

Not long after we finished eating, the bell rang and we were off to out next class. Just a little but longer until the very end of the day. I was walking Sophia to her last class when she laughed quietly at something she was thinking about. I smiled and poked her in the ribs, loving the sound of her laugh. She looked up at me and I she'd furiously. I stopped walking, and although she kept going, I tugged on her hand and pulled her back to me.

"What?" I asked her.

Her eyes were bright with amusement and embarrassment.

"After you left yesterday, my mom came up to my room. She gave me the talk, Cameron. Do you know how awkward that was? Even with my own mother? Oh gosh.." She put her hand to her forehead and gave an airy laugh.

"That's actually funny," I joked and she punched me without making eye contact to keep from making herself more embarrassed.

"I'm sorry if I gave the wrong impression," I told her. She looked up at me with guilty eyes.

"No! No, definitely not. We were just... cuddling. I was bound to get a boyfriend some time and get the talk. I'm just happy it wasn't from my dad." She laughed and stood on her tip toes to kiss me, "I'll see you later, okay?"

I nodded my head and watched her walk Into the room.

*

5:30 was just right around the corner and I was upstairs in my bedroom getting ready for this day when I heard a knock on my door. Feeling it wasn't too important, I checked my appearance quickly. Light wash jeans, plaid button down shirt, and my Nike shoes.

My sister was standing in the doorway holding Ella on her side. She put Ella down and she instantly jumped up on me. I smiled at her giggling and let Callie inside my room.

"So, you're going out on a date, huh?" My sister asked as she sat down on my squeaky mattress. I rolled my eyes and put Ella down so she could wander around.

"Don't act so surprised. It's not my first one, it's just the most important one." I said as I turned to my long mirror against my wall to check my shirt.

Callie laughed, "Aw, my baby brother is growing up!" She came over to me and planted a wet kiss on my cheek. I rubbed it off with my hand roughly. "Hey, watch it."

"So," she began after she stopped chuckling at me, "who's the lucky girl?"

I turned to her and stood there with my hands in my pockets. "Remember Sophia? The girl you met at the basketball game in like... January or February?" I asked her. She had a thoughtful look on her face and then one of recognition.

"Oh! She was really pretty! I'm so happy for you, Cammy." I groaned as she flung her arms around me. I hated it when she called me that.

"Yeah, thanks, Callie." I mumbled and watched as she picked up Ella and walked towards the door.

"By the way," she said just before walking out, "I might need you to watch her one day in the next couple weeks. I'm down here visiting with some old friends and I don't know where else to leave her. Mom and dad have work." I nodded my head. "Yeah, I'll watch Ella." I blew on Ella's stomach and made her giggle and squirm in her mom's arms.

After I got away from my mom and dad telling me to be safe and not do anything I'd regret later on in life, (har-har) I got in my truck with the blankets and pillows on the bed and drove to Sophia's house.

I knocked on her door and waited just a second before Sophia' opened the door with her beautiful outfit on I had laid out for her. She looked breathless and panicked. My eyes widened at her state and I pushed her hair out of her face, getting the pieces out that stuck on her glasses.

"Sorry, I wanted to get the door before my dad could." She chuckled at herself, "I'll be right back. I gotta put my contacts on." She darted up the steps without telling me to come in. I stepped inside and stared after her.

Mr. Belle stepped over to me and gave me a fatherly look. He was definitely about to give me his own little "that's my little girl" talk I'd gotten from other girls' dad's before. But, this one actually mattered.

"Hello, Mr. Belle." I said with confidence. I knew him, and was only a little scared of him. He is a cop, for the record.

"You better be good to my little girl." He said sternly just as Sophia's heavy sigh sounded beside him. He smiled at her and kissed her cheek.

"Have fun, okay? Be back by twelve and don't do anything stupid, Sophia. Bye, Cameron." Her dad said and we both waved goodbye before walking hand in hand to the truck.

Chapter Twenty-Two: Prom?

C hapter Twenty-Two:

Prom?

Sophia's POV

"Remember when I said that maybe you and me could go to the beach together?" Cameron asked me. We had been driving for only 15 minutes and I was getting really suspicious about the location of this date.

"Yeah. You said that when I came to your house for the first time." I smiled at the memory.

Cameron just let out a happy sigh and continued to steal glances at me like he has been.

I reached forward and turned the radio on with the little button on the dash. It made a noise that sounded like a man's voice and then shut off. I gave Cameron a weird look and he pressed his lips into a thin line before taking the heel of his palm and smashing it down on the top of the dash. I jumped, not expecting the loud noise.

"It's kind of broken. It will play for a minute -or more if you're lucky," he winked at me and I grinned, "and then it'll shut off for another minute and redo all that."

"I don't think smashing it will help," I smiled a toothy grin at him and scooted up further on the seat so I could look at it. The seat belt made it impossible to reach the radio fully but I managed.

"What are you doing?" Cameron with curiosity. I shrugged my shoulders and turned the dial so I could get a good station to come on the radio. You know, when I could hear it to know what song I liked.

Finally, I found a station I liked. It was playing "God gave me you" by Blake Shelton. Of course it was a love song, guys, that's what most songs are about today.

"Okay, when the radio is playing and we can hear the song, sing to it. Then, when it goes off, you keep singing to see if you can keep up it." I explained and Cameron narrowed his eyes at me, "what if I can't sing?"

I rolled my eyes at him. "I've heard you sing before. You aren't bad at all." I told him. It wasn't a lie. I went over to his house one other time to hang out to take a break from building the tree house, and he was singing in the shower.

He sighed heavily, not feeling arguing with me. The song came on and I started singing with it softly so I wouldn't make his eardrums bleed from my voice. I nudges Cameron's side to get him to sing with me. He glanced at me and started singing along with the song and then it suddenly went off. I continued to sing with and so did Cameron, the competition was on.

It went like that until that song went off.

"Whoever stops singing first has to.... has to give the other a ten second kiss." Cameron added to the game. I smirked at him, what kind of award was that? Even the loser would be rewarded.

"Deal," I smiled at him and we kept playing the song game for the next hour.

Eventually, Cameron did win. He must listen to country more than I thought he did because when the song "Little Moments" by Brad Paisley came on, he knew just about every word. I crossed my arms over my chest and popped my bottom lip out.

"I don't think it's much of loss, is it?" He asked smugly. I rolled me eyes at him.

"That'll be our song." A grin formed on his lips. I smiled at him and scooted to the middle of his truck so I could be right beside him. "I love you," I half whispered as I wrapped my arm around his and kept my eyes on the side of his face. I could have slapped myself for saying that.

Not that I didn't mean it, but... I felt weird. I can't explain the feeling.

"I love you so much more," he said, glancing over at me. I smiled leaned up to kiss his cheek softly. Goosebumps formed on his arm and I chuckled at my own power. He does the same to me.

"You have goosebumps," I stayed the obvious. He kept his eyes straight ahead at the road.

"It's cold in here." He told me. Such a lame excuse.

"We don't even have the air conditioner on," I made a "duh" face.

The weather was really nice for late April here in Virginia. I couldn't believe it was almost the end of the school year, either. This summer was going to be a good one, I could tell.

I let the subject of goosebumps go and leaned my head on his shoulder to pass the time. The radio continued to go in and out and eventually got on my nerves. As soon as I tuned it off, though, Cameron pulled into the beach parking lot. This wasn't Virginia beach. It was a smaller one that was much closer to our small town than Virginia beach was. We get more snow that the people that live near the big beach, this beach was called Mountain beach since there was a big hill beside it. Not a lot of people came here, it was kind of small and most people prefer Virginia beach. I knew a lot of kids my age came to this beach to hang out, but I never actually went.

I sat up and watched while Cameron slowly backed down closer to the shore line, the back end of the truck closer to the water. Of course, it wasn't that close, though.

He put the truck in park and sat there for a moment. He looked over at me and a smile formed on his lips, throwing my heart into overdrive.

"C'mon," he grabbed my hand and pulled me toward his door, helping me out onto the sand. I couldn't get the amazement off my face enough to stop smiling.

"Wanna go for a walk?" Cameron pulled me along beside him after I nodded my head.

"Wait," I unstrapped my sandals and tossed them onto the back of the truck so I could feel the sand between my toes, "I like to feel the sand on my feet." I explained to him quickly.

He gave me a warm smile and we started to walk down along the shore. The ocean water water was freezing cold and every time it touched my feet I jumped closer to Cameron since he was closer to the drier sand.

"Cold?" He asked in a playful tone, eyes bright with amusement. I nodded my head. He suddenly scooped me up in his arms bridle style and walked a little ways. I could feel my cheeks burning red from his sudden gesture. He chuckled and kissed my cheek.

Not much further down the beach, Cameron put me down and I walked along side him, his arm over my shoulder.

"Look," he gestured about ten feet in front of us. I squinted my eyes against the setting sun and we picked up our pace to get to the sticks I could see in the sand.

My breath caught in my throat once we got up to it and I'm sure the color drained from my face. I looked up at Cameron and he turned his head to meet my eyes.

In the sand, arranged in a bunch of tiny to huge sticks, was the word "Prom?". I smiled widely and threw my arms around Cameron's neck and wrapping my legs around his waist. I must've caught him off guard because we rumbled right to the ground, him landing on his butt and me on his lap. My face, once again, turned beet red.

"Yes, of course I will." I cupped his face in my hands as I said this. His smile grew wider, "mind if I have that ten second kiss now?" I nodded my head.

His lips connected with mine and he pulled me closer to him so that my feet were crossed around his torso. This kiss was toe-curling and heart fluttering a hundred times over.

"C'mon, the date's not over yet." I rolled off of him and he helped me up to my feet. We walked slowly back to the truck with mostly the waves as our background noise.

"Sorry I practically attacked you back there. It's just that no one has ever really asked me - or shown as much interest in me as you have. And I'm really blessed to have you, Cameron." I said sheepishly. I hated laying things on heavy and deep like they do in the books I read sometimes, but that's how I got my point across best. He squeezed my shoulder with the hand leaning on it. "That's okay, really. I like it when you get excited like that." He chuckled lightly and I blushed once again for the millionth and probably not the last time tonight.

We reached the truck and Cameron reached in the truck and turned his radio on. I was clueless about what he was doing until he put his tailgate down and pulled me up to him.

"We need some practice for next month, prom." He told me with a smile on his face. Lucky for us, a slow song came on. I wasn't sure of the name, but I could tell it was an older country song.

He pulled me close so we were chest to chest and our fingers laced together. His hand was holding the small of my back while I had mine on his shoulder. I couldn't believe he knew how to dance.

"You're just talented, aren't you?" I asked with a wide smile playing on my lips. This night was going amazing.

"Totally," his tone just made me giggle. The radio started playing its games, so, when it went off, Cameron continued to sing along to the song. He got them mostly right.

He twirled me a few times before the radio went completely off and Cameron had to turn the truck off so the battery wouldn't go dead.

"How about food? Are you hungry?" He asked me once he got back up onto the bed of the truck. He had laid a blanket out so we would have something soft to sit on. I noticed a few more blankets and some pillows piled in the corner of his truck for more comfort later.

"Hmm it depends on what you brought." I narrowed my eyes playfully at him. He continued to smile as he reached into the truck and pulled out a small blue lunch box.

"Oh, just some peanut butter and jelly sandwiches and some watermelon. Callie cut it for us." He added.

I nodded my head and made a mental note to thank his sister later. I haven't seen her in a while, hopefully she's remember me. The watermelon ended up being shaped like stars which made Cameron roll his eyes. I ate my peanut butter and jelly sandwich in silence as I dangled my feet off the tailgate and stared at the ocean and pink and orange sky.

"You didn't have to do all this stuff. I'm not high maintenance." I told Cameron softly. He was sitting beside me, eating and dangling his feet off the end of the truck as well.

"I wanted to. Do you like it?" He asked me with a serious expression as he looked over at me. I nodded my head eagerly, "yes! Of course I do. It's the sweetest thing anyone's ever done for me."

He shoved his last piece of sandwich in his mouth and stood up. I watched over my shoulder as he straightened the blanket out on the truck bed and piled the pillows against the back for us to lean on. He took my hand and helped me up. I straightened my dress out and sat down beside Cameron. The sun was almost completely down and it was getting a little dark. He pulled the blankets over our laps and we got comfortable.

"So, I have a question." I said after a while of waiting for the stars to come out.

"What?" He asked quietly, his fingers playing in my hair.

"What if Matt's cancer comes back?" I didn't move a muscle so I could focus on him answering. I felt his chest rise and fall one big time.

"Bloody noses are bloody noses sometimes, Sophia." He reminded me. His hand made comforting circles on my back.

"Sometimes," I echoed his words in a whisper. I have no idea where the dreadful subject of my baby brother. I instantly sat up and faced Cameron without actually moving.

"I'm sorry. I just brought down the happy mood." I told him shamefully.

I reached up and touched underneath of my eye with his thumb. I hadn't even realized I was tearing up. I grabbed his wrist and held it close to me for a minute, my face blank of emotion.

"You don't have to be sorry. You have that heaviness of Matt on your heart all the time. It's okay to let it out sometimes. Remember what I told you?" He held the side of my face with his hand. I was rolled over on my stomach pressed to his side while he was relaxed on his back with one hand behind his head.

"I don't always have to be so strong?" I asked quietly. He didn't have to answer me for me to know that's what he was talking about. I rested my head on his chest with my arms around his torso. Tears were sliding down my cheeks all warm and salty when the leaked past my lips. I made sure I wasn't making any noise so Cameron wouldn't try to be superman. If he would.

"Thank you, Cameron." I smiled even though he couldn't see me. His hand was running down over my hair like it has been for a while now.

"Anything for you," was his answer.

———————

I worked really hard on this chapter and I hope it's not bad, or too lovey dovey for those of you who don't like that! It's okay for me, but I don't like it when it gets too deep haha!

I have several more things planned for this book but it's coming to and end soon. I hope you like it!

Chapter Twenty-Three: Dazed and Red-Faced

- -

C hapter Twenty-Three:

Dazed and Red-Faced

Thursday came bright and early. The day before game day, and as I found out before, there are big events going on today. For the school newspaper, Emma and I (she's my new partner) are going to be taking pictures of the pep rally and writing an article on how we think we'll win. I have no doubt that we have the cat in the bag in this game, but every time I've started to oat before a game, I lost.

So I'm trying hard not to.

I got dressed for school in a dark purple shirt and a pair of capris with flip flops for the warm weather. My hair was pulled back into a ponytail that reached past my shoulder blades.

Texting Cameron and telling him I'll see him at school, I rushed downstairs to eat breakfast with Matt before my mom can take him to school. He's said he feels better after resting for the one day and now he's ready to go to school to get his missing work. He has to miss tomorrow since my mom is taking him to his doctor in Tennessee. Yes, that far away. It's several hours away from here which is why my mom and dad are taking off work and going right after work this evening. I'll have the house to myself after school. Mom wants to make sure it's nothing serious so she decided to go all out for this. She's not taking any chances. I guess I don't blame her, but I wish it wasn't so far away.

So I'm on my own tomorrow. All day pretty much unless I spend it with Cameron and then go to the game with Emma, which I'm very much considering.

"Bye, Matty." I grabbed him up into my arms and kissed his head before I darted out the door.

At school I found my friends and boyfriend in the usual spot. And I was told some news that Cameron knew I wasn't going to agree on.

"I can't skip school." I told him as we walked down the hallway. He had my books in his arms so I wouldn't have to carry them while his were stuffed in his bag. I already tried and failed to get them back from him until I said yes to this whole pre-game ritual. They only do it before Championship games every year and only the players and their girlfriends or really close friends can come. That's why I've never heard of it.

I may have been the MVP for a little while on my basketball team when I played, but that doesn't make me popular. It didn't make me popular, clearly.

"It's a simple bonfire, Sophia. It's at the same beach we went to on our date and plus, I'll be there with you. It's one half day of school you'll be missing.

Attendance doesn't count until next year, when we're seniors." He smiled down at me with a huge crooked grin stretched across his flawless face. It amazed me that I had a guy like him in my life.

"I don't know, Cameron. Emma and I were going to take pictures if the pep rally and everything." I reasoned with him. The last thing I wanted to do was go to a bonfire with a bunch of kids from school. I mean, it's not that I don't like any of them, but I don't know them. And half of the guys on the team have never even taken the time to learn my name and we've been classmates since kindergarten.

"The pep rally is right after lunch. So, whenever the pep rally's done, we'll leave which is the same thing everyone else is doing because the basketball players have to be at the pep rally. Sound good?" Cameron continued to talk enthusiastically about the idea even when we got to Mrs. Foster's class.

Cameron had been doing so well in this class now after I'd started tutoring him. You'd think that me now being his girlfriend would make him not want to work as hard, but I make sure he does. I go over this stuff with him right before a test. Because he usually doesn't pay attention during class, I have to pound the information into his brain before a test every time just about.

"Maybe. I don't want to miss school. Make up work sucks." I told him as I took my books from his hands and sat down at my desk. He sat down on the top of the desk beside me - which wasn't his by the way - and continued to look at me like he was planning to take me with him. The girl that usually sat there strayed away to one of her friends while her desk was occupied by Cameron's butt.

"It's only half a day since you're leaving after lunch." He stuck his bottom lip out this time to try and get me to agree. He dropped down to his knees and put his hands together on my desk. I sighed heavily, "I'll think about it." It was pretty much already decided for me.

"Yes!" He cheered and put his hands in either sides of my face and pressed his lips to mine roughly before walking back to his seat. He left me dazed and red-faced.

Lunch came quickly and past, leaving just the pep rally to tend to. Emma and I grabbed camera's and a notepad to take in all of our surroundings once the pep rally began. Emma took the liberty of writing down the events and describing the small details, something I couldn't do under pressure. I could take pictures, though. The pressure were both under is the while deal with Cameron and Adam wanting Tobago to this party-type-thing. I was still wary about the while idea. I knew my parents were leaving this evening after work so they'd wondering where I was if they got home and I wasn't there.

"What do you think about that pre-game party?" Emma asked me as we followed behind some of our classmates to get to the gym. I shrugged my shoulders at her question, "I don't really want to skip. I'm too innocent." Emma chuckled and agreed that she was also.

"I guess they'll just have to drag us out." I laughed lightly with Emma at her statement. That's exactly what Cameron would do if I said no.

I had my backpack with me, so if that was to happen, I'd at least have my homework fort first classes of the day.

"Hello, ladies." Adam spoke from behind Emma and I. I felt his arm rest over my shoulder and glanced over to see he was doing the same with Emma. He had both his arms draped around our shoulders and was walking with us towards the gym. He had his jersey on and was sporting a wide smile. I took the opportunity to snap a picture of this moment. In the picture, you could see most of Adam's face with a giggling Emma right beside him. I knew Emma would love to have that picture, so I made a mental note to keep it for her.

"Hey, Adam. Where's Cameron?" I asked him. He carefully took his arms off both of us and grabbed a hold of Emma's hand while we waited to get through the gym doors. Apparently the whole school was at this pep rally.

"He's in the locker room. I can here to deliver a message to the two of you." He told me. Emma perked up and I looked at Adam expectantly.

"What?" I asked him.

"Cam wants you to know that you have to be at the gym's back doors by the time the team leaves the gym." He said and pursed his lips out of boredom. I narrowed my eyes.

"And what if I don't?" I challenged. Emma smiled between Adam and me.

"Well, you'll have to find out. But if I were you, I wouldn't try." He winked at me before turning and leaving a lingering kiss on Emma's cheek. Her cheeks turned a shade of pink.

In the gym, no decorations were up because they'd just have to be taken right back down after the rally. But, there were pictures of the senior basketball players for both girls and boys. I saw Danielle's pictures pasted on a round paper basketball and taped to the wall along with other girls' from the team and some boys.

Emma and I sat down at the very bottom of the bleachers so we could get good shots and good views. Theist thing we wanted to do was travel up and down the crowded bleachers just to get a quick picture or ask a player a question.

"You could always interview Adam later. Then you'll have the interview part down." I told Emma as we waited for the players to come barging in. The band was playing loudly and it was hard to even think with the melodic music bouncing off the walls. Not to mention all the kids rambling all around us.

"Okay. Could you do Cameron, too? So we'd have another player?" She asked me hopefully. I nodded eagerly, "As long as you take some pictures at the beach -if we go." She smiled and nodded her head in agreement.

I began to snap pictures of the band in action, kids taking their seats, and the paper basketballs taped to the walls with seniors' names on them.

Then I heard cheering and looked in the opposite direction to see the boys team jogging out of the locker room. Most of them had on jeans or khaki short with their jersey's and basketball shoes on. The girls' all stars team was sitting on a bench observing the whole thing. Usually their games lasted through half of summer so the pep rally was only a quarter for them.

I snapped pictures of the guys running up and down the court shooting baskets and smiling and laughing and giving one another high fives. I smiled widely when I saw Cameron make a three-pointer. His eyes roamed the gym until they landed in me. I waved at him and gave him a thumbs up. He had a ball stuck between his hip and his arm and was smirking at me. I saw it as the perfect time for a picture. So I took one before he could move. He shook his head and smiled at me.

After the principal gave his little speech of how proud he was of the team this year for making it to the championships, a few meme bees of the team gave one also. I didn't expect Cameron to.

I noticed everyone leaving and made my over to Emma since she was taking notes from some of the players. I handed her the camera so she could take pictures at the bonfire. She gave me the note pad so I could interview Cameron later on.

"Hey!" I heard someone call out behind me. I turned around and was caught off guard when I was lifted off the ground. Cameron's arms were wrapped around my legs, right under my butt, and he had me against him. I felt my cheeks turn red from this PDA.

"Put me down." I said calmly. He let me slide down till my feet touched the floor and grinned at me.

"Ready?" He asked me. I sighed.

"Yeah, but I have a lot of work to do and I don't like skipping. I did once with you and that wasn't so bad but I still don't want to do it because I'll-" He leaned down and kissed me roughly on the lips and pulled back, only leaving me wanting more.

"Change your mind?" He asked, his forehead pressed to mine. I smiled - I couldn't help it.

"Emma! We have a party to go to." I called over my shoulder.

We all drove over in Cameron's truck, Emma and I had to share the middle seat while Adam sat in the passenger seat and Cameron drive. They insisted on only taking one car. We'd have to come back to get Adam's afterwards.

"I have to be home before my mom and dad, okay?" I told Cameron. I pressed myself closer to him so Emma and I weren't squishing each other.

She was fine with being squished against Adam, I could tell.

"Okay. You'll have to remind me when."

"What do you do at these parties?" Emma asked in general.

Adam spoke up, "we usually sit around a bonfire and tell stories, ghost stories, and play games. Some of the guys throw footballs back and forth or go swimming since we always do it at Mountain beach." He explained.

"Sounds like fun," I cut in. It seemed to not take near as long as it did when Cameron and I were going alone. Probably because we had more people to chat with.

We finally arrived at the beach and a lot of cars were already parked along the grassy parts before the sand starts. I jumped out on Cameron's side and waited beside him as he grabbed something off the back of his truck. It was a brown wool blanket.

"We'll need this later." He informed me. I nodded my head and walked close behind him towards the big bonfire they already had set up.

Adam and Emma were already over at the fire. Emma's eyes were darting around to look for anyone she was friends with. I felt the same as her. Even though I'm as nice as I can try to be to everyone I meet, I don't have a lot of friends at school. It doesn't really bother me, though.

Logs were placed all around the huge fire for people to sit on. This place was farther down than the place Cameron and I were at just the other day so it makes sense that I didn't see it before.

"Wanna play some football with us?" Adam asked Cameron and me. Cameron looked at me expectantly.

"Sure."

*

"Okay, so who wants to play Truth or Dare?" A girl from the cheerleading team asked. She was really nice to everyone, and a bit of a ditz.

We had all tossed a football back and forth and wrestled with one another all afternoon. It was really great and I had so much more fun than I thought I would. No one was saying anything about me - at least not out loud. I tried not to ponder in that thought for long.

"Okay," I said aloud. No one was objecting. I snuggled deeper into the blanket Cameron had wrapped around my shoulders. I was sitting on one of the logs they had laid out in the sand and Cameron was sitting crossed legged in front of me. The fire was warm, but I was still cold in the sun set for some reason.

I had also called my mom and told her Cameron would be bringing me home later tonight. She said it was okay, which surprised me. She and my dad were leaving with Matt in a little bit. Not very many people were left now. Some had curfews and some just got tired and left. A lot of seniors we left and plus Adam and Cameron, two of the three juniors left.

"What happens if you chicken out?" Someone else asked. I had the feeling it wouldn't be very good.

"Then that person has to..." The girl had a thoughtful look on her face.

"C'mon, Sarah. Pick something!" Someone called out playfully. So, her name was Sarah. How did I not know her name from school?

"Okay, okay," she said, "whoever doesn't do the dare or truth, has to take an item of clothing off. Sound good?" All around the fire, guys cheered. Some girls did, but mostly guys. I glanced down at Cameron and noticed he was grinning from ear to ear. I had one thought it my mind. I had to do all the dares people threw at me.

"Can I pick who starts?" An all too familiar voice said. Her voice was distant, but she came into view a short few seconds later.

Danielle Pierce stood in the light of the bonfire. There was a blonde head-ed, muscly boy standing beside her, their hands laced together. I stared for a moment. Her smirk got too much for me and I looked away. Since when did she have a boyfriend... that was from the school we were versing tomorrow?

"Uh... sure." Sarah said. She scooted over on her log to make room for Danielle and the guy to sit down.

"Thanks. This is Levi. He plays for the Tigers." Yes, the team we were versing tomorrow. Of course she'd bring him here. Levi smirked and I could already tell that he wasn't a nice person. They were perfect for each other.

"Okay, so, back to truth or dare? I get to pick." Danielle said. Everyone was silent. Cameron leaned his head back against my leg and I wished he hadn't. Danielle caught the movement out of the corner of her eye and looked at me, a grin spreading across her lip stick covered lips.

"I want Sophia to go first. Truth or dare?" She asked me. I felt my heart pick up. This could either be really bad or... who am I kidding? Of course it would be bad. It was Danielle we were talking about.

So, I picked the one option that I knew might embarrass me less. If I picked truth, she could come up with some embarrassing secret from middle school and announce it to these people I was just beginning to really enjoy being around. If I picked dare, the only thing I'd have to watch out for was some date that made me want to curl in a ball and hide...

"Dare." I said with less confidence than I wanted. I felt Cameron stiffen against my legs and he pulled his head up. He didn't look up at me but I already knew he was wary.

"Perfect!" Danielle said cheerfully, "I dare you to kiss the person to your left." I instantly looked to my left to find Adam perched on the log. He stared at Danielle with a shocked face and then looked at me. He gave me an apologetic look.

I shook my head. How does Cameron feel about that?

"She doesn't have to do that." Cameron spoke up for me. He pushed himself up and sat between Adam and I.

"Fine. Then she has to take a piece of clothing off." Danielle said bitterly. I rolled my eyes and bent over to jerk a flip flop off my foot. I sat down beside me on the log.

"Your turn," Sarah told me.

"Um... Emma. Truth or dare?" I asked quietly. This was definitely not my place.

"Truth." She answered a second later. I thought of something simple and easy, not embarrassing.

"Is it true that you have never been to a real party before?" I asked her. It was totally pathetic. Boo's erupted from random people's mouths and I frowned.

Emma gave me a relived smile, "that's true."

The game went on for a while. It was finally down to Danielle again and she had fire behind her eyes. But her gaze wasn't directed towards me. It was my shirtless boyfriend who was sitting beside me, one arm loosely hanging around my waist.

All around me people had 80% of their clothes off. I had managed to not get picked thankfully. The dares these kids came up with were all nearly impossible so they had no choice but to strip. Emma even had her jacket and shirt off, leaving her in a thing tank top.

"Cameron, truth or dare?" Danielle smirked. I looked down at my hands. The moment she set foot on this beach was the moment I knew I was not going to have a good evening. And I was right.

"Dare." He replied in a challenging tone. Danielle glanced at me for a moment before looking back at Cameron.

"I dare you to kiss me... for one whole minute." She said triumphantly.

So cliché right? I had writers block for the truth or dare part. I originally had another game planned but I didn't know what all to do with it and decided, hey, truth or dare is kind of perfect.

Thanks guys!

Chapter Twenty-Four:
The Night

C hapter Twenty-Four

The Night

————————

I was almost about to jump off the log and attack her. The thing is, I'm not a violent person. Then I realized the most horrifying part about this dare. Cameron was only in his boxers. Nothing else. Apparently, he doesn't like answering personal truth questions. Danielle knew he couldn't resist.

Everyone around the fire was silent. They all watched to see my reaction and Cameron's reaction. I didn't want him to be naked, that's for sure. I looked over at him.

His face was asking me "Is it okay?" and I simply nodded my head. He could barely tell that I did. I felt my face become frozen as he stood up in only his boxers, and his abs shining. Levi didn't even seem to mind all this.

Before Cameron hesitantly bent over to begin kissing her, I stood up abruptly and let the wool blanket fall to the ground. I turned on my feet and walked briskly back towards the truck. Even though it was kind of dark out and I had no idea what car was whose.

I did finally find the truck because it was the only truck there. I leaned my elbows on the hood of the truck and rested my head in my palms. It's okay, really. I told myself.

It's a silly kiss. It's a silly game. She's a silly girl who thinks she can get to me.

I suddenly felt someone touch my shoulder and I whipped around, expecting to see a rapist or something. Instead I found Cameron staring back at me. Blush rushed to my face when I saw he had only the wool blanket wrapped around his waist. He had his clothes clutched in one hand and my flip flops along with them.

"What are you-" Before I could get the whole questions out, he had dropped the clothes in his hand and cupped my cheek with it. His warm lips pressed to mine and I felt so dizzy I could have fallen. We must've kissed for nearly a minute before he finally pulled his head back and stared at me with bright eyes. I noticed his other hand was still holding up his blanket.

"You are the only girl I want to kiss for a minute long, understand that?" His voice was full of authority, but in a joking kind of way. I couldn't stop the smile on my face.

"I'm sorry that you had to get naked," it was nearly impossible to say that without giggling. He chuckled at my reaction.

"No biggy. Hold on, I'll change and we can head to your place." He told me before picking up his clothes and dashing behind the truck.

I sat in the truck while Cameron changed and decided to go ahead and turn the radio on as well as the truck. It wasn't even three minutes later that Cameron hopped inside and got his seatbelt on.

"What about Adam and Emma?" I asked him before he pulled out onto the highway.

"Adam said he and Emma would get a ride from someone else." He informed me. I nodded in understanding.

"I have to interview you. But I think I'll wait until tomorrow at lunch or something. Okay?" I told him as I scooted close to him and rested my head on his shoulder.

"Okay." He replied.

We were back at my house before I knew it. I don't know why but every time I have to stay home alone I get paranoid. I've always hated it. And now is not the time for me to start liking it.

I didn't want to keep Cameron back on a school night, and tomorrow is his big game. I inched over to the passenger side door and placed my hand on the handle. With hesitation, I decided to just ask.

"Do you want to... um... stay a while? I don't like being alone in there..." I told him quietly. I didn't even look at his face to see what it looked like. I just opened the door and stood there for a moment after hoping down.

"I would actually really love to," He suddenly said. I looked at him with wide eyes.

"Cameron, you don't have to. Tomorrow we have school and you have your game." I said in a rush. He rolled his eyes at me and jumped out.

"Typical Sophia. Always worrying about school. I'll leave later so I can get ready for school." He told me. I walked in front if the truck to meet up with him, a grin on my face. He put his arm around my shoulders and we walked up to my dark house. No lights were on and the only light we had to lead us to the front door was the moonlight. Dad must've forgot to turn the porch light on for me.

"How about we watch a movie?" I asked Cameron. He nodded his head and sat down beside me on our couch. I pulled a blanket over top of us.

"Why don't you go get comfortable and I'll find a movie?" He suggested and stood up to grab Matt's xbox 360 controller. We had Netflix on it and it seemed perfect right now.

"Okay. I'll be right back. Do you want a pair of shorts to put on or...?"

"Nah. I have a pair in my truck I can put on for now."

I rushed up the steps and into my bedroom. I grabbed a pair of short shorts that I always wear to bed. I would never wear these shorts out in public. I found an old t-shirt from basketball camp a few years back and tugged it on. I decided to go ahead and brush my teeth and hair while I was at it.

When I got back downstairs, I found Cameron sitting on the couch again, feet propped up on the coffee table. He had a pair of black basketball shorts on and no shirt. I forgot that's how a lot boys sleep.

"What movie is it?" I asked him as I sat down next to him. I had about three inches between us since I knew as soon as I touched him, my heart was going to beat out of my chest. He must've noticed because he smirked.

"What? Are you scared to touch me?" He asked smugly. I scowled at the coffee table. Cameron snaked his a around my waist and pulled me close to him. He snuggled his face into the crook of my neck.

"No..." It came out strangled. I grinned at him.

He fell to the side so he was now pressed against the back of the couch. He patted beside him and I laid down easily. He put his arm over my waist his head on the side of mine almost. I tugged the blanket over us and before I knew it, I was fast asleep.

*

I woke up the next morning in my own bed. The blankets were everywhere in my bed, upside down, hanging off the side half way.

I sat up and looked around. The clock read 7:00 so I knew it was time for me to get up and get ready for school.

Now that I think about it, Cameron had carried me up to my room. I remember him pulling the blankets over me and kissing my forehead. He left soon after. I stared out my window and saw his truck wasn't there so he definitely went home last night. I felt a little guilty. What if he got in trouble with his parents for being out so late?

I picked up my phone and sent him a quick message asking him if he did get in trouble.

I tossed my phone on my bed and went to the bathroom to take a shower. I scrubbed myself and my hair and hopped back out, brushed my teeth and hair. Once I was finished, I put my glasses on instead of contacts for right now and wrapped a towel around my body.

I flung the door open and stepped back into my bedroom.

Then I saw him out of the corner of my eyes. I nearly screamed and if I would have jumped anymore, my towel would have fell to the floor.

"Cameron!" I yelled, my face blazing red. He started laughing uncontrollably and collapsed to his knees in my doorway. I quickly slammed the door shut in his face and ran over to my drawer. I pulled out a homecoming t-shirt with our school colors in it. Along with a pair of shorts and whatever else, I ran back into the bathroom and dressed myself. I rolled the sleeves of the t-shirt up so they weren't so long.

After I was finished, I walked out into my room smelling good and ready to kick some butt.

"Cameron!!" I yelled with a parental voice. It reminded me so much of when my mother would yell for me after I did something bad.

"Yes?" I heard his melodic voice echo from downstairs. I stomped down the stairs, making sure to make a loud enough noise to let him know he was in trouble.

"What were you thinking? I was naked!" Humor was leaking through my voice because I couldn't hardly bare to be mad at him today. I was in a good mood and it was always hard to get me out of one.

"I thought I'd come pick you up and then I heard the shower running. I'm a teenage boy, can you blame me?" He smirked and wrapped his arms around my waist. I giggled and shoved him away.

"Yes I can blame you. Don't do that next time." I scolded and walked over I the living room. The phone started ringing and I picked it up.

"Hello?" I answered. The caller ID said it was my mom.

"Hey! Are you ready for school almost?" She asked enthusiastically.

I chuckled, "Yeah. Did you get good results?" I asked hopefully.

"We have the appointment this evening. Your dad thought it was at six in the morning and it's actually at four this evening," I could imagine her rolling her eyes, "I don't know where he got he six from." I remembered that she was an hour behind us so I'd find out at maybe 7:30 here. I'd be at the game. I made a mental note to remember to keep my phone on.

"Okay. Remember to call me. I have to go, bye, love you." I said.

"Love you too, Soph!" She replied and I hung up.

Now just to get to school and get ready for the game later tonight.

"How you feel when everyone is cheering you on when you play?" I asked Cameron. I've been asking him questions all lunch period about basketball. He hasn't complained once. Yet.

"I feel awesome. Like I'm a hero in my own little world." He answered honestly. I stared at him with loving eyes for a moment.

"Okay, that's all." I told him. He smiled at me and we engaged in a conversation with our friends. Emma was talking about Prom. What typical subject.

"Adam asked me the other day. Even though it's several weeks away." Emma told me. Adam must've heard her.

"I wanted to claimed her first." He hugged her close and snuggled right into her hair. She giggled at his action and pushed him away.

"Anyway, do you want to shopping with me, Sophia?" She asked me nicely.

"Yeah, of course." I had ready told her Cameron asked me and he must've told Adam because no one asked questions about it.

"Great. We can go this weekend, if you'd like." She suggested. I nodded my head. I needed some girl time.

"Okay, sounds great."

I turned to Cameron as he drank his milk silently.

"Are your mom and dad coming tonight?" I asked him casually. He shook his head.

"No. Dad has a business trip and my mom is going along. They only have to go to Winchester so they'll be back on Saturday. It's fine with me though. My mom always yells at the referee when he does something she doesn't like." He said. It didn't seem to bother him, so I didn't press the subject farther. His parents always seemed to be involved so it wasn't a big deal.

I had no clue what to write for this ending... I hope it was okay. Bear with me on the sucky ending! The next chapter is going to be intense sort of. I hope you liked this one! Thanks for reading!

When they "Okay" I was thinking "...Maybe Okay can be our always." JUST KIDDING HAHA

Chapter Twenty-Five: The Day

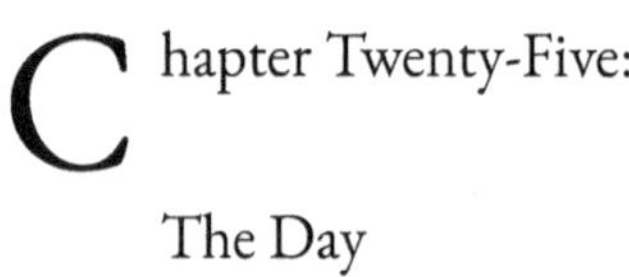

C hapter Twenty-Five:

The Day

The last bell of the day rang and I spring from my seat, rushing towards the door to get out if here. It was Friday and we had the big game later this evening. I was hoping to get a bite to eat before the game so we wouldn't starve and then rush back here so Adam and Cameron could get ready with their team.

People we rushing through the hallways and bumping into each other like crazy. I was squeezing through the tight spaces with my books in my hands when I finally spotted an open spot up ahead. I'll be able to breath!

I tried so hard to get up there, and I was making it, until someone charged into me so hard that I tumbled to the ground. My books luckily landed right in front of me and weren't spread out. I groaned and realized I had banged my elbow pretty hard when I fell backwards. I rubbed it and got to my knead so I could gather my books up when a familiar pair of sneakers were in my vision, right beside my books. Looking up through my lashes, I saw Cameron looking down at me with his eyebrows raised. I gave him a frown and accepted his hands. He pulled me up with ease and bent back down to pick up my books for me.

"Rush hour get to you?" He asked with amusement playing in his voice. I smiled a little at him and nodded.

"Yep," I told him, popping the "P".

We made it to my locker without running in to too many people on the way and Cameron shoved my books in my locker. I went hands on hips and cocked an eyebrow at him. "Since when did you know my combination?"

"Since I watched you put it in everyday." He said in a mock tone. I rolled my eyes playfully and grabbed his hand in mine. "Ready to hunt down Emma and Adam and get some food before the game?" I asked him. He nodded his head and we searched for their heads in the crowd. Of course, we heard Adam before we saw him. I haven't hung out with him outside of school before, but I'm guessing he's always loud and crazy. He's not like that in school, though.

After we found both of them, we got our bags and ran out to our cars. Adam and Emma in Adam's shiny red Dodge Dart and Cameron and I in his truck. He still hasn't fixed the radio.

We stopped at a Subway since we decided it would be the healthiest for the boys to eat. I waited with Emma to order while the guys got our seats. We decided to pay for theirs too, no arguments allowed.

Once we got our sandwiches and drinks, Emma and I sat down beside the guys and sorted the food. It was really delicious and I couldn't understand why I haven't eaten here more often.

"So, Danielle brought that guy with her that plays on the opposite team...
Seth? Was she trying to prove something or...?" Emma asked to start a
conversation.

"Who knows with her. She was being a brat that night." Adam piped in.
His eyes flickered to me when he said that. She always aims her wrath at
me.

"Amber's no better." Cameron added. That was almost off topic, but I
knew what he was talking about. Emma's eyebrows raised.

"What? I thought you two were like... best friends?" She directed her
question at me. I blushed and shook my head furiously.

"We used to be. Until she helped Danielle take my name off the all stars
team list after tryouts." I muttered and averted my gaze toward the doors.
I heard Adam scoff.

"Why didn't she get in trouble for that?" He practically demanded. I shook
my head.

"Because I don't really care anymore." There was an edge of anger to my
voice. I tried not to get worked up about this topic, but every time I
thought about it, I wanted to just take my anger out on something.

"You know, one day, you're just going to snap." Cameron said from beside
me. He was sipping on his drink and looking at me from the corner of his
eyes. I leaned my elbow on the table and looked at him innocently.

Of course I knew I would. But it wasn't any time soon.

"Hello, fellow classmates," A female voice spoke. I jerked my head to the
right and saw Danielle standing there. She was alone. I bet Amber and
what's-his-face were waiting in the car.

No one answered her. She kept her smug smile intact on her perfect full lips.

"I wanted to say good luck to you guys. I'm routing for the Tigers this year since Levi plays for them." She stated the obvious. I shifted my eyes to look at the table to keep them off of her.

Still, we all stayed quiet. The silence wasn't awkward, but it was intense.

"Well, I guess I'll see you at the game. Bring your A-game, boys." She winked in Cameron's direction and I had to rolled my fingers into a fist to keep from yelling. Not that I would, since I couldn't hurt a fly. Pathetic, really.

"Are you guys ready to leave?" I asked as soon as she was out of earshot. They nodded and we made our way back out to the vehicles.

"Can you drive? I have to have my uniform on by the time I get there. We're already running late for warm-ups." Cameron quickly explained to me. He tossed me the keys and I'd managed to catch them in mid air. He jogged to his truck and grabbed a duffle bag off the back of it.

I climbed into the driver's side and started it up while he said something to Adam before hopping in the passenger side. I noticed Emma was having to drive this time, too.

As I drove down the highway, Cameron started to get his uniform out. Before I even realized what he was doing, he ripped his shirt up over his head and shoved it into the duffle bag, leaving him shirtless for a second. I had to bite my lip to keep from giggling out of nervousness. If he noticed me blushing and acting all weird he'd never let me live it down.

"Are you... blushing?" Cameron asked in fake astonishment. I rolled my eyes and shook my head. He was such a tease.

He took his pants off and slipped his shorts on quickly. It's a good thing I was driving and had to force myself to pay attention. He could have had us killed and then where would we be? Hell, probably.

I was more than relieved when we reached the school and Cameron and Adam bolted into the school. Emma and I took our time. I was grateful that I didn't have to take pictures or notes during this game. Our teacher assigned that job to someone else this time.

We found some seats on the bleachers for the two of us and watched as the other people packed the gym. The players were all running across the court in big hurries, practicing with their teammates. I noticed when Levi darted across the floor. He went up for a layup and swished the ball. I noticed how big he really was. The muscles were so big, I swore he must've been on steroids.

Danielle and an anxious looking Amber sat on the opposing team's side with their school colors on instead of ours. I wondered silently why Amber wanted to be her friend so bad. Why did she want to be her friend, go to every length to do what she wanted, and then look so guilty about it later? She literally looked like she was dying inside from the guilt. I knew Amber as nice and caring person. I could still see that person in her, I just don't get why she would turn in an instant.

What really surprised me was that Danielle was a senior and was hanging out with Amber, a junior, like me. It was never like Danielle to hang out with people younger than her unless they were a cute boy that she could get a hold of like many others. I mean, who knows how she got Levi to agree to go out with her. She must think she's doing Amber a charity case.

*

With ally jumbled thoughts about my friends set aside, I was able to focus on the game. I watched Cameron move swiftly on his feet up and down the court, his sweat-soaked hair flipping in his face. His expression serious the while time, though you could tell he was feeling a bit smug when he could dribble around his opponents. He really had potential.

Only a few minutes remained in the third quarter and right now the other team had the ball. The boys had their best defense faces on and were on that basketball like white in rice. Coach did a wonderful job coaching them.

I looked over at the other bleachers consciously and saw that Danielle was staring at me. She had a smug grin on her face and kept her eyes locked with mine. Amber, on the other hand, looked like she was about to have a panic attack. She was rocking back and forth, biting her nails with anticipation while her eyes were glued to the game. A few seconds were left in this quarter and if the boys scored, they'd be six points ahead. I almost jumped out of my seat when I saw Cameron jumping up towards the hoop with the ball in his hands now. He was really going to do a slam dunk. He didn't quite get his hands all the way up to hoop as he would if he was doing a slam dunk, but the ball did go in. I shot up and clapped my hands together, a loud cheer escaping my lips.

It wasn't until I saw the look of horror on Emma's face that I knew something was wrong. I snapped my head around towards the court, right under the hoop. My hair smacked me in the face but I couldn't feel the slight sting of it. The only thing I noticed was Cameron laying on his back, hands clutched around his throat. He almost look like a fish out of water the way he was gasping for air.

"What happened?!" I asked Emma with so much demand in my voice that if I were her, I would have flinched.

"H-he hit him in the throat." She pointed towards the one person that wasn't standing near the wall to give the coaches some space. Levi was standing there, his yes locked on Danielle up on the bleachers, a small smile playing at his and her lips. They had succeeded in destroying me. Almost.

I darted out of the bleachers, anger building inside of me that was ready to come out at any second. I saw paramedics swarm around Cameron and they were talking to him calmly. He was still squirming. I felt my heart crack a little as I ran over to him, ignoring the yells I was getting from he referees.

Cameron's eyes locked with mine for a short moment. He was turning blue from the loss of oxygen. How sick can you be to do this?

I didn't even realize I was crying until I felt a salty tear touch my tongue. I quickly wiped it away and reached up to touch Cameron's sweaty hair, pushing it out of his eyes. I didn't care if his sweat was on me or that people were pushing me out of the way.

He suddenly stopped moving just as the paramedics had him on a stretcher. I felt my heart beat quicken and I could only the thumping of it in my ears. Emma was suddenly by my side. She was gripping at my arm and I realized I was trying to follow the paramedics out of the back entrance of the gym. That's probably where the ambulance was. I was thankful for the hospital being a minute's drive away. How did someone call them that fast, though?

I jerked my arm out of her reach and followed them out the door.

That's when my phone rang. I pulled myself together quickly and pulled it out of my pocket with frustration. The time read 7:30 and the caller ID said it was my mom. She must have the results. I quickly composed my shaky voice so she wouldn't suspect anything bad and pressed answer.

"Hello?" I answered.

"Sophia?" My mother's voice was heavy with exhaustion and even through that cover up, I could hear her heavy breaths. Something was wrong. Very wrong.

"What, mom? What is it?" I demanded. I was still moving my feet outside of the door. And as far as I knew, the game was going to go on for now.

"Matt had a relapse" was all she had to say for me to sink to my knees and allow the tears to flow freely.

____

Oh my goodness. Such a sad chapter. It's probably really short.

I don't really know what to say here so...

Oh wait! now I do.

Please be patient with me on the small details. I've done my research on what happens when you get hit hard in the throat and I'm going to try and keep it as real as possible. Don't get worked up if something doesn't sound right.

Tell me if think it's wrong - nicely.

Thanks you guys!

Chapter Twenty-Six: After

C hapter Twenty-Six:

After

———————

I found myself curled up in a ball in the corner of Cameron's hospital room. I had my knees pulled to my chest, arms wrapped around them, and chin resting on top of that. My eyes were just blue swirls of emptiness as I stared ahead. I didn't even have tears to cry anymore I they were dried up. It's been three hours since the incident and all I could do was think about how I wanted to literally kill Danielle. I wanted to make her feel this.... this emptiness.

My other half of my brain was thinking one thing and one thing only: I needed to see Matt. I knew this was going to be a tough road. I had to worry about Cameron waking up and having speaking problems on top of worrying about my little brother dying.

It won't happen, I told myself. I won't let Matt go. But those thoughts weren't as heavy right now. My mother would be the reason for that. She told me that the doctor said he'd be okay if he worked well with the treatments. She said it would hopefully be a quick recovery. She also said that I wouldn't be able to see him until next Friday, when they get back. They wanted to start treatments right away so it would be a week before they could come back. Then they'd have to go back soon once again. Just like last time. Except, last time, we had the money for it. This time, I don't think we do. The last treatments and checkups drained our bank account. How would we do it this time? I had already decided to go downtown and get a job at the Dairy Queen or something like that. Anything I could do, really.

Mom told me to concentrate on Cameron. And now I could say I really could because my mom didn't sound worried. Whether she was just being strong for me or she really was confident in the situation, I believed he'd be all right.

So, I sat here, for the last three hours as doctors came in and out, Cameron's friends came in and out. His parents weren't picking up their phones for me so there was no way to tell them. I called as soon as I possibly could, but there was no answer.

Another three hours passed, leaving me at 1:30 in the morning. My eyes refused to shut and I refused to eat or drink anything until I heard his voice again. Or even just his green eyes would make me happy.

I now had a blanket draped over me, courtesy of one of the lovely nurses. My legs were stiff when I stood up to stretch them. I had been sitting in a ball for so long that my legs were wobbly from the pressure.

I covered back up and sat down on the chair, making myself comfortable for the next long hours I'd have to endure.

I thought about what to tell Cameron's parents. The doctor said he'd be fine. He wasn't hit hard enough to cause death, but it was darn near close enough. They had to put a tube down his throat to help him breath since he wouldn't be able to that on his own. His voice would be gone for a couple of days due to the sourness and they put IV's in his arm to keep him hydrated and fed.

I didn't want them to rush home if they were on a business trip all the way in Winchester, so I wanted to let the doctor talk to them quickly and explain everything. I would then let them know that I won't be leaving his side.

So, to pass time, I stared at him. No matter how creepy it sounded, I stared at him. His jersey was no longer on him. They had ripped it off as soon as they got him in the ambulance and stuck heart monitor things (I guessed that's what they were called) on his bare chest. His color slowly came back after the put the tubes in his nose and down his throat, widening his air passage. They left his shorts on him and draped a hospital gown over his bare upper body.

I couldn't believe it was actually happening then. I couldn't stop rocking back and forth with worry once we got to the hospital. No one hardly noticed that I followed them hastily into the emergency room and watched everything they did. It was enough to give me nightmares. Event nightmares nowadays didn't involve anything that serious from when Matt was in his treatments. I never had to see any of that stuff.

I watched as the doctor put a defibrillator to Cameron's chest and yelled "Clear". He pressed down on the square objects and Cameron's body bounced from the electrical shock. I learned later from a nurse that escorted me from the room that his heart wasn't getting oxygen and stopped beating. That set me over the edge. I didn't want anybody touching me. I didn't want them to talk to me or anything.

That's why I wouldn't sleep. I was afraid the nightmares would come and I wouldn't be able to get out of them.

But I eventually did sleep. I wanted to be awake when he finally awoke, alive and alert.

Around four o'clock in the morning, I heard movement coming from the bed beside me. The small uncomfortable wooden chair I was in creaked when I moved my head. I had fallen asleep in it. The light above Cameron's bed was shining down on his face illuminating every feature.

Suddenly his eyes fluttered open like he had been trying to open them for hours and they just wouldn't budge. His neck was in a brace so he could bend it. Due to the tubes in his throat, that probably wouldn't feel to good when he craned his neck. So that he could see I was here, I grabbed his hand and squeezed it as well as standing up and showing him my face.

I tried really hard to hide the tears falling again so he wouldn't be worried but it wasn't working as well as I wanted it to.

"Cameron," was all I could mutter when I saw his face. He had a worried expression on his face the moment he saw me crying. I wanted to go her a nurse or the doctor, but I couldn't let go of his hand.

He reached up with his hand that wasn't hooked up to any machine and wiped a tear off my cheek. I held his hand there for a moment with mine and lifted it to my mouth. I was sobbing when I kissed his palm, pressing it to my chest so he could hear my heart beating.

I smiled through my tears and set his hand back down on his chest. He pulled at the material of the gown and I immediately got the point. He was hot. I carefully pulled it off his chest, leaving him bare with only his basketball shorts on. I smiled at him warmly. My eyes felt swelled up.

"I'll be right back, okay?" I told him. My voice sounded so... odd. It was stale from not being used for past several hours. I planted a quick kiss on Cameron's forehead and forced myself to find a nurse.

I spotted the same one that covered me up with a blanket last night and all but sprinted to her. She smiled at me when she saw me, happy to see I wasn't dead.

"Cameron's awake." I sputtered out. I couldn't find it in me to be too happy yet. I still had other things to worry about. And I found it hard to be happy when I had my baby brother in a nearby state, dying from a sickness.

She nodded and came with me back to the room.

I watched her work on Cameron. He was staring at the ceiling while she took his blood pressure, checked his IV's and tubes.

"Now, honey," the nurse started with her thick country accent, "your throat is probably going to be sore once we take this tube out, okay? So keep the talking at a minimum." She told him. I studied her. She had long curled dark red hair and brown eyes. Her freckles were small and spread over her nose and under her eyes. I looked at her name tag for the first time in several hours and saw her name was Jessie.

"Thank you, Jessie." I told her before she walked out to get the doctor. I assumed they were about to take his tube out of his throat. Was he even strong enough for that yet?

"Anytime sweetheart," she smiled brightly at Cameron and I.

*

It was seven in the morning and they had just taken out Cameron's tube a half hour ago. I was surprised he hadn't said a word yet, but I was sure his throat was killing him. Since I wasn't extremely tired right now, I decided to start a conversation. I grabbed a pen and note pad off the desk right outside his door from a nurse and handed it to him. The neck brace was no longer on him so he looked half normal again. The only problem was that he was a giant purple and blue bruise on his throat, close to his Adam's apple.

He raised an eyebrow at me when he noticed the things in my hand.

"Talk to me. I need to talk to you." I said as if I was dying without conversation.

He slowly took the paper and pen out of my hands and propped his knees up. He rested the notepad on his knees and began to write something while I sat back down.

A moment later he handed me the paper by nudging the top of my head. I was fighting my eye lids from sleep.

'Go to sleep. Your eyes are bloodshot.'

I rolled my eyes at his message.

"I don't want to sleep." I pouted and rested my chin on my arms on the side of his bed. He made a disapproving look and took the notepad from my hands. He jotted something down quickly and handed it to me. It was kind of hard to read since he had chicken scratch for handwriting.

'Did you tell Callie or my mom and dad?'

I shook my head before answering. "I can't get a hold of your parents and I don't know Callie's phone number."

I remembered Callie once from the basketball game a few months ago. She was really sweet, and I remembered her daughter, Ella. She was the cutest little girl ever. How could I forget them?

'Ok'

He nodded his head glumly. A few moments of silence went by as we both had our eyes on the TV watching Spongebob. At least, I thought we both were. I felt a tap on my shoulder and looked up at Cameron. He had scooted over to the opposite side of the bed and was patting the empty space next to him. A small smile formed on my lips tiredly, not reaching my eyes quite. Instead of arguing, I climbed up onto the bed and wrapped my arms around his torso. He had his arm behind my head. Cameron lifted my fingers with his and laced them together, playing around with them.

This was all I wanted to do, hug him tight and not let go.

Oh yeah. I remembered. I never told Cameron the news about Matt. He probably forgot he had an appointment today.

Just the thought of it made me shudder. I never Cameron felt it but I ignored his stares as a tear slipped down my cheek. Reality was suddenly punching me in the gut and I couldn't think about how I could handle this. There was no way I was going to Tennessee. My parents would never allow me on a trip like that all by myself. What if something horrible happens? What if the treatments don't work this time?

"What's wrong, Sophia?" Cameron's raspy voice asked. My eyes widened and I looked up at him with alarm.

"You shouldn't be talking." I scolded him. My voice was thick was grogginess. He rolled his eyes and reached forward to wipe a tear off my cheek with his thumb. And I couldn't hold it in any longer. It was pathetic really. Cameron had enough on his plate and I was a burden to him with my problems.

"Tell me, please." He said pleadingly. His face contorted into something of horror and worry as he watched my sob. I nodded my head and squeezed my eyes shut in attempt to stop the tears.

It was a few minutes before I could tell him.

"Matt's c-cancer relapsed and m-my parents a-are in T-Tennessee with him for a w-week." I said through sobs. His eyes widened at my reply. I felt his arms tighten a round me and his lips press against the top of my hair.

He softly whispered, "it'll be okay, I promise" next to my head. I could tell he was upset but was refusing to show it. Without anymore words spoken -which I was grateful for- I slowly fell asleep happily wrapped up in Cameron's limbs.

*

"Oh, I'm just happy you're okay." I heard a familiar female voice say calmly. There was no trace of sadness, just pure relief and joy. Was that Mrs. Bridges?

"You're a tough kid, I'm proud of you, son. I heard your team won the game, too." Mr. Bridges added. My eyes were glued together from sleep and I automatically wondered how they got here and what time it was.

"She looks like she was crying," a third voice piped up. It sounded like Callie... I made sure not to flinch or move. This was the hardest part of eavesdropping.

"She was. In her sleep, too. It's her brother..." Cameron sighed heavily and I felt him push a strand of hair behind my ear. I held my breath at the mention of Matt and slowly let it out. I hope nobody saw that...

"Her brother's cancer came back." He said slowly and carefully, quietly because his throat was probably in fire. I could tell by the way he sounded. I had a feeling my cover was blown.

"We'll make sure to add her family to the prayer chain at Church." His mother said.

"I'm starving. Let's go get a bite to eat." Mr. Bridges announced. I heard someone chuckle and some shuffling around before the bed sunk in and I made the assumption that they were hugging him. If they were coming back, why were they giving him hugs now?

As soon as the door clicked, I slowly opened one eye to peek around. Then I felt someone jab me in the side and I jumped, squealing in response. I barely got a smile on my face even though he was trying to tickle me. I made a serious face, suppressing a grin and stood up from the bed. He had the blankets kicked down to the bottom of the bed and had a different pair of basketball shorts on. I assumed he had to take his others off since the uniforms were usually handed down year after year for so many years. The jersey was definitely ruined...

"Don't mess around too much, you'll pull your IV out." I told him quietly. I saw him grin out of the corner of my eye.

"Sophia Belle, were you eavesdropping?" Cameron tried to say in a humorous voice but epically failed due to his hoarse voice. I cracked a smile at that one.

"It doesn't matter anyways. And you should stop talking. You're gonna lose your voice and I won't like that very much. It's going to be very lonely at my house for the next few days and I need someone to talk to on the phone." I spilled out. I didn't mean for that much to spill.

Cameron shook his head. "Yes mother. And what's this about the phone? I'm staying at your house." I felt my eyes widen and jaw drop. My arms dropped to my sides from their spot around my torso.

"You can't. My dad would flip-"

"Your dad called and asked me to. Well, he asked my parents because I can't exactly talk." He groaned in frustration. I wonder what he was going to do when he saw Danielle or Levi again.

"Well..." I honestly didn't know what to say to this. I leaped up onto the bed and grabbed Cameron's face between my hands and smashed my lips to his.

I was happy for the moment while my mind was elsewhere...

____

Chapter Twenty-Seven: Alive, Barely

- -

C hapter Twenty-Seven:

Alive, Barely.

"Are you ready to go home?" Jessie asked Cameron as she unhooked his IV's. He said his throat felt much better and he could breath perfectly fine. I think he was just saying that so he could get out of that closed space.

I concentrated on grabbing his stuff together and shoving it in the duffle bag his parents had brought him the first day they got here. So far, Cameron had only been in the hospital for two days. It was great considering the awful condition he was in. I had a flashback of how I saw him squirming on the ground with his hands around his throat, eyes squeezed shut. He looked completely helpless.

I cringe from the thought and turned to watch Jessie unhook everything from Cameron. Anything to distract myself. I knew that as soon as we left here, Cameron and I would go our separate ways for a little while and I'll be alone to think about everything. This is going to eat me alive. I closed my eyes and sighed heavily for a moment. Cameron has to go home to his family for a little while. Although I wished so bad that he didn't have to, I knew he needed to and probably wanted the comfort of his own bed.

Then the thought of him staying with me while my parents were away, it still stunned me. How could my dad give in like that? I'm sure, him being a cop, he weighed his options carefully. Who else did he have to trust in town or anywhere close that didn't have to take off work to stay with me? He knew me well enough to know that I wouldn't be able to handle being alone. Cameron was his only choice, and he trusted him.

Cameron told me that my dad set rules as well. Cameron had to sleep on the couch downstairs to be near the phone and the door and what not, he wasn't allowed to sleep in the same room as me, and he had to respect me. He even told me that my dad said this, and I quote, "her body, her rules. My house, my rules". I laughed at that. That's my dad, always over protective.

"Ready?" I heard the door creak open and my eyes darted over to see Mrs. Bridges step inside. She was if in her son a happy smile and her light eyes slid over to meet mine. Her smile grew warmer as she approached me, arms stretched wide. I could hardly manage a smile at that point, but I made sure to make up for that with a tight hug.

"Thank you, Sophia. We don't know what we'd do without you." She gushed to me in my ear. I nodded my head and gave her a small smile. She grabbed Cameron's duffle bag and slung it over her shoulder as she approached the door.

"I'll be in the car out front." She waved goodbye to me and I retired the favor as she walked away. Cameron stood up from his bed and walked over to me. The room was now silent, only the two of us there to break it. I didn't left my head to meet his gaze as he stalked over to me. He had finally put on a pair of khaki tan shorts and a blue Nike shirt.

He wrapped his arms around me and I automatically slid my arms around his waist. His hands went to my hair and held my head in place against his chest. I could hear his heartbeat against my ear and it seemed to be in rhythm with mine. I was happy for the sound of his heart. I didn't want the silence to surround me. It will only give me time to think.

I fought back tears as I clung to Cameron's shirt with my nails. I wasn't going to cry. I had plenty of time to do that alone, later. And to be perfectly honest, I don't know what I would be crying about. Cameron is fine and healthy. Matt is... okay, so far. Mom called me and informed that the first treatment went well, it was definitely a little painful for Matt, though. Maybe it was that. The fact that my baby brother was going through all that pain and I wasn't there to hold his hand or even read him a bedtime story. It sucked. Majorly.

"I'll see you soon. Hold yourself together for me, please?" Cameron asked. He backed up about an inch from me so he could look me in the eyes. He was forced to hold my chin up with his fingers since I couldn't bring myself to look at him. He kissed my forehead and them took my hand in his, pulling me towards the door of the room.

I hadn't had a shower in two days and I was still wearing the same clothes as Friday. Talk about feeling like crap.

I kept my head down as we walked towards the exit. Cameron had decided that it would be best for me to drive his truck home and he'd have Adam or somebody drop him off later to get it. And not to mention he was supposed to be staying with me, so it worked out good. Tomorrow was Monday, the most dreaded days of the week for most people. No, everyone.

My fingers were limp and Cameron's were tight on my hand. I couldn't find the strength to hold on tight.

I hadn't even realized we were at the front entrance until Cameron's hand slid from mine. I immediately missed the warm ness of his palm against mine. My head shot up and I saw him digging in his bag for his truck keys. He dangled them in front of me and I slowly grabbed them.

Cameron grabbed my face between his hands and made face, "I'll see you soon, okay?" His voice was laced with worry. I don't know why I worried him so much.

I nodded my head and leaned in to kiss him first, to prove that I could still function a little bit. He kissed me back immediately and then broke it off. His mother was growing impatient. I waved bye to him as he got in the car and wished that I could quit acting like this. It was a little while to be alone. Only a little while.

But I couldn't bring myself out of this mood. I was in too deep.

I watched them drive away before I went looking for his truck in the parking lot. I guessed that someone brought it up here as favor to him. I hopped inside and started it up. The radio came on at first and then shut back off. I sighed and backed out of the parking lot before driving towards my house.

The driveway was empty of my mom's car and the cruiser (my dad's police car) wasn't there either. Another pang hit me. I think that if someone asked me what I was most scared of, it would be to be alone. I can't take it. And I don't get why.

It wasn't this bad the first time. I was always with Matt then, though. Except for when he had treatments when I had school. Chemo was a rough thing for him.

I pushed those memories away and rushed up to my front door. I found the key easily and unlocked the door. It flew open after I shoved it open and I stood there in the open doorway for a long moment, just staring at everything. I tore off my shoes and threw them in the living room, the sandals landed on the couch, and slammed the door behind me.

And that's when it happened. I thought about how so many people on TV and in the books I always read say that screaming and breaking stuff can make you feel so much better. And I think I can. Because the next thing I knew, I was picking up a random picture off the stand closest to me and slamming it on the ground. The glass shattered all over the floor and I let out a shriek so loud that I hoped the neighbors didn't hear me. Feeling like my chest wasn't as tight, I ran through the glass without a care that it probably just stabbed my foot to pieces and ran up the stairs, each step stinging the bottoms of my feet. I ran to my bedroom and grabbed a pair of shorts and a shirt to slip on and headed to the bathroom.

I got a quick shower and examined the bottoms of my feet while I was there. My right foot had a long scratch on it that, to me, looked like it was gushing blood. It would need to be wrapped.

After I got dressed, I slid down against the wall in my bathroom, door locked, with a roll of bandages in my hand, and wrapped it around my foot. My hair was wet against my back and was probably making my white t-shirt almost see through. I didn't care.

I threw the bandages across the tiny bathroom and frowned. My vision blurred and I realized I was about to cry. And I didn't stop myself. I let myself sob. I bawled with my knees pulled up to my chest and my arms wrapped around them. I stuck my head between my knees so the darkness could comfort me and cried as loud as I felt the need to.

I shouldn't have to cry anymore after this. I've been crying a lot lately, and it was time I stopped. I will, I promised myself, right after this time.

*

Cameron's POV

As soon as I got home I pulled out my phone and made arrangements for Adam to come pick me up. Turns out he can't because he was being forced to now the lawn or else be'd get grounded. I decided to call Emma and she said she was happy to take me over to Sophia's later. The plan was for me to get a shower and everything else and then call Emma.

She got me not long after and I didn't hesitate to meet her outside of my house. She had a small, black car that was really quiet when it was running.

"You can come in, but I don't know if she'll be in a mess or not." I said truthfully as we travelled toward Sophia's house. My throat was still throbbing with pain, but I pushed it aside so I could be here for Sophia.

"I was really worried that she would just... explode or something. She's acting like a time bomb, Emma." I told her. Emma flashed me a worried look.

"I want to talk to her, let her know I'm here for her." She insisted. I didn't argue. Maybe Sophia just needs to know that she has friends that are willing to help her through tough times. A friends shoulder to cry on is worth more than anything most of the time.

We finally reached Sophia's house and saw my truck parked in the spot the Mrs. Belle usually parks her car, in the garage.

I hopped out, in a hurry to check up on the shaken Sophia. Emma was right behind me when I knocked on the door. I waited a moment and there was no answer. My eyebrows pulled down in confusion and I knocked again on the door. It was still silent. Was she sleeping? I slowly turned the doorknob to find it was unlocked.

The scene right inside the door shocked me. I was sure my mouth had dropped the floor. Broken glass was everywhere it seemed. The culprit was a picture lying in the ground face down. I saw the bloody footprints leading all the way up the steps and didn't even wait for Emma before I darted up them in a hurry. The footprints grew darker when I reached her bedroom. The first led over to her dresser and I followed them to her bathroom door. I turned the knob, not even caring if I was disturbing her privacy. It was locked, and she was in there. For sure.

"Sophia?" I kept my voice calm even though it hurt like I poured lava down it.

No answer.

I banged on the door this time.

"Sophia?" I asked a little bit louder. I was joined by a frantic looking Emma in less than a minute.

I looked at Emma for a moment and had to think about how to get this door open. I wasn't busting it down because her parents not appreciate that. Yet, it might be worth it. Instead, I headed to her closet to pick out a metal coat hanger and bent the top to make it straight instead of a hook. I stuck the pointy part into the tiny hole that led to the lock on the other side of the door.

It wasn't long before I heard the clink of the lock and I twisted the door knob. I slowly pushed it back just in case she was sitting there behind it and I ashes her with it. Instead, I was shocked at what I saw.

————————

Aahhhh Cliffhanger! What do think she did?

Hmmmm...

I know I gave Cameron a short Point Of View, but I thought it would be nice to see inside his head.

Hope you like it! Thanks, readers!

Chapter Twenty-Eight: Always There

C hapter Twenty-Eight:

Always There

―――――――――

Cameron's POV

I rushed over to Sophia's side and kneeled down. Emma sat at Sophia's head with a panicked expression. I could only imagine what I looked like.

"Sophia?" I asked softly.

"It's okay, Cameron," Emma began, noticing the panic in my sore voice, "she's just asleep. Check her feet real quick." I picked up her feet and looked at them carefully. She had them wrapped up good, so she must not have been in too much of a crazy mood.

"It's fine." I informed Emma; she seemed like she knew what she was doing.

"Okay, pick her up and put her on the bed, if you can. I'll get some ice for her foot and some for your throat, your voice sounds horrible and it's still bruised." She made a face and darted out of the room.

I put my arm under Sophia's knees and under her back and lifted her easily. She was a small girl. I sat her down gently on the bed and pulled a blanket over her. Her hair was still wet from her shower, so I decided to put her on her side so maybe Emma could braid it.

Not even two minutes later, Emma came through the door quietly and gracefully with two bags of ice and dish towels to wrap the bags in. I took one from her hand and wrapped it in a dish rag. Then I lifted the bottom of Sophia's blanket and pressed it to the bottom of her foot. Hopefully this will help it. If it bled that much coming up the steps, it must be deep. I decided to take a look at it when she woke up.

"Here," Emma said calmly. I took the bag of ice from her hand and pressed it to my throat. It felt good on the bruises. I felt like such a wimp, the next time I see that kid, I'm not holding anything back. That goes for Danielle too, just not in a really violent way.

"Can you braid her hair? It's wet and she usually hates it when it dries all poofy, or so she says." I shrugged my shoulders.

"Yeah. Where are her hair ties?" She asked me and I realized she has never been here before. I gave her a soft smile and pointed to the bathroom, under the sink.

I settled down beside Sophia on her bed and put one arm under her neck, careful not to get in the way of her hair so Emma could get to it.

I remembered in the hospital when she fell asleep in the hospital bed with me before my family came. My arm had fallen asleep along with her and I wanted to move it badly but I kept it there so I didn't disturb her. Just those little things... Holy sh*t. I'm becoming a mushy romantic. What is Sophia doing to me? Not that I minded... that much.

Emma came back with a brush and a purple hair tie. She brushed out Sophia's hair and started to braid it which didn't take her long.

"Sophia's house is really pretty." Emma mentioned. I smiled at her.

"You should see the tree house in her backyard. Both of us built it, with some help from her dad, for Matt, her kid brother." I explained.

"Wow. I'll have to-" Her phone must have buzzed because she dug it out of her pocket and looked at it, frowning.

"I have to go. My mom wants me home for some dinner with her clients." She told me with a sad smile.

"Okay, well, thanks for helping me with her." I told her as she inched toward the door.

"Welcome. Take care of her."

I nodded in agreement.

Sophia budged about twenty minutes later. She had been talking in her sleep, frowning and gripping my shirt with her nails like I was going to leave at any moment.

Her eyes were squeezed shut now and we were face-to-face. I was laying on my side, barely touching her except for her fingers gripping my shirt, and she was laying on her side.

I stared at her closed eyelids and her long, brown eyelashes. Then they popped open. Her blue eyes were wet with tears and she just stared at me wide eyes for a moment. I kept my facial expressions under control. Her eyes eventually went to normal and her grip on my shirt loosened. I raised my eyebrows in worry and rested my palm against the side of her face, playing with a strand of her hair.

"Ow" was the first thing she said. I sat up and looked at her blanket-covered body in alert.

"What? What hurts?" I asked her.

"My foot. Did I cut it?" She asked me as she sat up. Besides her puffy red eyes and sniffling nose, she looked normal again; happy.

But then the smile she had on her face vanished. She stood up from the bed and walked out of her room. The sun was setting outside and I was sure she was hungry by now. I followed her downstairs hoping to make her some food. I found her standing on the bottom step, staring at the broken picture frame on the stand. Emma must have cleaned up all the blood and the glass because it was like it didn't even happen.

"I broke the picture that my mom took of Matt and I. The first picture of us when he was born." Sophia turned to me and continued. "I didn't mean to." Her voice was full of regret. I walked down closer to her and past her, picking up the broken frame.

"It's okay, Sophia. The frame is broken, not the picture." I carefully unhinged the back and took the picture out if it and handed it to her. She smiled at me and it reached her eyes.

"Are you hungry?" I asked her. She nodded her head slowly and followed me into the kitchen.

"I want lucky charms." She said out of no where. I watched her grab a box out from under the cabinet and she reached up to get a bowl as well.

"Get me one, too." She reached up and grabbed another bowl for me.

I got the milk out of the fridge and met her at the table. She poured cereal in to both our bowls and I poured the milk. She grabbed two spoons and put one in each bowl.

"What are you doing?" I asked her as we both ate silently. She grinned at me. "I always separate the marshmallows from the other cereal and eat the marshmallows first." She said sheepishly. I laughed and for some reason, I belly laughed. I clutched my stomach as I laughed.

"It's really not that funny!" Sophia pouted. I shook my head. Of course I knew it wasn't that funny but I needed the laugh. It was hurting but throat like crazy though, so I had to stop.

"I miss laughing." I said through chuckles.

"The last time we laughed was literally three or four days ago." She deadpanned. I smiled a crooked grin at her and she couldn't resist a smile.

*

Some time later, I found myself sitting on the edge of the tree house with Sophia right beside me. She was so distracted by her own thoughts that she didn't realize she was digging her nails into my arm. I didn't move though, so I didn't scare her. For some reason it felt like she was going to break at any second. This wasn't the Sophia that I fell in love with, this was the Sophia that was breaking and no one could help her.

I was going to change that.

"Sophia? You're going to draw blood." I said quietly, touching her hand.

She flinched and jerked her eyes towards my arm. Her eyes widened and she had a guilty expression on her face.

"I'm so sorry!" She said quickly. The only damage done was five red marks from her nails.

"It's okay. Hey, talk to me," I put both my hands in either side of her face over top of her hair. She frowned at me wrapped her fingers around my wrists.

"About what? I'm fine."

"No, you're not."

"Yes, I am."

"Sophia!"

"Cameron!"

I groaned in frustration. She was going to play hard to get. I glared at her and she laid back on her back, feet dangling off the edge of the tree house porch.

"Sophia, it's not good to keep these things bottled up. I know I sound extremely... parental. But I'm being serious." I said, venom in my voice. She only glared at the tree above us.

"Gosh, Cameron!" She suddenly stood on her feet. "I can handle myself, okay? You are ways telling me that I don't have to keep to myself with my problems but I do! And I am! Please," she took a deep breath, chest rising and falling.

"I'm just showing I care." I said calmly. I've been known to have a temper. Being around Sophia all the time has definitely calmed me down, but it's starting to again.

"I already know you do! I know it." She shouted and almost whispered the last part. Sophia climbed down the ladder and landed on the ground roughly. She recovered and began pacing back and forth in her yard.

I leaned against the single-board railing we put up and stared at her. Her long, now curly do to the braid she took out, brown hair swayed every time she walked. Her lips were pressed into such a tight line that they were white. I had to resist the urge to smile at her. When she was mad it got pretty intense. Maybe I should get her fired up more often.

"I didn't mean to make you mad," I told her. Though I was slightly happy I did. Most of the time when people are mad, they spill their guts.

"I just... I want to stop feeling like this and go that to happen, I need to do it myself! So just... leave me alone!" Her eyes were bright with confusion when they looked up at me. I could tell she didn't know what she wanted. And knew how to make her figure out what she wanted.

"Okay, I'll leave then." I backed down the ladder and landed swiftly on my feet. Without a word from either one of us, I walked through the back door and towards the front door. Sophia followed me.

I could already tell she was going to think she made me mad.

She didn't say anything when I placed my hand on the door knob and froze. Maybe she really did want to be alone. But I knew better than that.

I opened the door and walked out onto the front porch, closing it behind me. I think she pushed on it to shut it as well.

I turned towards the door and stared at the door knob. Come on, Sophia.

It felt like hours to me, but it had only been a minute when the door cracked open. Her beautiful face was there, only half of it. I stared at her for as long as she was there. Her eyes were wide with shock, probably not expecting me to still be right there.

She finally opened the door all the way and stood there, hand still on the door knob, shoulders slumped and head down.

"I'm sorry," she forced out and looked up at me. She really meant. Though I didn't doubt her when the words first came out of her mouth. Sophia Belle always meant an apology.

She was suddenly flinging herself at me. Her arms went around my neck and she squeezed me so right that I had to hold on to her waist to keep us both up.

"Really, really sorry." She whispered to me. "I'm not to hopeless. Promise." She backed up to grin at me. I smiled back and walked inside the house with her.

____

Hope it's not too short! I had to brainstorm for this one... much more exciting chapters next! I'm honestly not sure when it's going to end. Soon, probably. It depends on how many more ideas I get!

I had a pretty good ending for this and then I forgot it. Wow.

Must be my bad luck. I broke a mirror a while back and apparently I had "7 years of bad luck" blah blah. But then I broke another mirror and yeah. So it's 14 years of bad luck now.

Chapter Twenty-Nine: Rules Were Made To Be Broken

Chapter Twenty-Nine:

Rules Were Made To Be Broken

Sophia's POV

I wasn't ready to wake up in the morning. To return to my life would be a downgrade compared to the amazing dreams I had.

I didn't want to live through seeing how some people saw my overreaction to everything these past couple days. Cameron continued to tell me that it wasn't an overreaction. That's a lot to go through and I should stop being embarrassed by myself.

But I can't. Who would smash a picture frame and get her feet all cut up and fall asleep on a bathroom floor? I guess I was sort of out of it at the time, and that's my only excuse.

I will admit, waking up with Cameron's arms wrapped around my body protectively is probably the best thing ever. No wonder I had good dreams. I could escape reality for a little while.

Even though school started in an hour and we needed to get out of my bed and get dressed, I didn't want to move. I was turned toward Cameron - face to face - and our legs were all tangled together. He had the faintest smile on his face. He could pass for an angel.

I ran my fingers down the bruises on his throat that were disappearing it seems as soon as they formed. That was a good thing, I guess.

Then his eyes popped open and I almost screamed at the sudden movement.

I felt my heart hammering against my chest from getting caught touching him. I was still in shock that he was allowed to stay here with me alone. My dad trusted both of us, I know that. And I wasn't about to let anything happen. The thought made me blush even more.

A smirk came across his face and his arms tightened around me.

"Did I scare you?" He asked smugly. There was nothing to be smug about.

"Nope." I answered, popping the "P".

He sighed heavily before taking his arms from around me and cupping my face. He kissed me gently for a few seconds before rolling over and right off the edge of the bed. I laughed to myself when he got back and groaned.

"Way to go." I joked. My blush came right back when I saw he was shirtless. I knew he took it off last night, but I'm still not used to it.

"You know, we broke the rules last night." He told me as he looked around for a shirt to put on for a little while. His basketball shorts were rolled a little at the bottom from him sleeping in them.

"Why?" I asked, almost in a panic. I didn't want him to think I was going to freak out that he broke a rule in my house. The rules that my dad made. I composed my face and smiled at him.

"We slept in the same room. Your dad told me on the phone to sleep in the living room, on the pull-out couch." He smiled a crooked smile and got down beside his bag on the floor. We both took showers last night, so there's no need to take one this morning.

"Rules were made to be broken." I murmured. Cameron cracked up laughing and fell onto the bed, making me flop from the movement.

"I can't believe you just said that, Miss I don't break rules." He said after he got his laugh.

"I don't remember ever saying that!" I smacked a pillow against the side of his head and waited for his reaction.

"Yes, but you were thinking it." He mumbled before he pounced on top of me, hovering over me, inches between our bodies. I giggled on accident which ruined the serious moment and made Cameron laugh, the smile in his face wrinkling the corners of his eyes.

He rolled off of me and onto his back before he jumped off the bed and grabbed a set of school clothes.

"I'll go to the bathroom down the hall to get dressed while you do." He called to me as he sauntered out of my room. I huffed, disappointed that I have to go to school.

I tossed the covers off my toasty body and stood up on my morning jelly legs. I walked slowly to my closet and grabbed a pair of shorts and shirt from some store at the mall my mom went to.

I slipped them on and went to the bathroom to do my rats nest mess of hair. After brushing it out and letting it fall straight down my back, I brushed my teeth and went downstairs for something to eat. Cameron was already down there pouring cereal into a bowl for me and him. He poured the milk into mine and dipped a spoon in it before handing it to me. I took my seat at the table and started eating slowly. I was in no hurry to get to school, that's for sure.

Cameron stared at me while I separated my cereal from my marshmallows in the bowl. A habit I would never break most likely.

I saw him smile, shake his head, and look back down at his own cereal. Good. I don't need a stalker.

"So, about these rules. What exactly did my dad say?" I asked. I took a break from separating my cereal and just shoved a spoonful in my mouth.

"Your body, your rules. His house, his rules." Cameron recited. I smiled a little.

"You're really going to follow those rules?" I asked him with a raise of my eyebrows.

"Of course. I don't want your dad to hate me. Last night I broke them because you needed me." He spoke the last part more quietly, knowing I didn't want to hear about it. "But I'm not breaking them anymore."

I gulped my cereal and kept my gaze on my bowl of milk.

"Um, is it okay if we stop by my house this evening? I wanted to get more clothes 'cause I forgot to bring the others and I'm sure my mom wants to see me." He changed the subject. I nodded my head.

I honestly didn't care that we had to stop by his house. It'll be nice to get away from here even though I wasn't even here for two days barely.

The phone rang and broke off anything Cameron might've been about to say.

"Hello?" I said into the phone after I saw it was my dad.

"Sophia? Hey, how are you?" He asked me, sounding wore out.

I yawned right then and he chuckled.

"A little tired. I slept good, though." I looked at Cameron through my eyelashes, phone stuck between my ear and shoulder. He smirked.

"How's Cameron? He doesn't mind staying with you does he?" His voice went from tired for alert. Typical dad.

"Yeah, I don't think he minds. That was cool of you to have him stay with me, dad. Thanks." I said as sincerely as I could.

"Well, I'm gonna let you get off to school. Your mom and Matt say they love you. Me too." He added in quickly. I smiled to myself.

"I love you guys, too." I replied in almost a whisper. We hung up then and Cameron had already stolen my bowl to wash it out. He finished and grabbed my hand, pulling me towards the door.

*

When we got to school, all eyes were on us. Well, maybe they were more on Cameron since he's the one that got hurt. But I couldn't help feeling a little self-conscious since I'm the one that had a meltdown in front of everyone Friday night.

Cameron's arm tightened around my shoulders and I held my hand up to intertwine it with his. I kept my eyes on the ground in front of me while we walked into the school. Emma and Adam met us not long after and I could tell Emma was trying hard not to shower me with questions about how I was. Did she even see me make a fool out of myself?

All I could think about was how my strong on the inside ego was down the drain. I probably looked like a zombie as well as felt like one right now.

But once lunch came around and it was just Emma and I at the table, I knew she was going to ask me. Her wary eyes lingered on me every other second and I could tell she was debating on whether or not to ask.

The boys had a basketball meeting or something like that. So that gave us a boy-free lunch.

So, I got this over with. "Go ahead and ask." I said with a small smile to let her know I wasn't going to be mad if she asked.

"Are you okay?" She immediately asked. An expression of concern crossed her face.

"Yeah. Worried, but fine." I told her and pushed my broccoli around with my fork.

"But... how's your foot?" She asked warily. I felt my face drop and my gaze went to my foot subconsciously. There was a layer or two of gauze wrapped around my foot from where I cut it. Did Cameron tell her? Aw man....

"Did Cameron tell you what happened?" I asked, biting my lip.

Her eyes widened with realization.

"No! No, I was there. I braided your hair." A smile formed on her lips. "Did you think Cameron braided it?" We both laughed at the thought of him attempting that.

"You were there?" I asked her.

She shrugged. "Yeah. Cameron asked me to drive him over since you took his truck. I saw the broken picture and everything... I was worried all night." She told me.

"I promise, I'm fine." I said, feeling a little ashamed. I didn't want my best friend seeing me like that.

We were both finished with our trays soon enough and were about to get up and dump them when someone walked up to our table.

Danielle stood there with a smile in her face. A pleasant one.

"Can I help you?" Emma asked through her teeth. It wasn't normal to see her mad.

"I was just wanting to ask Sophia something." She directed her creepy smile at me. "How's Cameron? Is he breathing or what?" I snorted. Like she hasn't seen him around today.

"I want to ask you something, too." I laced my fingers together on the table to keep them from tightening into fists.

"Why would you try to hurt the person you liked?" I asked her. Her smile faded and turned into a flat line.

"I don't like him. I was hurting you, of course." A smirk took the flat line's place.

I couldn't deny that one. I felt the anger boiling to the top and was about to boil over. I know I can usually hold it down. But maybe it was time for a change.

When I stood up, I felt several pairs of eyes on me and Danielle. Yep, this was going down in history. "Sophia Belle standing up for herself!" I could already hear it in my head.

"Well, now it's my turn to hurt you." I said with anger laced in my voice.

Her expression turned confused right before my fist connected with her nose.

Not so perfect now, is she?

____

Dedicated to my best friend because without her, Danielle wouldn't have gotten punched!

Love you girl!

Chapter Thirty: Anxious

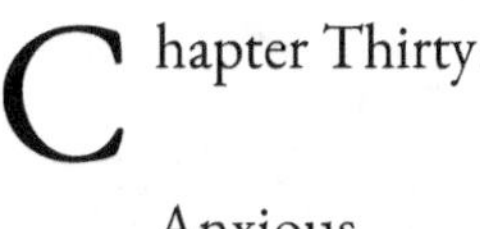

C hapter Thirty:

Anxious

My leg wouldn't stop shaking from me being so anxious. I sat here in the front office, waiting for the principal to come out and start telling me I'm kicked out of school.

The funny thing is, I don't feel bad for punching Danielle. Not one but because she deserved it.

I clenched and unclenched my right fist to keep it from going too stiff. It hurt like hell every time I balled it up, but I didn't care. My eyes lifted to stare over at Danielle. She was on the opposite side of the office holding a bloody paper towel to her face. She had a scowl on her face from what I could see and her eyes never left her lap.

I remembered her ear piercing scream after I nailed her. I never smiled, that would be a stupid thing to do. I should've kept my anger under control like usual, but I didn't want to. I just didn't feel like it anymore. Oh well.

The door suddenly opened and squeaked. Cameron peeked in and saw me. I had to hold back a huge smile since Danielle was glancing up at the door to see who it might be.

Cameron suddenly vibrated and I realized he was laughing. He had to cover his mouth and shut the door for a moment. I let the smile break through and I looked down to keep Danielle from seeing it.

"Okay, ladies." Vice principal Sherman came out of no where. I guess the principal wasn't handling this.

"First, go back to class, Danielle. You're not needed here at the moment." Mrs. Sherman said. I waited patiently until Danielle reluctantly left the room without seeing that I got in some big trouble.

Mrs. Sherman looked back at me. "Sophia, what got in to you? You've always been a good kid." She told me. Mrs. Sherman has always been a loving vice principal. Everyone seems to like her.

"I don't know." I told her. Though I really did know. I wanted to show her how I felt.

"Well..." She scratched the back of her neck. "I'm going to let you off easy. You've never gotten in trouble a day in your life. Let this be a lesson. You could have broken her nose and her parents wouldn't be happy."

She stood up. "I'm going to talk to her later. You're not in trouble, just don't let it happen again. Go on to the kitchen and get an ice pack for that hand." I nodded my head and stood up, anxious to get out of there and happy that I wasn't getting in trouble. My parents would not be happy if they got a call from school.

I walked out of the door and saw Cameron propped against the opposite wall. I smiled and walked over to him, wrapping my arms around his waist.

"So, you punched Danielle, huh?" He laughed and I couldn't help but laugh with him. I pulled Cameron along with me to the kitchen with my good hand.

"I did. That was the worst thing I've ever done." I cringed at my horrible action. Here comes the guilt.

"You're fine. I don't blame you. Emma told me what happened. You did what you had to do." Cameron squeezed my good hand in his.

"I could have just walked away. You know, done the mature thing." I mumbled.

"Sophia, you always do the mature thing. You can slip sometimes-" He stopped after he realized he was about to lecture me like the other day. I kicked him out of the house for less than a minute before I realized I was being dumb.

I looked over and smiled at him. He grinned his crooked grin back at me.

The cook wasn't hesitant at giving me an ice pack after she saw my hand. It wasn't too bad. Just bruised knuckles and some of Danielle's blood. But the ice made it feel better. I thanked her and Cameron and I began walking back towards our classes.

"Um, my mom called me after our basketball meeting." Cameron started. He had his hand pressed to the small of my back.

"And?" I asked, impatiently. Was this good or bad?

"She wants you to have dinner with us tonight. And she wants to ask you something. Suggest it, really. And I agree with her." He had my heart beating out of my chest. After all that happened today, I could have a heart attack right now.

"Is it bad?" I asked him. He chuckled and reached around for my hand.

"No, of course not. Will you come? Right after school?" He asked me hopefully. I didn't have any reason to object.

"Yes. I'll be there." I smiled up at him

*

I thought about the Danielle situation all day. That and the situation of having dinner with Cameron's family. I've met them before and this should be a piece of cake; except they want to suggest a few things to me. I mean, what am I supposed to think to that?

The last bell rang over ten minutes ago and I've been sitting in Cameron's truck that long waiting for him. I finally spotted him sauntering out the doors of the school and towards the truck. Must've forgotten something.

"What took you so long?" I asked him as soon as he got in. He looked at me and shook his head.

"Stupid teacher and her stupid rules." Cameron grumbled under his breath. He put the truck in drive and started to back out of his space.

"Seat belt," I told him. He glanced at me and reluctantly put his seat belt on. More like jerked it on. He was definitely annoyed at something.

"Should I ask?" I asked him cautiously.

"No. I'll probably tell you later." He gave me a small smile to reassure me. It was all I could ask for right now.

"What is it that your mom wants? I've just about chewed my nails all the way down." I chuckled at my actions.

"Don't worry about it. If it was something that I knew you would be uncomfortable with, I wouldn't be taking you to my house right now. I forced it out of my mother after she said she wanted to have dinner with you. She's just being protective." He informed me.

I raised an eyebrow. "Protective? Over me?" I asked him. He smiled proudly at me.

"Sophia, have you ever seen me stick with a girl as long as I have you?" He said a little sheepishly, like he was disappointed in himself. "She thinks of you as her own already."

I felt the blush creeping up my neck and lingering on my cheeks.

"It'll be fine. I promise." He told me.

We arrived at his house not long after and I slowly stepped out of the truck. Cameron was at my side in a second, lacing our fingers together.

He pulled me along with him up the steps of his front porch. We walked right in and the smell of steak and baked potatoes filled my nose. I know that smell so well since my mom makes that meal often. It's my favorite. Cameron must've had a part in that.

Cameron smiled when he saw the grin on my face. We both tore our shoes off and made our way into the living room where his dad was watching a basketball game. His eyes were glued to the TV with a look of concentration on his face. He noticed out presence and his head snapped up with a huge grin spreading across his face.

He stood up and grabbed me up in a bear hug so tight that I thought my head was going to pop off.

"It's great to see you again, kiddo!" He patted my back.

"You too!" I replied just as cheerfully.

"Dinner will be ready in twenty minutes!" I heard Mrs. Bridges say from the kitchen. I looked around at the familiar living room and back to Cameron who was already staring at me.

"Okay, we can go to my room, then." Cameron grabbed my hand again. His dad never protested about it, so I went along willingly.

Once we got to his room, Cameron went straight to his bed. He collapsed on it on his back and put his arms behind his head. He used one hand to pat the free space beside of him.

"I'm not as anxious now." I said to him once I was comfortable beside him.

"Good. You don't need to be." He told me quietly.

I started checking out my knuckles and the weird purplish-blue bruises scattered on them. I didn't think I punched her that hard.

I lifted my fist to Cameron's throat and smiled at him although he wasn't looking. All I could see was his closed eyes short eyelashes.

"We have matching bruises, babe." I blushed at the word I used. It quickly went away, though. He lifted his head just barely to look down at me.

"Huh. Match made in heaven... babe." He smirked at me and laid his head back down and closed his eyes. My nostrils flared.

"You're never going to let that go now, are you?" I asked him with slight humor. I already knew his answer.

"'Course not, babe." He smiled again.

I rolled my eyes at him.

We only laid for what seemed like a minute before Cameron's mom was calling us for dinner.

"Cam..." I whined when he hopped off the bed. I was feeling so awfully lazy today.

"Yes, madame?" He asked with a sarcastic smile hinted with a real one. He knew I didn't feel like walking.

"My hand hurts," I rubbed my knuckles softly and made a puppy dog face, "can you carry me?"

"Your hand hurts so you can't walk?" He asked me. I chuckled at him.

"Of course. Hop on." He backed up to the bed and I stood up. After securing my arms around his neck without choking him, I jumped and wrapped my legs around his waist. Our heads were pressed together and I could hear his breathing really good now. I pressed my lips to his temple as he carried me carefully down the steps.

I made him put me down at the bottom of the stairs and we walked into the dining room. The food was smelling even better now.

"Hi, Sophia!" Mrs. Bridges hugged me tightly before we sat down. I already had an empty plate in front of me. Cameron and his dad had already begun scooping food into their trays before I could get a scoop of corn. Geez.

"Thank you for having me over for dinner," I said to Cam's parents. They both smiled at me while getting their food.

"We love having you over!" She said.

"Cameron, say the blessing?" Cameron nodded at his dad and reached for my hand and his mother's. I took it without hesitation and closed my eyes, bowing my head. Cameron made it short and sweet but he said a way that seemed like he really meant it. It made me love him more that he has a good relationship with god.

In the middle of our dinner, between laughs from funny stories from when Cameron was little, Mrs. Bridges decided to drop the bomb I had been expecting.

"So, Cameron tells us you've been staying at him alone? Well, when he's not there." She smiled at me. I nodded my head, feeling nervous.

"Yeah. My mom and dad are gonna be in Tennessee at least until next week. They'll probably have to go back again." I took a sip of my sweet tea. "They always want the best for Matt, and me, ya know? They go all out. But I'm so happy they do."

She smiled at me. "Yes, you are blessed with amazing parents."

She continued after chewing her bite of steak. "I wanted to ask you something very important. I already called your parents and asked if they would like this more, and they agreed. But I want to ask you too since it involves you mostly." I felt my heartbeat pick up even though it had no reason to.

Cameron's hand squeezed my knee under the table reassuringly.

"We were wondering if you'd like to stay with us while your parents are away? Every time they go away, actually. You're parents think it would be much better to have a home with guardians in it and to be honest, we would too." She gestured to herself and. Her husband. My heartbeat retired to normal.

"Wow..." I whispered to myself, shocked. "I'd love to. If I wouldn't be a bother..." I started worrying again.

"No! No of course not! We have a spare bedroom since Callie no longer lives here. She's coming back tomorrow, though. Only for a few days to visit with her old friends. You can room with Cameron for those days." She gave her son a stern look as if to say "no funny business".

"That's... that's great. I don't know how to thank you guys..."

"You don't have to, honey. We're doing this for you and your family as a favor that doesn't need to be repaid."

I grinned at Cameron then.

"Well, thank you so much." I said to them all.

"If you'd like, you can stay tonight. I'm sure Cameron has clothes you can wear since his sister took all of hers with her when she left." She had a thoughtful look on her face. "And you could stop at your house in the morning. Just a thought." She added sheepishly.

I was genuinely surprised at her eagerness for me to stay. And I was so happy about that.

"Yes, I'd love that. Thank you."

____

Wow. Thank you guys so much for all the reads recently! It's making me so happy and more eager to write more!

P.s. I might be writing a sequel! Tell me what you think, if you'd like!

Also: Follow for Follow! And if you have any book suggestions then let me know! I'm always looking for a good book!

Thank you so much!!!

P.p.s. I realize that Cameron's mom's name used to be Emily. I went back and changed in the beginning chapters and hopefully fixed it!

Chapter Thirty-One: What Am I Going To Do?

C hapter Thirty-One:

What Am I Going To Do?

After dinner was over, I helped Mrs. Bridges clean up the table. Even though she continuously reminded me that it was her job and she could do it, I ignored her requests for me to go relax and helped her anyways. She seemed like she enjoyed my company, actually.

After I called her Mrs. Bridges for the 100th time, she told me to just call her Andy. Her real name was Andrea. I didn't mind calling her that. And Mr. Bridges to me was now Chad.

"Thank you for helping me clean up, Sophia!" She told me when I was almost to the stairs to go up and find Cameron. I was so tired and it was only six-thirty. I was eager to get out of these clothes and into something more comfortable.

"You're welcome! It was the least I could do." I replied and darted up the steps before she could deny my favor to her. I would feel guilty if I didn't help her out while I stayed in her house for however long.

I found Cameron on his bed, phone in hands and her was scrolling up and down. Probably on Facebook. Not something he usually did.

"I'm so sleepy." I mumbled when I leaned against his door frame.

"I have a pair of jogging pants and a t-shirt for you." He pointing to his dresser and I spotted the neatly folded clothes. Clean ones, thank goodness.

"Thank you so very much." I walked over to the bed and crawled up next to him, "love you." I mumbled against his lips when I leaned in to kiss him. He smiled into the kiss and I jumped back off the bed. I grabbed the clothes and walked to the bathroom, completely exhausted. I didn't do much today, so I didn't get why I'm so tired.

After exchanging my clothes for Cameron's, I went back to his room to talk to him before bed for a few minutes.

A few minutes turned into a few hours.

"So you're taking me to my house before school?" I asked him. We both sat on his bed, backs propped against the head board.

"Yep. You can take a shower and get ready for school. Then we can stop by on the way home and get your clothes for you to stay here." He said and tightened his arm around my shoulder. He kissed the top of my head.

"Holy cow. I just remember that Finals are tomorrow." I mumbled when the idea of school came to mind.

"Oh yeah." Cameron said nonchalantly.

"I know most of the ones I have to take anyways, I'm good. What about you?" I asked him. My eyes were drooping and I was yawning every seven seconds. I counted.

"I know it too. If you wouldn't have tutored me then I probably would fail them. No doubt. Thank you, babe." He smirked. I rolled my eyes.

"Yeah, yeah." I grinned sleepily.

"I think I'm gonna go to bed." I turned sideways so I could kiss his lips. "I'll see you in the morning."

He pouted.

"I'll see you later, babe." He said as I was walking out the door. I laughed out loud and he did too after hearing me.

Callie's room was painted a light pink color. The pink was so light that it almost looked white. Her bed was mostly three colors: blue, pink, and green. Most of her room was neat and tidy, too.

I switched the light off and pulled her covers back before climbing under them. I then realized that I was way too hot to sleep in sweatpants. So, I pulled the sweatpants off and tossed them off the bed, still covered in the blankets of Callie's bed.

I closed my eyes, but I knew I wasn't going to be able to sleep anytime soon.

The digital clock beside the bed read eleven-thirty pm. I'm so tired, yet I can't sleep. Ever had that problem?

Then I heard the door open. I turned my head to look at whoever it was creeping on me, half expecting to see Callie. I hope she didn't mind me sleeping in her bed...

"You're still awake?" Cameron's voice rang through the darkness. I smiled a little.

"Yeah. Can't sleep but I'm so tired..." I mumbled. He walked over to the bed and without hesitation, climbed underneath the covers. His cold skin touched my hot legs which instantly cooled me down.

"Do you have pants on?" He asked me incredulously. I instantly felt my cheeks burn red and silently thanked the good lord above it was dark. I pursed my lips.

"Um... I got hot." I said sheepishly.

He laughed and wrapped his legs around mine, pulling me closer.

"Get some sleep, babe. You're out of it." I could practically hear his smile.

Then, I was out like a light because he was here.

In the morning, I reached my arms around on the bed to find that it was empty except for myself. It was kind of disappointing.

Now, the clock read 7:00. Uh-oh. I had a half an hour to go home and get ready. I had jump start out of bed and ran to Cameron's room, not even knocking.

He was sitting on his bed, laptop on his lap.

"Hello?!" I said, almost shrieking.

"Let's get going! I'm not gonna be late!" I grabbed his laptop and closed it, grabbed his wrist and took off down the stairs.

It felt like a year went by by the time we reached my driveway. Cameron has been quiet this morning, which was sort of unusual for him. He talks to me a lot when we're together, which is pretty much all the time. I didn't let it bother me too much since I needed to hurry up and get ready.

With Cameron still stuck in the truck, I darted into my house and up the stairs in record time. My shower was legit three minutes and I quickly threw on a pair of jeans, flip flops, and a t-shirt. I pulled my wet hair up into a messy bun and put on some light makeup, like I do some days.

I saw Cameron sitting in the truck when I got down locking my front door. He was leaned back into his seat and staring out his window. What was up with him today?

"Ready to get your smarty pants on?" I asked in attempt to make him laugh. His lips twitched like they were going to pull up into a smile.

His eyes met mine for a second before they turned back to the road and he started his truck. He kept both hands on the wheel intentionally, I think, so he wouldn't have to hold my hand.

That's it. He knew something that I didn't.

Once we reached the school, I got out first since he was being slow as a turtle and walked over to him, almost fuming.

"What's going on with you?" I demanded. He shut his truck door and locked it with his key. I liked how this truck was so old that it didn't have one of those remotes. It was nice.

"Nothing," he said. I was surprised that he didn't walk around me since he didn't seem like he wanted anything to do with me this morning.

I started to panic. "Did I do something wrong?" I asked him. I was mad, so naturally, tears came. Gosh, I was such a girl.

"No." He simply answered, looking everywhere but my face.

"Cameron, there is. Just... why do you suddenly want nothing to do with me?" I asked him while my hands dropped limply to my sides. He gave me one hard look before answering.

"I don't know."

I stood at his truck in the same place for about five minutes before someone waved a hand in front of my face. I shook my head to clear it and my vision came back.

It was a boy I knew from my math class in Freshman year. He asked me if I was okay.

"Yeah, I'm good." I answered half heartedly before turning my

Back to him and walking towards the school. I needed to get my head in the game and ready for these finals.

Grades were my priority right now.

But I couldn't think about school when all I could think was "what am I going to do?"

____

So, why do you think Cameron is mad/upset?

Let me know below!

That rhymed...

Chapter Thirty-Two: Love You, Night.

C hapter Thirty-Two:

Love You, 'Night.

Finals were easier than expected, that's for sure. Or maybe that's a bad thing. If it was easy, I probably did everything wrong.

I wouldn't be surprised.

I'm still having trouble figuring out what I did wrong. With Cameron, that is. Last night we were just fine, joking and everything. It was this morning that he seemed so different.

A light bulb almost blew up inside my head.

His laptop! What was he looking at before I put it down for him? What could him I have given him a reason to be mad at me for... on the internet? I honestly don't know. But I'm going to find out.

It's 2:57 pm and I'm counting the seconds until I get out of here. I needed to get out of here and back to Cameron's place. As soon as possible or this is going to bug me all day. It couldn't be anything too bad, right?

I got out class as soon as the bell rang and ran to my locker. I waved at Emma as I darted past her. I barely talked at lunch. Cameron didn't even come to lunch today and Adam wouldn't spill the beans. Even Emma was on edge sort of.

I packed my clothes at the house this morning and put them on the back of Cameron's truck, so we didn't have to go to my house after school today to get my things. Unless he doesn't want me at his house...

I became even more saddened by that thought.

As soon as I had all the right books to study for tomorrow's finals, (the last ones) I walked out if the school and to Cameron's truck without another glance behind me. I felt like I was sneaking around. But I wasn't. I was a girl on a mission.

Cameron was just opening his truck door when I got there. I knew he noticed me but he decided not to look up. He looked totally out of it. What could be bothering him so much?

Instead of being a good girlfriend and hounding him with questions, I decided to wait until I got home to stalk his computer. I tried to tell myself that this wasn't a bad thing I was about to do.

As soon as we got to his house, I grabbed both my bags off the back of his truck and walked up to the house. Both us were quiet the whole way home. Nothing surprising considering the circumstances. Cameron thankfully took my bags from me like the gentleman he was and walked to the door.

But when we got to the door, it was unlocked. Cameron and I both knew his parents were at work so why would the door be unlocked? He had his hand out as if to tell me to not go inside yet. I obeyed. Though I had to bite my tongue. Sure, ignore me all day but act like a hero now.

"Callie?" Cameron asked in surprised. I raised my eyebrows and pushed past Cameron through the door. A little Ella came waltzed up to us and she smiled a toothy grin up at me. Callie stood up from the living room couch, her expression guilty.

"Um, hey guys. I need to ask you a favor. I know it's sudden, like really sudden, but I need you to watch Ella for me tonight until about 9:30." Callie was pleading although there was no need. Of course I'd babysit for her.

"Don't worry, Callie. We can watch Ella." I told her before Cameron could respond. She looked between the two of us warily before nodding her head. Sisters always know what's up.

Callie had to rush to get out of here because she was apparently late.

Cameron immediately started playing with Ella. He dropped his stuff in the doorway and grabbed Ella up, raising her above his head. Her soft giggle erupted through the house and I found myself smiling. She was so cute.

I lugged my stuff up to Cameron's bedroom since Callie was no here and was probably wanting to sleep in her own bed. This was going to be awkward tonight, then.

I came back downstairs as soon as my stuff was in his room to find the two of them pulling blankets off the couches and chairs along with the cushions. A fort!

"Help us, Sophie!" Ella smiled up at me. I grinned when she called me Sophie.

"Okay, where do I start?" I asked her as I kneeled down beside her. I didn't even notice that Cameron had slipped out of the room for a moment until Ella and I had gotten a wall for our fort put up and he was coming down the stairs, arms filled with blankets.

"Cammy put the roof on!" Ella ordered. Cameron smiled a small smile at her -also unusual around his niece - and gently laid a blanket over the top of the fort.

We all huddled inside the little fort, Cameron was squished because he was so big and the fort wasn't.

Ella sat between us and had a little flashlight she got from the kitchen and was shining it on the blanket in front of us. She put her fingers in front of the light and made bunny ears, giggling when Cameron made a dog and barked at her bunny. I saw this as the opportunity to leave while he was occupied.

"I'll be right back. Gotta go to the bathroom." I lied. Gosh I hate lying.

As soon as I was up and out of the tent, I did a little dance to show that I had to pee. I bounced up the stairs the same way until I was hidden by the wall in the hallway at the top and sprinted to his bedroom.

His laptop sat in the same spot that I put it in this morning. I walked over to it, checking over my shoulder just to make sure he didn't catch me, and popped it open. The screen was black at first. Then it came on and the Facebook log in page was up. He was on Facebook? That's what made him so mad? I don't get it... I don't have much stuff on my Facebook. I mean, my profile picture is of Matt and I taken when he was probably about six years old. I don't get on often, so there can't be anything for him to be mad about.

At first I thought about why he could be. Is he mad because I haven't changed my relationship status on here...? No, he wouldn't get mad at me for something as stupid as that. Then... why?

I'll check it later, tonight when he's in the room. I'll get on my Facebook and look around while he's here, just to show that I know what's on my Facebook and that he doesn't have to be mad about anything. I can't take it when he's mad.

I'm so used to his company anymore that I hate it when he's not talking to me or laughing with me. Or laughing at me.

I put the computer carefully back in it's spot and raced back down the stairs. I'm sure my facial expression gave me away to Cameron, but I didn't care right now. He was barely looking at me anyway.

The rest of the evening stretched on for what seemed like forever. Cameron made Ella and I grilled cheeses, the best meal ever, and we all laid down in the living room to watch Looney Toons until Cameron's parents got home. After that we were free since Ella'd fallen asleep on the couch.

I went upstairs with Cameron silently and was about to take a shower when my phone buzzed. I glanced at Cameron to see him on his bed, phone in hand, not paying attention to anyone else.

I pressed answer on my phone and put it to my ear.

"Hello?"

"Sophia!" Dad's deep voice sounded through the phone. I small smile appeared on my lips as I leaned against an empty place on Cam's wall and slid down it until I landed on my butt.

"Hey, dad. How are you? How's Matt? Is everything okay?" I asked him, almost in monotone.

"He's great, I'm great, and so is your mom. How are you? Do you like it staying at the Bridges'?" His question threw me off.

"You knew? Holy cow I forgot to call you!" I gasped horrifyingly.

Dad just chuckled. "No, I asked Andy to ask you. I didn't want you alone." Then it dawned on me that Andy did say something about my mom and dad knowing. My heartbeat went back to normal.

"Okay. Um, I like it. It's better not being home alone even though I always had Cameron with me." I glanced up at him through my lashes. Still wasn't paying attention. "Is Matt really okay or are you just telling me this?" I queried.

"He's doing good, Soph." He answered me. The sound in his voice sounded otherwise. It was tired, stressed, worried. He was lying to me.

I decided I should go before the waterworks come.

"Well, dad, I gotta go. I have studying for my last finals tomorrow. Love you, bye." He said he loved me and goodnight and I hung up. I had to keep myself from throwing the phone down on the floor so I sat it on his dresser instead. I grabbed up my clothes and practically ran to the bathroom. I felt a pair of wary eyes on me as I left.

Once out of the shower, I dressed quickly and brushed my teeth as well as my hair and went back to Cameron's room. He was in the same position as he was when I left. I knew my eyes were red and blotchy from crying in the shower but I didn't care if Cameron noticed. Maybe he'd talk to me if I was in pain.

"Can I borrow your laptop?" I asked him with a stuffy nose. His eyes lifted to look up at me and I could already tell what he was feeling. He was confused, definitely. And sad.

He nodded once and that was all I needed. I grabbed up his laptop and sat on the edge of his bed. Opening Facebook and signing in, I went to my profile page and clicked on my settings. I don't know if that's why he's mad, (it probably Isn't) but I need to feel somewhat better.

After changing it from single to in a relationship, I sent a request to Cameron's Facebook so he'd accept it and be happy.

I put the laptop on his dresser and found my phone. My next step was to turn around and lay down in the bed but then I realized that he was there. Why did Callie have to come back tonight?

"Cameron?" I asked in a somewhat hoarse voice. I turned around and sat Indian style beside him. He put his phone down and looked at me expectantly. I was sure I was about to hit him or slap him or something. Instead I clenched my fists together in my lap.

"Why won't you talk to me? Or acknowledge my existence?" I added through my tears. He sat up on his bed with an almost angry expression on his face while he grabbed his laptop. He sat back down and flipped the top open.

I waited patiently since I couldn't see what he was doing.

Then he turned the computer towards me and I saw what he was mad about. It was on Facebook, his Facebook messages, and it was Emma. My best friend Emma. She asked him a question.

Why is Sophia's house in the paper for sale?

She asked him. I looked between that message and Cameron for a moment. What?

"What?" I voiced my thoughts.

"She asked me to see if it was true. That you are moving away probably to... Tennessee or something? Why else would your house be for sale?" He asked accusingly. I stood up from the bed, raging.

"I had no clue about this! Oh my gosh... I'm calling my mom. Cameron, I didn't know about any of this." I went to grab my phone off the bed but he got to it first.

"You didn't know your house was for sale?" He asked a little more in control of himself now. I nodded my head, face turning red out of anger.

"No! I would have told you myself..." I felt tears sting at my eyes again and my bottom lip quivering. What a day.

"And you were mad at me all day because of that? Oh..." I wanted to scream at him. "Why didn't you just ask me? You jerk! I thought I did something so bad that you were going to just.. end it!" I made sure not to raise my voice since there were other people in the house trying to sleep.

Cameron sprang out of his bed and was now standing in front of me. He wasn't touching me, just hovering so close that I could feel his body heat.

"The truth?" He asked more quietly. All I could do was nod my head and keep my eyes on his chest instead of his face.

"If you're moving away... then how can we be... us? How are we supposed to do that, Sophia? While your over in Tennessee and I'm stuck here, without you." His voice cracked at the end by his expression stayed blank when I looked up.

"You want to break up before I leave?" I said quietly. Our eyes were now locked in a way that couldn't be broken.

Cameron nodded his head slightly. "I don't think it would be good for us... so far from each other for so long. Matt is having treatments. That could take a while, right? How would we be able to do that?" I hates that he was right. This was probably the reason why my parents were moving us. To be closer to the hospital without having to travel back home every week.

"Yeah, you're right." I agreed so quietly that I didn't know if he heard me or not.

"I don't want to. I love you so damn much, Sophia." He put his hands in my shoulders to steady himself. I wrapped both my hands on either of his biceps. "You and I both know it's what's best."

"I know." I squeaked. Of course I knew. If there's a will, there's a way. Does he have no will to be with me?

"I'm tired." I said after removing his arms from my shoulders.

Cameron walked over to his closet and grabbed a blanket from the top of it and took one pillow from his bed. I stared at him.

"Where are you going?"

"Your dad told me to sleep on the couch. And I am." He answered without looking at me.

I didn't reply. He turned out the lights and stood at the door for a moment, staring at me through the darkness.

He walked over to the side of the bed and leaned down so his lips could touch my forehead.

"Today, I tried to convince myself that I wasn't in love with you anymore so that I could let you go. It didn't work. At all." He whispered. His breath fanned my face.

"I love you." He whispered before walking out the door. I waited for almost ten minutes for him to come back and mend us together again.

But he didn't.

———————————

Aww yaaassss!

But wait, more surprises to come!

I hope the long-ness of this chapter makes up for the shortness of the last one!

Chapter Thirty-Three: Bad Luck

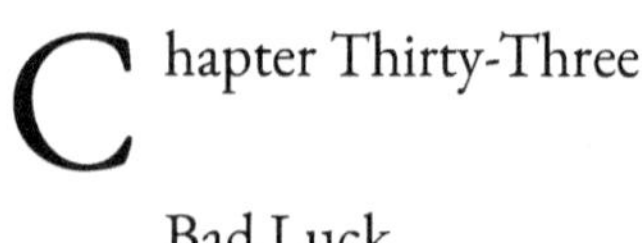

C hapter Thirty-Three:

Bad Luck

You could say I was mad. Just a little.

How could you break up with someone and then afterwards tell them you love them? What was he thinking?

When morning came the next day, I was more than happy to get out of that house. I got up, got dressed before he was even up, and started walking to school. I decided against breakfast since that would make it easier for him to catch up to me and I needed to get to school before him.

The sky was clouded over when I walked out the door of the Bridges' residence. It was probably going to rain so I was happy I went with skinny jeans today. I had to be as quiet as I possibly could since I got up at 6:00 to get ready. I knew Callie and Ella were still asleep in her room and didn't want to disturb them or wake up the monster that slept on the couch last night. I brushed my hair and and pulled it up into a bun to make it quick. I didn't even brush my teeth. Nope, I stuffed my toothbrush and toothpaste in my bag and planned on brushing them at school.

Call me stubborn, it would match me perfectly.

I unlatched my arms from around my torso and grabbed my phone out of my pocket to call Emma. I had to rant to someone before it all came out to someone who didn't need to know about my problems.

"Hello?" Emma's sleepy voice answered. I almost forgot it was only 6:30. Oh well, she'd be getting up soon anyway.

"Hey, Em." I said through gritted teeth. I've never seen myself so mad before.

"Sophia? Are you okay?" Emma replied, her voice more alert. I clenched my fingers around my phone and walked faster.

"Yeah. There is." I grumbled.

"What?" She asked in an almost scared voice. This was very unusual of me.

"It's nothing important. Cameron. Yeah, it's about him." I didn't even want to say his name. That's how mad I was.

"Okay, I'm almost done getting ready so I'll meet you at school and we can talk before class." She shuffled her phone around and I could tell she was getting ready now.

"Okay" was all I could say before hanging up. My normal response would have been "No don't go to school early for me!" or "No It's okay". But I didn't care at the moment.

I reached the school just as it turned 6:45. I must have really been walking fast. Emma kept her word and was waiting by my locker when I got there. I stomped up to her and twisted my lock to unlock my locker.

"What's up?" She asked me, biting her lip nervously.

I didn't want her to worry. My best friend. So I took a deep, deep breath and let it out through my nose. My temper was controlled now.

I turned to her with a blank expression.

"He broke up with me." My whisper came out strangled from the force. If I didn't whisper, I would scream.

"What? Why?!" She exclaimed so loud that I was taken aback. She's never that loud. She must have noticed too because her face turned blood red and she covered her mouth. We were both discovering sides of ourselves we weren't used to.

"Evidently I'm moving. And he thinks it would be better for both of us. I don't get it. And then you know what he said right after that?" When I looked back at her and away from my locker, her face was ghost white, all blush gone.

"Oh my gosh." She said under her breath. "Sophia! I told him that! I just wanted to know and I didn't want to ask you because I just... I didn't want to make you uncomfortable. You know," she twisted her fingers together nervously, "I thought you'd want to tell me later." She sputtered.

"It's okay, Emma. I know you asked him. It's fine. I found out that way and I haven't talked to my parents to figure out what the heck is going on yet." I rushed.

"I fe at fault here." She had a sick looking expression that made her look like she could puke.

"No! Don't. Seriously, if he felt that way this time then he would've felt the same way when he found out later. No worries." I reassured her. She nodded her head but I knew she wouldn't forgive herself.

"What did he say to you?" She asked suddenly.

I cocked an eyebrow. "What?"

"What did Cameron say to you after he broke up with you?" She explained more.

"Oh. He told me he loved me. Still." I said as if it didn't matter. But it did. It really, really did. Emma's arms were around me in a second and it didn't take me long to hug her back. She's a real friend. And here came the tears stinging at my eyes. I didn't want to let them fall.

"It'll be okay. He'll come around. I know he will." She told me as she rubbed my back comfortingly. I nodded my head and wiped a tear out of the corner of my eye before it could roll down my cheek.

"I don't know if I want him to." I said in such a low whisper that I'm positive she didn't hear me. I don't know how true those words were, so I didn't want to say them out loud again.

"Here he comes. And he looks kind of mad." Emma told me in a warning tone. I quickly let go of her embrace and turned to my locker to close it and lock it.

"I'll talk to you later. All right?" Emma asked me as she started towards her locker. I nodded my head and tried to look happy even though I could taste a salty tear touch my top lip. I scowled at myself.

The hallways were beginning to full up now and more students were flowing through the halls to there classes for the last day of finals. It was a gloomy day for everyone. Bittersweet, really.

I spun around to head towards my first finals class but ran into someone. Just a stranger and it made me jump. I didn't see Cameron any where. I thought Emma said he was coming? I thanked the good lord above and stared walking along the wall to go to class.

The janitor's closet door was cracked open a little in front of me. I didn't think much of it until I was pulled inside by someone's arm. I didn't even have time to scream before the door was shut and I heard it click, indicating it was now locked. Someone had to see me get kidnapped in here! C'mon, why me?

Then the light snapped on and I was face-to-face with Cameron. It reminded me of the time after he found out I was his tutor. He warned me not to tell anyone, if I remember correctly.

"What do you want?" I asked quite bitterly. I kept my eyes on my shoes instead of his beautiful face.

"Do you know how worried I was this morning? I didn't know what happened to you!" He almost shouted at me. That was it. I was on fire now.

"Why do you care?!" I shouted back, letting my anger out. It felt good. Like taking your bra off for a shower at the end of the day. Great comparison, yeah?

"Sophia..." He started but I cut him off.

"No. Don't even start. I am so furious with you, Cameron. Just leave me alone and we'll be fine." I tried to walk past him but he blocked my way. Of course he did.

I crossed my arms over my chest childishly.

"I do care. You know that. And you also know I did what I did for a reason." He told me. It seemed sincere. But I didn't care about sincere right now.

"Do you realize what you're doing to me? Cameron, we were in this for the long run." I was now anything but a sobbing mess. "You broke my heart. You dumped me, and then said you loved me. What the heck?" I said through the thick tears. I was glad I didn't worry about makeup today.

"Don't say that." He shook his head, referring to the word dumped. His eyes were squeezed shut and I could only guess what was happening behind those lids.

"It's true. Now, if you'll excuse me, I have finals to ace." I said and shoved past him forcefully this time.

He didn't come out of that closet even after I'd gotten to the end of the hall.

*

"Hey." Emma greeted me.

"Hi." I replied glumly. I sat down across from her at our usual lunch table. She didn't look too happy herself.

"What's wrong?" I asked her, genuinely concerned.

"Adam and I had a fight. It was about you and Cameron. It's okay. We're okay." She reassured me. I quirked an eyebrow, not believing her at all.

"What happened?" I asked.

"It's really nothing. We just disagree on what you guys are broken up for. He agrees with Cameron, of course, and I agree with you. But the thing is, I don't think Cameron agrees with himself." Her words spoke to me and I had a glimmer of hope run through me. Maybe he really did regret ending us.

But did I?

I didn't reply to Emma's observation. I didn't know what to say, so I shoved a French fry in my mouth and let the voices all around us fill the pause in our conversation. I didn't feel comfortable nor was I used to speaking my true feelings to my friends.

I shrugged my shoulders more to myself and finished eating my food. I told Emma I'd talk to her later and went to dump my tray. School was almost over.

Thank The Lord.

*

When the last bell rang, I darted out of the classroom with the rest of the students from my class. I already had my books that I needed in my backpack and ready to go so I didn't have to make a stop at my locker.

I was avoiding any communication with Cameron and his attempts today made me feel like I would really have to worry about talking to him. I caught him staring at me multiple times during the classes we had together. Every chance he got he was at my locker. I was glad that I had all my books needed in my backpack.

I was not about to let my attempts come crashing down now.

Swiftly, I made my way down the sidewalk towards Cameron's house. Sadly, I had to live with him for a few days. But, maybe I could change that. Or at least speed it up.

I grabbed my phone out my pocket as I continued walking down the sidewalk. It only rang a few times before someone of the other line picked up.

"Sophia?" My mom asked, surprise in her voice.

"Hey, mom. Um, what's this about our house being up for sale?" I demanded. This was the core of my problem. Them not telling me caused Cameron to grow distant in the first place.

"I was just going to talk to you about that tonight. We have to move here for a while, Sophia. It's too hard traveling back and forth. Your father and I have both found jobs down here since we couldn't be at our old ones." I could tell she was worried about my reaction. "I'm so sorry you found out before I told you, honey. I hope you understand why we had to."

I sucked in a sharp breath and let out a shaky one.

"I know, I know, mom. Gas money and plus me being here alone... I get it." I said in a defeated tone. "So who's coming to get me then?"

There was a silence on the other line before she finally spoke up.

"I was thinking Cameron could bring you. With Matt being sick and having us with him at all times, I thought it would be easier to have him drive you." When she said his name, I flinched physically. She doesn't know about us.

I would have to travel to Tennessee with someone I couldn't stand at the moment. He made things so much more difficult. I couldn't tell my mom now, she has to stay with Matt, my sick baby brother. The one I should be thinking about right now. I just now realized how selfish I've been. And right now, I was willing to do anything for him. I was willing to put up with Cameron for a few days.

"Okay." Just as the word slipped from my mouth, Cameron rackety old truck pulled around the corner.

Speak of the devil.

———————————

Chapter Thirty-Four: A Long Night

C hapter Thirty-Four:

A Long Night

I couldn't believe that I had to travel all the way over to Tennessee with the boy who just broke up with me. I was having a hard enough time trying not to think about him and now being stuck in a car for however many hours was going to be even harder.

That Saturday, Cameron glumly took me over to my house and helped me pack up all my clothes and belongings. The rest, my mom said, would be packed up by the movers. I didn't know they would pack it up for us, but I didn't argue.

The remaining days of that week, I managed to hang out with Emma and tell her goodbye for a while.

We agreed to text, call, and FaceTime all the time. Emma is my first honest best friend and I didn't want that to end.

Once all my stuff was on the back of Cameron's truck, he stood at the opposite side of the truck and we looked at each other for a moment. I was the first one to move over to get in the truck. He followed afterwards. I made sure to get my iPod and headphones and kept them with me because I had a feeling I'd need them.

"I can't believe you're actually moving away." Cameron said. It was low and I thought he was talking to me but it was more to himself since he never looked at me. I felt guilty for a moment before realizing I don't need to feel guilty. He did this. He broke us up and now we can't be together.

But the butterflies I got every time we touched or he said my name never disappeared for a second. They were always there, haunting me of my feelings I still have for him.

A small part agrees with him. How in the world could it have worked? I don't know how long Matt's going to be in the hospital. All I knew was that I was willing to make every arrangement I could to see him as much as possible. But it seems that he wasn't as willing.

I decided to keep quiet. A conversation would be awkward right now. So, I leaned forward with my seatbelt holding me back and turned the radio on. That was much better. The next step was to plug my headphones in and put them in my ears before turning the volume halfway up.

I could see Cameron glancing over at me warily as I propped my elbow on the door and stared out the window. I wasn't in the mood for a conversation.

I flipped through the songs I had on my playlists and noticed that the battery was halfway down. I had my car charger, thank goodness, because I knew I would need it. But then I realized that Cameron's stupid truck didn't have a plug in. That was disappointing. I guess I don't get to play flappy bird now.

I had went through my one playlists of fifteen songs titled 'Favorites' one and a half times when Cameron started to pull over to the side of the road. I hadn't even noticed where we were at until now. Hay fields were surrounding all sides of us now with no sight of human life for next five miles or so. This grass had yet to be fully grown into hay for the farmers to make so it wasn't too high. A river was on the left side of the road which, for some stupid reason, is the way Cameron pulled off. Normally a person would pull off on the side they were driving on but Cameron here had to be difficult about it.

"What's wrong?" I asked after I pulled one earbud out of my ear. Cameron gave me a look of annoyance before he quickly and hastily jumped out of the truck. It was then that I noticed the black smoke coming out from the cracks of the hood. Alarmed, I threw my iPod down on the seat and jumped out the truck. Of course this would happen to me. Of course it would.

"What happened to it?" I whined, obviously annoyed as much as Cam was. He leaned both his elbows against the truck and covered his face with his hands in a stressful way.

"I'll have to check on it. Do you have cell service?" He asked me. I took my phone out of my pocket and sighed heavily. "No."

This was beyond suckish.

"Wait, I do. I have one bar. I bet if we were higher up it's be better." He stated. Then he looked at me and smile wickedly. It's weird how he can act as if nothing was wrong even for just a quick seconds.

"What do you think I can do? You're taller than me." I argued. He shook his head planted his phone in my palm.

"Climb on the back of the truck and get on the hood if you have to. I know it'll work better. Then you can call a row truck." He explained nicely while ushering me to the back of the truck. I sighed, feeling defeated.

On the top of the truck cab, I took in the sky. It was getting clouded over with rain clouds already and I knew right away that wasn't a good sign at all.

On the bright side, I got two more bars on Cameron's phone so that was a good sign. Before I searched a number to call, I asked Cameron where we were.

"Um, I think we're in Cascade, Virginia." He told me as he searched around for a tool. He was focused on his truck now.

I searched on his phone until I found the nearest number from the nearest town. I didn't know where this small town was with a towing company in it, but that was the only option I had. I dialed the number and held the phone to my ear.

After explaining where we were, which wasn't hard since there was only hayfields surrounding us. The disappointing news was that he'd be here in about two hours. I could have cried. Two hours in a truck with Cameron? I say truck because just as I got off the top of the truck, rain came down from the sky.

There goes my luggage.

Cameron hurriedly ran to the back of the truck with a trash bag he found behind his seat. I watched through the back glass as he covered my bags with the bag as much as he could. I have several bags since most of my stuff was back there. I just hoped my clothes wouldn't be soaked. Plus, his bag of clothes was back there too. I noticed that he put his under the bag last.

Oh, how sweet, I seethed.

He climbed back in and I watched the raindrops tap against the windshield periodically. I didn't think it would rain very hard right now.

"Thanks for covering my stuff." I mumbled, half distracted by the raindrops racing down the glass in front of me.

"Welcome. How long will it take for the tow truck to be here?" He asked. I could feel his eyes in the side of my face but I didn't dare look over. Instead, I grabbed my iPod and plugged my ears with the headphones.

"Two hours." I told him solemnly.

But when I went to pick a song, the screen went black. It was dead. Groaning in frustration, I yanked the headphones out if my ears and tossed my iPod onto the seat between Cameron and me.

"Stupid truck." I grumbled. This made my bad mood soar.

"I guess you'll just have to talk to me for the next few hours." Cameron said with a little bit of triumph. He liked having me cornered.

"What makes you think I'll talk to you?" I raised an eyebrow at him. He smiled a little.

"I don't know. Maybe because we have two while hours to endure." He answered back before crossing his arms over his chest. I scowled.

"That makes it easier not to talk." I deadpanned. It was a lie, I didn't like silence for that long. But I was willing to put up with it right now. Cameron frowned now.

"This isn't like you at all, Sophia." He said with a regretful tone. It was almost a sad ton.

"Gee, Cameron. I wonder why I don't want to talk to you." I snapped and turned my head to look out the window.

"Don't be like that. You know I was only thinking about what was best for us." He tried to pound his point into my head.

"How do you think that would help? You know what? Just drop it. I don't want to talk about it right now." I growled and leaned my head on the window. I forced my eyes shut to keep myself from crying hot, angry tears, but it didn't work. Although my face was relaxed, I felt a tear slide down my cheek and right over my lip. I hastily wiped it away and tried not to look like I was as a mess in the outside as I was on the inside.

Cameron didn't speak from that moment on. I could tell he was getting fidgety and he hated the silence. I did too; my ears were ringing from the silence.

Thankfully, I soon heard a truck roaring near by on the highway. I craned my neck to look out the window into the rain. I saw headlights and soon enough, the two truck was backing up to us and and hooking the front of he truck up to the back of his.

"Looks like you guys have a problem. Probably a spark plug..." The man trailed off. I sighed and shook my head. I didn't know much about cars, but I've heard guys talk about spark plugs before. And this doesn't look good.

"Okay. How about we take it to the nearest garage and we can get it in the morning?" Cameron asked the guy. He pulled his wallet out of his back pocket, about to pay for the towing.

"Yeah I can do that. Where do you want me to drop you guys off? There's a hotel in the next town up the road a few miles." He accepted the right amount of money from Cameron and tucked it in his pocket.

"Okay. Sounds good." Cameron glanced at me and I nodded my head. My mom would most definitely pay him back the money he spends. But I was planning to pay for the room tonight, he wasn't.

As we climbed up into the tow truck with me squished in the middle, the man who I saw was named Paul from his name tag started to talk to us.

"I'll warn you now, it's crowded in town. People are starting to go in vacation for the summer." He said.

"Why do they stay here?" I asked him, talking about the town we just entered.

"They're mostly on their way to the beach." Paul told us. I nodded my head in understanding.

Once we got to a hotel, Paul gave Cameron the directions to the garage he'd be taking the truck to. We'd inly have to walk there. Slinging one bag of my clothes off the back of the truck, I followed Cameron into the lobby of the small hotel and I saw just how crowded it was. People were piled in the pool even at this hour of eight o'clock.

"Can we have one room please?" I asked the person at the front desk. He nodded his head and I paid before Cameron even realized what was happening.

"Wait, did you just pay for the room?" He asked me. I simply nodded my head and strutted off towards the elevator. It didn't take long for Cameron to catch up to me. This was going to be one long night.

———————————

If you guys see any spelling or grammar mistakes, point them out! I'll get to editing it once I'm finished with the story!

Thank you all for reading!

Chapter Thirty-Five: Chimichanga!

- -

C hapter Thirty-Five:

Chimichanga!

____

"You've got to be kidding me." I mumbled to myself as soon as we stepped inside the room. When we flipped the light on, fear shot through my spine. Maybe it was more of annoyance...

Either way, this was not good news.

There was one single bed in this hotel room. The person at the front desk never told me it would be this small. I assumed that there would at least be two beds.

"I'll sleep on the floor." Cameron automatically said. He slid past me and into the room. He was clearly pooped.

I had a moment with myself. I could either be a mean ex-girlfriend or the kind that is still nice to you and wants to be best friends. I chose the middle option. To be both.

I didn't get a word out before Cameron started stripping in front of me. I couldn't help but stare, even though I've seen him shirtless a million times. Shaking my head clear, my eyes dropped and I knew I was tired.

Once I got out of my pants, I pulled on a pair of soft shorts and left my t-shirt on. Cameron was grabbing towels and some extra pillows out of the small closet that we had. I sighed, knowing what I was about to do.

"Cam, just get up here." I told him, too tired to care. I could freak out later. Right now I think we both needed our beauty sleep.

He was hesitant at first, but eventually gave in and crawled under the covers beside of me. There was an inch of space between us since the bed was so tiny and both of us were on the edges of the bed.

I rolled over so that I was laying on my arm and facing him, bracing myself for what I was about to say.

"I'm sorry I've been such a brat lately." I whispered. The room was pitch dark except for the moonlight shining in through the window behind me. Cameron's face lit up from the light when he turned to me. I could tell he was tired, maybe he wouldn't remember this in the morning.

"It's okay. I deserved it." His words were slurred from sleepiness but I knew he meant them.

"Maybe just a little. But I shouldn't be so mean to you." I told him back. He had a lazy smile on his face, eyes closed, and he turned to face me before he cracked his eyes open just a slit.

"Yeah, maybe just a little." He chuckled sleepily. I smiled at him, missing this so much. Even though we just broke up barely two days ago, it felt like a lifetime.

I reached my hand up to run my fingers through his thick hair. He seemed to be sleeping, but he opened his one eye just a little to stare at me. I dropped my hand down to his face; remembering all his features from his long eyelashes to his nose, to his lips. Oh those lips.

I think I still lived the boy. A year slipped from my eye. I didn't bother to wipe it away. It was dark, he wouldn't see me.

Without a second thought, I reached under his pillow where his one hand was and laced our fingers together.

I finally fell asleep, with Cameron on my mind.

*

When morning came, I was the first to wake up. Cameron was sleeping silently beside me, taking up most of the bed. At one point last night I found myself tangled together with Cameron. I didn't move because he'd wake up and it would be awkward. Plus, I missed it. Already, I'm missing how we used to be. Never angry at each other.

Sitting with my arms wrapped around my knees, I had plenty of time to think since I woke up at seven and we needed to leave at nine.

I had decided that I can't do this. No matter how much I love the boy sleeping next to me, I can't make him think I still love him when he doesn't want to be anything other than friends. Maybe if one day I came back to our hometown, then we could get back together. But not right now. I'll spare us both the pain.

When eight o'clock rolled around, I didn't even have to wake Cameron up. He turned his head toward me, who was sitting in the same position since I woke up, and opened his eyes. He still looked pretty tired to me.

"Hey," he blinked his eyes as if to see if he was dreaming or not, "how long have you been awake?" I turned to him with an emotionless face.

"Not too long," I lied. I could lay back down and take a nice nap if I wanted to. I'm sure Cameron wouldn't mind.

"Okay. You wanna get your shower first?" He asked as he sat up in bed, revealing his bare chest. I left my empty gaze on the end of the bed while I nodded.

I walked straight to the bathroom, too ready to get the warm water on my tired skin.

After washing up, I wrapped a towel around my body and stood in front of the mirror. Then I realized that I didn't have any clothes to put on. Frustrated with my tired brain, I put the towel around my body even tighter to make sure nothing was showing.

"Um, forgot my clothes..." I mumbled to Cameron when he looked at me with wide eyes. I felt warm blush ram using from my neck to my cheeks.

After running back in the bathroom with my clothes in hand, I slipped them in a brushed my hair out. Cameron took a shower next, and then we ordered breakfast up to our room. It was short and awkwardly silent.

"Ready to go?" He asked me once we were both dressed and ready.

"Yeah." I answered with no emotion to my voice. I was eager to get to my new home to see my parents for the first time in what seemed like years. And Matt! Oh, Matt...

I followed behind Cameron as we made our way to the elevator. No one was in the halls of the hotel so it was quiet. And everything was quiet between Cameron and I.

We stepped into the elevator and Cameron pressed the number one to get us down to the lobby. The closer we got to Cameron's truck, the closer we got to my mom and dad and baby brother.

My sky high hopes fell to the ground, six feet under, when the elevator stopped. The lights went out for a second but then came right back on. That didn't make it better when the elevator jerked to a stop.

"What's wrong? Cameron?" I rambled in a panic. This cannot be happening...

But it was. Using his cell phone, Cameron called down to the front desk to have them come get us out of this elevator. I've never been stuck in one before, but I've also never had a panic attack before. There's a first time for everything.

"Calm down, they're working on it right now." Cameron told me. I slid down the wall of the elevator and sighed heavily. This seriously sucked.

"I just want to get home, Cam... away from this elevator, away from this hotel..." Away from you...

"I'll sing to that off your mind." He grinned at me. My eyes widened and I tried I say no but it was too late. He started singing wrecking ball in a loud, obnoxious, high-pitched, girly voice. If I didn't t need hearing aids before, I definitely needed them now.

I couldn't help but laugh at least a little bit. Cameron made a horrible situation into a good one just like always. How was I supposed to stop loving him if he kept feeling me back in like this?

Finally, I started to sing along. Except this time I sang Dark Horse by Katy Perry. While I sang the chorus and everything that Katy sang, Cameron came in on the rapping parts. At one point I laughed through my parts to sing because it was just a ridiculous situation we were in.

Here we are, sitting in an elevator singing to each other in our worst possible voices at the top of our lungs.

I feel bad for the people outside the elevator who can hear us.

Cameron stood up and held a hand out for me to take. Me being stuck in a far-away happy yet delusional place, I took his hand and we laced them together.

As we danced in a every which way, I giggled and laughed as Cameron did the same. No, not just slow dancing, but we were doing the salsa. If that dance looked something like someone having a seizure, then we were dancing right.

"Are we doing the Chimichanga?" Cameron asked me, his tooth paste breath fanning my face. I let out a loud laugh as he said that and he had to hold me up so I wouldn't fall over laughing.

"No!" I said once so could catch a breath. "Chimichanga is a food!"

We both had a pretty good laugh at his silly mistake.

When the doors to the elevator opened, I had a weird feeling inside me that didn't want to go away. I thought it would feel better after we got outside and I wasn't so close to him, but that didn't seem to help.

We walked along the sidewalk on our way to the garage when Cameron was suddenly beside me. I wasn't walking fast, but I ended up in front of him some how.

"You okay?" Cameron asked me. I looked down at the sidewalk and thought, am I okay?

"Yeah." I answered softly.

He sudden grabbed my hand and intertwined our fingers together. Our hands fit just right, like a puzzle piece to another.

The feeling was back and it didn't go unnoticeable. It made me feel like crying. I slid my hand out of Cameron's and held my hand to my chest while keeping my face turned the opposite way of Cameron's. I had a feeling that maybe it was just my heart breaking. I would have to leave him behind.

But which was more important? My family or my first love?

"Sophia?" He asked me, shaking me from my thoughts. This time I turned to him.

"Why, Cameron?" I asked him with absolutely no trace of sadness in my voice even though I had a few stray tears sliding down my cheeks. With a small smile on his face, he lifted his hand and wiped the tears away with his thumb.

"Why what?"

"Why are you doing this to me? I thought we broke up for a reason? Why do you act like we didn't?" It all came out like a rush, but I was sure he understood by the way his face fell. His hand dropped down to my waist and then he found my hand, holding it in his like it was about to fall off.

"I-" He started but was interrupted by a distant voice. Then I saw Paul jogging toward us waving his hand in the air like a crazy man. Biting his bottom lip, Cameron let go of my hand and turned towards the man count toward us.

"You're Cameron right?" He asked Cameron. He nodded his head at Paul and waited for him to continue.

"Your tuck is done. I saw you and thought I should come tell you so you didn't pass the shop. Here's your keys." He dangled the keys in midair until Cameron out his hand underneath of them. He dropped them and nodded to Cameron before walking back to the garage.

"Thanks!" Cameron called after him. He waved over his shoulder as if to tell us you're welcome.

I didn't even give Cameron time to finish telling me what he wanted to say before I started walking quickly to the truck. I was so happy to finally be closer to seeing my family. I couldn't wait to see them again.

———————————

So the book is coming to an end guys! Song is If These Sheets Were States by All Time Low, my all time favorite band!

I hope you all liked it as much as I enjoyed writing it! Thanks for all the reads, votes, comments, and follows! and the amazing experience I had while doing all this.

Thank you soooo much!

Oh, and this isn't the last chapter! There will be one more and then an epilogue! They will be up as soon as possible and them editing will start!

Yay. (Note the sarcasm.)

Chapter Thirty-Six: Home Sweet Home

C hapter Thirty-Six:

Home Sweet Home

Deuteronomy 5:16"Honor your father and your mother, as the LORD your God has commanded you, so that you may live long and that it may go well with you in the land the LORD your God is giving you."

"Turn here,"I pointed to my right and Cameron pulled the truck into my new driveway. My mom gave us the direction on the phone and I hung up with her just as we pulled into our road. Just as she said there would be, a one-story tan house sat where I would now call home.

I liked it; there was a wide garage door where the short driveway ends, connected to the house. There was already red flowers planted in the front from the previous owner, I guessed.

I looked over to see Cameron swallow and look out the window. This house was beautiful. Not as big as my old one, but it was good. It already felt like home because wherever my family was, that's where home was.

I hopped out of the truck as soon as it was put in park and grabbed the few bags I could. Without taking a second glance back at the truck or Cameron, the last piece of Virginia I had, I zoomed up to the front porch. Mom said it would be unlocked, so I wrapped my fingers around the doorknob and twisted it.

Inside, the house was bare. I walked down the short hallway that passed the bare, wood floor, living room and another door that was open. It was the bathroom. In the kitchen were a few empty McDonald's bags on the counter. Mom and dad must've come home at least once.

A note on the island in the middle of the open kitchen caught my eye. Maybe it was the bright pink sticky note, or the big 'Love Mom' written at the bottom. I grabbed the note like I couldn't live without it and read it carefully. It told me that my bedroom was third back the hall and to meet them at the hospital, third floor.

"What's that say?" Cameron's voice made me jump. I smiled a little at him, not wanting to rub it in that I didn't have to go back to Virginia and he did. Cameron gave me all the smile he could muster which was just the stretch of his lips.

"Um, my room is third back the hall. And mom wants us to meet her at the hospital after we get all my stuff in here." I said quietly, my energy level suddenly dropping. The look in Cameron's eyes kept me from moving for a moment as we stared at each other. Maybe I was feeling guilt?

Cameron looked down at the luggage in his hands and raised them up as if to tell me c'mon. I jerked back to reality and rushed down the hall. There were empty beds in each of the three bedrooms I passed. As soon as

I reached the end of the hall, I took a right and there it was. My new bed-room. The walls were painted a light cream color and the bed was a canopy bed. I had a closet with those wooden sliding doors and a big window that looked out over the backyard. I sat my bags down and collapsed on the plastic-covered mattress. Someone must not have wanted this canopy bed. I didn't mind it.

I stood up and got a look of myself in a round mirror that hung on the wall.

"Ew. I need a shower. Do you wanna take one when I'm done?" I asked Cameron. He nodded his head as I grabbed some new clothes from my bag.

"I'll go grab the rest of the stuff and then check out the rest of the house." He said dismissively as he walked out the door. I forgot about the other bags. There should only be two more, so I'd thank Cameron later for helping me carry them in.

I hopped in the new shower and stood under the hot water for a few minutes. I couldn't wait to see my family again in just a little while. I wanted to hug them all so tight.

Once I was done in the shower, I put my good smelling clothes on a pulled my hair up so I wouldn't hair to worry about it. I found Cameron laying in my bed with his hands behind his head, feet crossed. His face was peaceful so I assumed he was napping. I decided not to wake him up since he was probably still tired from all the driving. It's almost dark now, we'd been driving all day. I drove a few times but we both figured out that he was a much better driver than me. I had rode rage.

I sat down at my bags and unzipped my biggest suitcase. It had a few of my favorite belongings in it that I didn't want strangers handling. The picture on top is what made me stop. It was my framed picture of Cameron and I. I forget when this picture was taken, but it was in his house. Maybe his mom or sister took it. I had my arms around Cameron as he leaned back on me. I was kissing his head while he smiled at the camera. It was such a precious moment in my life. Even if we weren't together, I wanted to keep the picture anyway. He was my first love, I wanted to remember that forever.

As I gently placed the photo on the white carpet, I heard the bed squeak. Cameron sat up, stretching and yawning at the same time. I smiled at him even though he didn't see me for his eyes being closed. He stood up and walked over to me.

"You can take a bath now." I told him and pointed down the hall. "The water feels awesome." He barely got a smile out as he disappeared down the hall. How could I do this to him? Or myself? I can he not see that I'm in love with him and I can't just suddenly stop because I'm moving away? I can't make a move, though. He was the one who broke it off with me. He might actually be over me although his body language says otherwise. I hated assuming things, though. It would be embarrassing on my part to tell him I can't let him go while he already let me go.

Instead of emptying the rest of my things, I grabbed the picture of us again. The more I stared at it, the more tears began to fill my eyes. Why was I crying?

I rubbed my knuckle under my eye to catch the tears before the fell. The last thing I felt like doing was crying right now. This was supposed to be a happy time. I was going to see my family in only a few hours. But I was fooling myself. I wasn't happy. I miserable. I had talked myself out of having such strong feelings for this boy that I thought I was happy with the situation I was in. I was moving away from him; I was never going to see him again; I wasn't going to be in love with him anymore.

That was enough to make me really sad.

I didn't notice Cameron standing in the doorway until he dropped the towel he was using to dry his hair. His face was emotionless which made it hard to see what he was thinking. He picked the towel back up and hung it over my bed post before sitting down beside me Indian style. His hair was soaked and black looking and disheveled.

I suddenly cracked a smile.

"What?" Cameron asked me with a smile tugging at his lips.

"Nothing." I chuckled. I couldn't tell him he looked sexy. That would do me over; I'd start kissing his face all over.

"I remember that picture. He said after staring at me for a moment. I looked down at the frame in my hand.

"Yeah, I really love this picture." I sniffed. I'm sure my eyes were puffy and my voice sounded like I was sick.

He took the frame from my hands and held it in his for a minute, staring at it intently. His eyebrows knit together and he looked up at me, eyes pleading.

"I love you, Sophia. I just..." he scratched the back of his head nervously, "I can't leave here without knowing you don't hate me. I know you probably do, but please. Please, just don't." When I heard his voice crack, I couldn't take it anymore. I cupped his face with my hands and forced him to look me in the eye.

"I love you too." I said before crashing my lips to his. I smiled into the kiss and moved my hands up to his wet hair. With hands tangled in his hair, I pushed him back so he was lying in the floor and I was on top of him.

"Sophia, Sophia." Cameron said against my lips. I frowned and my heart dropped, did I do something he didn't want? I lifted my head to look at his face, ready to yell at him. When he noticed my expression, he smiled and wrapped his arms around me to keep me in place on top of him. When I tried to wiggle free, he simply rolled us over to he was the one crushing me.

"This isn't funny," I warned him, my voice strained from him crushing my ribs. He lifted himself up on his knees and hands and smiled down at me.

"Does this mean what I think it means?" Cameron asked me with a smile still on his face. I stopped frowning and raised my eyebrow. He continued. "Sophia, I am willing to do anything to keep our relationship together. I hate that it's taken me this long the figure out that I can't live without being able to kiss you everyday." His face turned serious as he stared at me.

"I really want it to mean what you think it means." I told him honestly. "Because it does to me." He leaned down to kiss me softly on the lips before jumping up in his feet. I groaned and frowned at him and his hand that was stuck out for me to grab.

I liked what we were just doing.

"Don't you wanna see your family?" He asked playfully. There was no need to say anymore. As soon as the word family came out of his mouth I was up. My good moods always made me do weird things, so when I did what I did, I had an excuse.

When I jumped up off the ground, I went high up and just clung to my boyfriend. My legs wrapped around his waist, arms locking around his neck, and my face pressed against his.

"Let's go!" I pointed towards the door.

Cameron laughed and out his hands under my butt to hold me up. I quickly pushed his hands up to the small of my back.

"Watch it, buddy." I narrowed my eyes and pointed at him, touching the tip of his nose in the process. He scrunched it up and stuck his tongue out at me.

*

At the hospital, I waited behind one other person to get to the front desk to ask what room my brother was in. Mom left out that one specific detail.

Cameron put his arm over my shoulder and I reached my hand up to link fingers with his. He squeezed them reassuringly as the nervousness hit me. I haven't seen Matt in about a week and his appearance could have changed drastically.

"Can I help you?" The front desk lady asked. I moved up a step with Cameron still at my side.

"Yeah, I need to know what room my brother is in. Matthew Belle?" I told her. I could feel the anxiety building in my chest as my heart beat a little faster. Now I was minutes away from them.

"I need your name and relation, please." She asked as she typed something on her computer. I knew there was a family only policy when it's later than 8:30 pm.

"Sophia.. Bridges. Sister." I stuttered. Cameron smirked from beside me. He knew what I was doing.

"And you young man?" She asked him.

"Cameron Bridges. Brother-in-law." He said cockily. The lady eyed us suspiciously before telling us to go up to third floor and knock on room 5-C.

We got in the elevator and I had find memories of earlier today.

"If this gets stuck, I am not singing with you again." Cameron said as he leaned in the opposite wall as me.

"Why?" I asked.

"Because you ruined my melody." He joked and I laughed, shaking my head at his silliness.

"Mrs. Bridges." Cameron muttered under his breath. I laughed at his expression and went over to hug him right saying, "Maybe one day, in your dreams." He shoved me off playfully and then the elevator door opened on our floor.

I didn't even have to find room 5-C because as soon as I stepped off the elevator, swinging mine and Cameron's linked hands back and forth, I spotted him. Even without his hair, I knew it was bright-eyes little brother. Mom and dad were standing behind him watching him walk or talking to another mother or father with the same situation as them. My heart leaped and my hand broke from Cameron's. He let me go easily or he knew he'd lose an arm.

I found myself flying down the hall towards my family, past all the other people who gave me dirty looks. Right now, I didn't care that I was making someone else mad.

"Sissy!" Matt's voice made my smile grow wider. When I reached him, I stopped abruptly and got down on my knees, hugging my little brother like my life depended on it.

"I missed you so so much, little booger." I kissed his bald head and realized I was crying when a tear fell from my face and landed on my knee.

I looked up to see my parents giving Cameron a hug and thank you's.

Matt caught me staring at his shiny white head and giggled.

"We shaved it off since it was starting to come out a little. Do you like it?" He made his fingers into a gun and pointed at me to be cool.

"I love it." I laughed through my happy tears.

While we all sat in Matt's room eating pizza my dad went out to get, I couldn't help but stare at everyone of these people around me. As cheesy as it sounds, I'm totally blessed to have family like them. If there was one thing that I learned over these past few months, it's life's too short to sit on the side lines. You gotta get up and play the game to win.

So when my mom asked me to take a group picture with them all to remember what challenges God brought us through, I jumped right in. And although we were in a hospital under horrible circumstances, I could say that with my family, I was finally at home sweet home.

____

Ahh.. this is the last chapter! Don't worry, the next chapter will be the Epilogue!

[Video is I Love You More Than You Will Ever Know by Never Shout Never]

I can't believe it! God has definitely given me his blessing through all this writing! To be honest when I started writing this story, I never thought I'd actually follow through with it. I'm so happy I did.

I wanna thank you guys soooo much for reading, voting, commenting, following, oh, and breathing! haha.

I now know that I'm capable of completing my very own story and I'm definitely going to continue doing that.

Remember, I follow back, so follow me!!

Thanks again!

Epilogue: My Everything

Epilogue:My Everything

One year and four months later

Is sucked in a deep breath and prepared myself to walk back into my new home for the next year.

Just moments ago I was telling my parents and cancer-free little brother that I'd miss while I was away at college. I really would miss them while I'm away. After living with the same people for eighteen years you kind of get attached to them. I could barely let Matt out of my hug because I'd miss him coming in my room at random to play with my hair or tease me.

I actually had tears building up in my eyes for the first time when he handed me a little wrapped box. He told me to wait until I get to my room to open it, sonI crossed my heart that I would.

I found out that Emma was my roommate after she called me. We had both requested that we room with each other since we decided to go to the same college.

After so much arguing over the phone, it was settled that we would be roomies for the next year of our grown-up lives.

As for Adam, he is also going to Virginia tech. He decided that if his love was going to be far away from home then he was too. I thought it was sweet.

I saved the best for last. Cameron called me last night and told me that he'd see me today. Sadly, I'm not sure if he's even going to college. He hasn't said anything about it and I haven't pushed the touchy subject. We have went to each other's houses for the past year for holidays and just about every night we stayed up on Skype and FaceTime talking about our days. I think we both fell a little harder for each other.

I even had Mrs. Foster call me, after not seeing her for a while year, and tell me that she sent a good recommendation in to this school for me. I remembered she told me that to get me to tutor Cameron at the time. I was so happy that she didn't forget, although it wouldn't have mattered if she did.

Finally, I took a step into my new home for the first official time since we got here today. After unloading and rearranging all my things in the dressers along with Emma's, we went out to get some dinner at 6:30.

Inside our apartment, there was a flat screen sitting on too of one of the dressers with our clothes inside and a couch directly across from that. A mini fridge was in the corner of our small living room. We had no kitchen, but I heard there was a cafeteria close by on campus. There were two rooms on the other side of the room, one for me and one for Emma. Although they were small enough for a twin-sized bed and a small desk and chair, it was okay.

I stripped out of my jeans and nice shirt to trade them with more comfortable clothes. I sat down on the couch and flipped the TV on, pulling out my phone to find something to do.

Then, my phone buzzed in my hands and I saw I had a call from Emma. She was supposed to be out on a date with Adam, why would she be calling me?

"Hello?" I answered, my eyebrows knitting together.

"Sophia! Hey, um, I need you to meet me down in the parking lot." Emma said breathlessly. I instantly stood up off the couch and rushed to get my shoes on.

"Emma? What's wrong? Are you okay?" I asked into the phone as I rushed out the door, in only a tank top and cotton shorts. She hung up. I started to panic thinking that something was going terribly wrong with my best friend.

When I pushed through the double doors of the school, I ran over to the parking lot, jumping over brushes and what not.

"Emma?" I shouted through the people-empty parking lot. Cars were in every parking space since it was move-in day. But most people were out to eat dinner.

"Hello?" I said again, panting. I put my hands in my knees to rest and catch my breath. I think I just broke the speed barrier.

I pulled out my phone to call Emma and tapped my foot impatiently as it rang. I waited the whole time until her voicemail came on. Yet, I still didn't hear the distant ringing of her phone. She always has her phone's ringtone set as the beginning of the song "California" by Phantom Planet. And it's always loud, so if she was close by, I would've heard it.

So when I looked up from my phone in frustration, I didn't expect to see him there. He had on a New York Yankees t-shirt and black basketball shorts. I could've sworn I heard my heartbeat in my ears for a second. After not seeing his crooked smile for almost a month, I took off running again down the parking lot and jumped into his arms. He swung me around with his arms holding me tight. I took a deep breath to make sure he still smelled the same, as weird as that sounds.

"Holy crap! Where did you come from?" I half screamed. Cameron beamed at me and kissed me. He started at my lips and trailed his kisses down my neck and to my shoulder. I laughed and pushed him away from me enough for me to see his face again.

"What's with Emma?" I asked him seriously. He smirked and held me tighter to him.

"I met her out here in my way to my apartment-" He started but my screaming cut him off.

"You're staying here? Oh my gosh! With who?" It's Adam, isn't it? That little sneak.." I trailed off.

Cameron nodded to confirm he's in the same apartment with his best friend. "And she said she'd get you down here for me so I could surprise you. Here I am!" He held his arms out wide to show me he was here.

"Yes, I see that." I poked his shoulder and turned around, strutting back towards the building.

"What are you doing?" He asked and I heard his hands slap against his thighs.

"Back to my apartment." I turned around and raised my eyes seductively at him. He smiled and raced towards me. When I felt his hands in my shoulders, I braced myself for his weight to be on my back. He hopped up in my back, even though I was smaller than him, and held on tight and I struggled to walk right.

"You're so strong." He purred like a woman would a man and squeezed my invisible muscles. He rested his chin on the top of my head.

"Thanks, babe." I said in a low voice.

"Oh, we're calling each other babe again?" He laughed and I felt him vibrate my back. I dropped his legs and landed on his feet on the ground. I hooked my arm through his as we continued walking towards the front doors.

"Yep, babe." I stood on my tiptoes to kiss his cheek.

Once we got back inside and up to my room, I tore my black bed spread off my bed and drug it out to the living room. On the couch sat a shirtless Cameron shoving his face with some left over pizza I brought back with me and put in the mini fridge.

I plopped down on the opposite side of the couch and threw my legs up over his. He looked at me and winked before looking back at the TV. A basketball game was on.

"I got a basketball scholarship." Cameron told me absentmindedly.

"Cam! That's awesome!" I smiled at him tucked my foot under his leg. My feet were freezing.

"Thanks. I actually can't wait. What all stuff do we need for classes? Mom is coming by next week to get me school supplies." Cameron told me as he watched the game.

My face fell. "Holy crap! I forgot about school supplies! How could I forget about school supplies? I need my books and pencils! Oh my gosh..." I put my hands up to my face and groaned.

"Sophia?" Cameron asked. I split my fingers apart so I could see him through the slits. His eyes captured mine in one glance and I lowered my hands.

"Hm?" I asked him, feeling less panicky now.

"Will you marry me?" The words startled me so much that my body went numb and the only thing I could feel was my heart.

"Where did that come from?" I squeaked. My cheeks were burning with blush now.

"I don't know. I didn't expect to ask you so soon, to be honest. Will you?" His eyes never left mine once which meant that he was being honest. He really wanted to spend the rest of his life with me?

"I do. I will marry you." Even though my heart was steaming yes, my mind was telling me to wait a little while. "Why don't we get married when we're actually settled in?" I suggested so casually. I felt like I was about to have a heart attack, why were we talking about marriage so casually?! We're barely adults yet!

Seeing the disappointment on his face, I leaned up and poked his stomach with my finger. He lunged at me and straddled my body between his legs.

"Of course I can wait." He leaned down to kiss my lips a million times before finally keeping them on mine. Our lips moved in sync for a little while until he broke us apart and we both panting.

"You're my everything, Sophia Belle." We both grinned before kissing me again.

———————

I can't believe I actually finished it...

Thanks guys for everything! I've pretty much said all I can say in my previous chapters' author's notes.

Next page has news about my brand new story that I'm very excited to start writing! Let me know what you think about it!

He Stole My Bandana (So I Stole His Heart) Preview!

Hello! I'm so excited to tell you I have another story in the works! Here is the preview for my new story "He Stole My Bandana (So I Stole His Heart)". I know, it's a long name. Shameless self advertisement here! Thanks to my best friend for coming up with that catchy name - xfanxgirlx.She's helped me a bunch with all of my stories and I really appreciate it! Love ya Meg!

Anyway, here's the description:

"You just don't belong in my world, Jasey."

Jasey Eldridge didn't expect to have a good senior year. She knew it would be rough with all the complications in her life. Living with her two brothers and dad, Jasey was used to rough. But she didn't expect it to come in bad boy form. When Jasey loses her bandana, the bad boy doesn't want to give it back. So, she decides to get it back herself. Sneaking into strangers' windows wasn't really a normal thing for her and her amateur ninja skills.

Will she succeed in whisking away her special bandana or will she also whisk away a few hearts while she's at it?

And now for Chapter One! Tell me if you guys like it! I'm going to post it soon if you like it! Thanks in advance for reading!

——

"Jasey, you drive like a grandma!" My twin brother yelled at me. Lilly laughed beside me in the passenger seat, thinking my brother's joke was hilarious.

"The kid's right." Lilly said when she was done laughing. I scowled at my best friend beside me. Taking my hand off the wheel, I flipped both Reese and Lilly off.

"Wow, that hurt." Reese said in mock hurt, holding his hand over his heart. My brother was such a pain in the butt. I didn't understand why he couldn't just tag along with one of his friends everyday. Instead, he had to ride with me.

"Maybe you should get your own driver's license and you won't have to ride with me." I suggested sassily to Reese. He smirked at me.

"Why? I have you to drive me everywhere when I want you to. You're my personal chauffeur." He said with a bright grin.

"You can't make me do anything for you, idiot. I'm older than you." I shot back at him.

He rolled his eyes at me. "You're older by what, five minutes?"

"I don't act like a two year old," I pointed out, "therefore that makes me older."

"Okay you two." Lilly cut in. She was usually our referee when Reese and I fought. Which was 90 percent of the time. And 80 percent of the time, Lilly was with me.

I live in a household full of boys. There's my dad, Grant, Reese, and then there's little old me. My mom and dad divorced a few years back and she married a rich man from Miami. She ran away with him like we were nothing. Not that it bothered me.

Grant is in his second year of the United States Army, he just turned twenty-one not long ago. He tries to come home on holidays but when he can't, it's a skype date for the three of us kids. Plus dad, when he's home. He's a truck driver and has to drive all over West Virginia for his job. He gets home late and wakes up early, making it hard to see him everyday. When he is home early, Reese and him usually throw football and tackle me into the game.

"Lilly, why don't you drive your own car?" Reese asked as he propped his chin on the back of her seat. I frowned at my brother.

"Reese, why don't you have your seatbelt on?" I asked him. He grumbled and sat back, knowing I'd release my wrath on him if he didn't listen. I had all the boys in my house wrapped around my finger, except my twin.

"Because I don't have a car. Would you like to buy one for me?" Lilly batted her eyelashes at him before turning around and pretending to gag. I couldn't help but laugh at that. Lilly shoved her blonde hair behind her ears to get it out of her face while she texted someone on her phone.

"Hey Lilly, do you know how to drown a blonde? Put a scratch and sniff sticker at the bottom of a pool." Reese chuckled at his own cheesy joke and just as I suspected, Lilly was out of her seat and reaching back to smack my brother on the head. There was a little bit of struggle since the car was small, but Lilly laughed when Reese cried out in pain.

"Want to tell me another blonde joke?" She asked him intensely. I knew she was just joking around. I don't know if Reese did, though.

"No!" Reese sighed in defeat. Lilly plopped back down in her seat and buckled up before I could nag her to put it on.

"What did you do to him?" I asked her with a smile playing on my lips.

"I twisted his ear until it turned red." She told me nonchalantly. I laughed at her and glued my eyes to the icy road ahead of me. I was way too eager to get to school today. All I wanted was to get off this icy road. I wouldn't be surprised if I got out of the car and kissed the ground.

A sigh of relief escaped my lips when I saw the tall brick school building up ahead.

"Lilly, make sure you don't kill my brother when you take him home tonight, okay?" I reminded her as I pulled into a parking space behind the school. She smirked at me and then turned around to show her smirk to Reese. He shook his head at her before hoping out of he car.

This evening I had to work at Danny's, a local diner that I've worked at for the past three years. At Danny's, I have to wear an apron over my normal clothes, have my hair pulled up, and have a navy blue bandana wrapped around my head as if it were a headband. I don't mind working there. The only problem was the kids from school always come there after school or on weekends to eat. They're the one that harass you if you aren't like them.

I followed behind Lilly with Reese right behind me, stepping on the backs of my boots with his feet. I swiftly turned around when he least expected it and drew my fist back. He flinched and leaned away, he knew I'd tackle him if I had to. But, instead of punching him in the face, I brought my hand closer and flicked him on the forehead.

He made an unamused face at me. I smiled at him and caught up with Lilly in the hallway. Oh, how I loved picking on my brother.

*****

Wrapping my favorite coat around me tighter, I continued to walk down the plowed sidewalk towards Danny's Diner. This Jacket was given to me last year by Lilly, and I haven't been able to take it off. The sleeves and hood were made of a heavenly soft gray sweatshirt material while the rest of the body of the jacket was made of jean material. It was the most comfortable jacket ever.

My boots crunched the ice under them as I walked up the sidewalk that led to Danny's Diner's back door. When I swung the door open, the smell of funnel cakes and coffee hit me like a freight train. It was a perk to working here. The air in here was warm from the stove running most of the day and from the heat being on. It was just a great aroma that I love sucking into my lungs everyday. Besides the having to be here everyday part, I liked this job.

The main cook, Brian, looked over to see who had walked in and grinned when he saw me. He was the fun old guy. Probably in his early 50's, he has the heart of a child. I waved at him and proceeded to strip of my outerwear. Hanging my backpack and coat up on the old wooden coat rack, I grabbed my apron out of the closet and put it on. My name was written in cursive on the front of the apron, Jasey Eldridge.

I quickly pulled my thick, straight hair up into a ponytail and grabbed my navy blue bandana off of my hook. I wrapped the bandana around my head and now my uniform was complete.

Just as I was about to take my position in front of the cash register, my name was called from the back office where Danny himself worked most of the day.

"Yeah?" I peered around the wall and in to see Danny holding his phone up for me to grab. He was trying to write something down. Silly man, always trying to do two things at once. And they were never for himself. I grabbed the phone in my hands and pressed it to my ear.

"Hello, Jasey speaking." I said as I held the phone between my ear and my shoulder and went to the cash register. People were still eating but no one had come in to order so I was good to talk for a moment.

"Jasey! How are you?" Amanda asked me. I silently groaned. Amanda was my dad's long-time girlfriend ever since a year after my parents' divorce. She was probably the best thing to ever happen to him, but acted like she was my mother already. Don't get me wrong, I like the woman but she can be a bit nosey sometimes. She doesn't even live with us, yet. I was happy about that part. I liked having my dad and my brothers home with me. We were a family. My dad hadn't even popped the question yet.

Plus, I'm the one that cooks and cleans for them. I feel like the mother of the house.

"Hey, Amanda. I'm good. How about yourself?" I asked her. She loved it when I made conversation with her. It meant something to her.

"I'm great! Oh, honey. I'm supposed to tell you that your daddy needs you home right after school. He wants to speak to you and Reece about something. I don't know what it is, so don't ask." She chuckled at her little humorous ending. It wasn't even that funny. I decided to humor her. "haha, okay. I'll be there. Thanks."

"You're welcome sweetheart! Talk to you later!" She hung up. Amanda had a southern accent on some words and you could tell where she was from. Right along with my dad, all of us kids were born and raised here in West Virginia. Now, before you go judging me or the state of West Virginia, you should know that not all the people here act like the kids that were on that tv show called Buckwild. Most parents raise their kids to become hard workers and respectful. Heck, I wasn't even allowed to watch that show because of how protective my dad is. He doesn't like me watching shows or movies with cussing or anything inappropriate.

I still watched it, though. What he didn't know wouldn't hurt him.

I quickly took Danny's phone back to him and ran back to the front of the diner to watch for customers. The bell to the front door sounded and my head snapped up from the little doodles I was drawing on an old recite.

"Hello, Charlie." I waved at the older man who was making his way to the bar where he could sit and order his dinner. He smiled his normal smile at me and scooted up to the bar on his stool.

"Hey there, Jasey. How's it going with that daddy of yours?" He grabbed a laminated menu out the stack on the counter and flipped through it, though he and I both already knew what he was going to order.

"He's doing great. He's been out late the last couple of nights since he had to go to Charleston." It was easy talking to Charlie considering he and my dad were good friends and I saw him very often. Charlie owned the local garage in town and every time my dad needed an oil change in his rollback work truck, he went to Charlie. Evidently my dad worked for Charlie when he was younger. It was weird to think Charlie was around his mid-sixties. He doesn't look that old or act that old.

"Good, good. How about your brother?" Even though he didn't specify, I knew he was talking about Grant. He's been away for two years and the only communication my big brother and I have had was through Skype.

"He's good as far as I know," I sighed and rested my elbows in the counter, chin in my hands. "I think he might be coming home for Christmas." A smile grew on my face from ear to ear at the thought. Grant and me were closer than close. He was one of my best friends, and, he and I got along much better than Reese and I.

"That's great news." He smiled at me and the corners of his eyes crinkled.

"Now, what can I get you?" I asked him.

"I'd like to have Dippy Egg with some toast and bacon, and some if that peach jelly Sue makes so well." He smiled past me at the black-haired woman standing at the counter. She was in her late thirties and could make a mean peach jelly. She cans it each year at summer time and we have it all year round.

"And some syrup for my bacon, please? Thank you." Charlie sat the menu down with the others and grabbed a paper out from beside the cash register.

This is what he does every evening. He orders breakfast for lunch with syrup for his bacon to be dipped in and reads the paper. He was good company.

After I got the whole order, including a steaming coffee he forgot to tell me to get, I sat the hot plate of food down in front of him and his eyes twinkled.

"So," I pulled the stool out from behind he register and sat it in front of him, "anything new happening?" I liked talking to Charlie. He lived alone in the small log house beside his garage with his little beagle dog, Sam. Charlie and I had a granddaughter-grandad relationship. And since both of my grandparents were gone, it was nice to have.

"My grandson is supposed to be paying me a visit here soon. Tonight, I think." He said without looking up from the paper.

"Oh, and what's the special occasion?" I asked him with a small smile.

When he looked up at me, I could tell by the look in his eyes that it wasn't for a good visit.

"His parents couldn't handle him anymore, so, they're sending him to me. I don't know what good I'll do." He shrugged his shoulders.

I was about to ask who his grandson was, but the bell rang again and in came my brother. My twin, my look-alike, my arch-nemesis. I glared at Reese until he got up to the counter and he hopped over the counter instead of using the small swinging door. Just because I work here, he thinks he owns the place. Not because everyone loves him, but because he gets free food. I usually fix dinner when I get home, but when the opportunity presents itself, he catches a ride to the diner to "pay me a visit" as he would say.

"How did you get here?" I asked him with annoyance written across my face.

"Lilly brought me. That girl can drive, let me tell you. Why don't we let her drive everyday to school? We'd never be late then. Oh, hey Charlie." Reese babbled as he stuffed his face with some bacon Sue had just laid on the plate that she had finished. She laughed at him and nudged him in the chest to get him to stop.

"Jasey," I heard Lilly say. She took a seat next to Charlie as he ate.

"I thought you were taking him home. You know I hate when he comes here!" I whined to Lilly. She grinned at me and I knew she did it on purpose. What a bestie, right? She's the friend that would help you prank your brother but then go behind your back and help him prank you next. I still loved her.

"Have you ever thought of getting your driver's license, for real, Reese?" Sue asked him the simple question.

"Yep. I thought about putting a wig on Jasey and making her take it for me. I suck at tests." I managed to say after swallowing his mouth full of bacon.

"No way." I said in a sing-song voice.

"You have to drive. That's all. Besides, don't all your friends have their license? Why not you?" I loved Sue for trying to get him to take the dang thing. I hated driving him to school.

"What friends?" I asked with a grin pulling at my lips. Reese shot me a glare before turning to Sue again.

"I'll take it soon, promise. Besides, I hate riding with granny over here." He jabbed his thumb at me. I rolled my eyes at him and turned back to the cash register. Lilly couldn't help but chuckle. I glared at her, too.

Not long after, Reese and Lilly left since my dad would be home soon. I sent dad home some friend chicken and mashed potatoes, his favorite meal from Danny's. Since I didn't get off until nine tonight, my dad would probably want some food when he gets home at six.

"I'm leaving, I'll see you guys Monday. Same time, same place." I waved bye to Danny, Brian, and Sue. There were only a few other workers, but these three were my good friends.

"Okay, have a nice night!" Sue called out. Danny probably didn't hear me and Brian was busy cooking.

The clock on my phone said it was 9:01, perfect timing. With my jacket and backpack on my back once again, I trudged out the door and prepared myself to be freezing. The cold didn't bother me at first, but I knew I would be froze by the time I got home. Hopefully dad has the wood stove fired up.

I realized I still had my bandana on my head and decided to leave it there, but when they cold air hit my neck and ears, I tore it off my head. Tilting my head over, I stared to pull my hair band out of my hair when I saw a pair of headlights heading straight towards me.

————